THE HUNCH

The Ant Murders series

VOLUME ONE

BY

Marion Lindsey-Noble

CASHMERE PUBLISHING

First published in Great Britain in 2021 by Cashmere Publishing

Brompton Regis TA22 9NW, Somerset,
marion.lindseynoble@btinternet.com

A CIP catalogue recorded for this book is available from the British library.

ISBN 978–1–9168859–0-5

Cover Design by Print Guy

Printed by www.Print Guy/books.co.uk

CHAPTER ONE

She has finally reached the top.

'Oh shit!' Ant, a woman in her forties, small, wiry, her thick, brown hair gathered in a ponytail reaching down her back, is slipping around in a mixture of the same claggy soil and rotting straw. It doesn't help that it has been raining heavily all night. Typical October weather! Ant's Wellingtons, stuck ankle-deep in muck, are splattered, and her baggy, faded-navy-blue jumper is sodden with the constant drizzle. The pigs look at her in anticipation, then, as if she hadn't got the hint, at the tin bowl she is carrying, full of apples, bananas, carrots and cucumbers, pigs' delights.

'Sorry girls!' She puts the bowl down on the muddy ground, so vast in diameter, that she can hardly clamp it under one arm. She had done well not to drop it, slipping and sliding, on the way up. The hungry grunts of Iolanthe, Agatha and Persephone turn into furious squeals, as she puts the bowl out of their reach.

'Be back in a minute,' she mumbles apologetically. As she stands upright, she hears the telephone ring faintly again in the distance. There is no signal, so bringing a mobile up here is futile; it would only get plastered in muck like everything else; apart from that, trying to catch a signal on this remote Exmoor farm is a rather hopeless task.

Ant slips and slides down the hill as fast as she can without falling over, shrugs off her Wellingtons on the patio of her house, and runs in through the doors on thick socks – more holes than wool. She reaches the telephone just before it switches to the messaging service.

'Yes? Who is it?' she catches her breath.

'Is that Antonia Bell?'

She takes a deep breath. She would recognise that voice anywhere, in spite of not having heard it for well over a year.

'Yes,' she confirms brusquely.

'Ant, it's me.' He sounds relieved. Was it, because he has caught her in; or because he had dared to ring her, or because she didn't put down the receiver immediately?

There is a long silence before she manages to say:

'I know. What do you want?'

'Can I come and see you?'

'You must be joking. No!'

'It's about Lucinda.'

'Have they found her?'

'No.'

'So what?'

'I want it solved.'

'Don't we all?'

'I am retiring at the end of the year, but I would hate to leave it like that.'

'…why not? Someone else will take over from you.'

'It will haunt me for the rest of my life!'

'Good luck then!' Ant wants to end the conversation.

'She was your colleague, too,' he reminds her, pushing his luck.

'Don't you come with this emotional blackmail crap!' she snaps.

'No, of course not...' He sounds chastised.

'Can I just come to see you and talk it over? Two heads are better than one.'

She thought, obviously in vain, that she had left all that behind. 'No!' she repeats firmly. 'I am busy.'

She suddenly remembers Iolanthe, Agatha and Persephone, waiting for their breakfast. 'I have to go.'

'Ant, don't hang up!' he begs, but she has already replaced the receiver.

CHAPTER TWO

Two hours later, the pigs are fed, watered, and their pens have been cleaned out and given fresh straw. Nobody who cares for pigs would ever call them dirty! They would be most disgruntled if they were neglected and kept in filthy conditions. The last thing Ant has to do is to check the electric fences. Pigs are great escape artists, often more imaginative in their methods than their human counterparts.

Ant sits down at her roughly hewn long kitchen table which doubles up as her office. She pushes a pile of bills and unrequested catalogues aside and puts down her cup of sweet, milky tea. She takes a sip and nibbles on a piece of ginger cake, when she remembers the phone call. She hadn't thought neither of Bex for a while, nor of Lucinda Sheridan. It's an odd sensation to remember the past, her work, cases she has left behind. She doesn't want to be reminded: she has a new life, as demanding as the previous one, but more personally rewarding. For one, she isn't answerable to anybody but herself, and she avoids the bother of team work as much as she can. She always thought team work a fallacy; she much prefers to do things herself; only then will she know that they are done properly.

Lucinda was one of very few people Ant had ever trusted without regretting it later. They got on; they had an affinity. The first time they had been introduced was years ago, when the Wiltshire Police Force had exhausted all the checks, tests and lines of enquiry in a nasty child murder case which had hit the headlines. The investigating team had reached   a dead-end and the public was baying for someone to blame.

Lucinda was seconded from her usual rural Yorkshire police force and came with a reputation of being a dab hand at solving cases. She was an unlikely pathologist – tall, straight-backed, almost regal with a head of thick blond hair, cut in a Princess Diana style. Her eyes were as vibrantly blue as a sunny Mediterranean sky, and she pronounced her posh name with an even posher accent. Lucinda was everything, Ant wasn't. Not that Ant had ever been prejudiced, but, at the time, she had to look twice before it sunk in, that Lucinda was her new partner in the case. As it turned out, Lucinda might have been an unlikely pathologist, but a damn good one! Her authority, based on reputation, calmed nerves and even mollified the frenzied Press men into respectful silence which provided her colleagues with some much needed breathing space. They had gone over all the evidence once more, had pursued alternative paths of research and had finally cracked the case.

Ant grabs the handle of her mug and takes another sip. That's when she remembers the joke between the two of them when Lucinda insisted on bitter, black tea. 'I'm sweet enough!' she used to say, pointing as Ant ladled three spoons of sugar into her cup. They were good times!

After the case, they had stayed in contact and met up whenever they could, simply because they liked each other and seemed to think about things in a similar way. For a start, they were both living on their own, after having broken up numerous relationships which had got in the way of their passion: their jobs. They decided, that most of the time, they were too dog-tired in the evenings to feel lonely without company.

Ant grins to herself with a tinge of bitterness. Men had always found it at first alluring to go out with a tough girl, someone who investigates murders, but eventually, when the novelty wore off, the daily routine set in and they rarely saw each other, the men began to feel overshadowed and neglected. Each and every time! Ant and Lucinda had laughed until tears were streaming down their faces as they compared notes, while people around them looked strangely or disapprovingly at them. They agreed that it might be a good idea not to hope for a lasting romance.

They always met in London, usually in pubs to have a meal and then to go to a show in the West End afterwards. Ant never travelled up north to visit Lucinda, and they never saw each other's home turf. Occasionally Ant mentioned something about her tiny, unloved flat, and on a rare occasion, Lucinda offered a brief verbal glimpse into her luxury apartment. Meeting in town, on neutral ground, suited them both.

Ant shrugs her shoulders. She is not ambitious in that respect: flats, cars, clothes are there to be useful, not a beautiful status symbol.

When had she seen Lucinda last? The intervals between their meetings had suddenly lengthened without either of them noticing, and finally they had stopped altogether. Both were drowning in work anyway: so much crime; each day a disaster in somebody else's life.

And one day, to Ant's utter amazement, she and her entire crime squad received an invitation to Lucinda's wedding.

It turned out to be a lavish affair as both parties brought their own wealth into the relationship, according to guests whose comments Ant had overheard. It wasn't really of interest. Ant was far more preoccupied by the distinct feeling that her tidy, black trousers, white blouse and black blazer with brass buttons were not anywhere close to the attire expected for such an occasion, but then she simply didn't possess a pretty dress, and she had long loathed skirts which were either too short, too tight or swivelling round her waste in times when she was so immersed in a case, that she forgot to eat for days. Clothes were a bother, and she rarely bought anything new.

'Have you given up your job?' she had asked when she finally had a chance to speak to the deliriously happy, blushing bride, flushed with alcohol and excitement at the end of the reception, when most people – including her colleagues from the Wiltshire police, were stumbling about on the dance floor, drunk and uninhibited, with the glow of a successful day. Lucinda seemed glad to sit down and shrug off her white silk covered, high heeled Jimmy Choos.

Lucinda avoided an answer. 'How have you been? I haven't seen you for ages!' she gushed instead.

Ant could only grin and pointed out, unnecessarily: 'No change.' An awkward pause had ensued, both women staring past each other. 'How long have you known Piers?' Ant wanted to be pleasant and happy for her friend.

'It seems ages,' Lucinda spouted breathlessly and with a strangely theatrical wave of the hand. 'I am so lucky, Ant, finding love at my age. Piers is such a sweet man, romantic, charming, well-mannered and…' she leans forward whispering: '…and good-looking, don't you think so?'

Ant could only nod and smile. Piers definitely would not be her cup of tea, but who was she to rain on Lucinda's parade. To her, Piers was average looking, tall, lanky, a sharp nose, glinting eyes behind stylishly round glasses, slightly balding, greying at the temples. Not bad, but no George Clooney.

It was, as if their bond had been broken, and there was not that much left of what they had had in common.

'Piers and I shall go on a long honeymoon. After all, I haven't taken a holiday for years,' Lucinda rambled on: 'We shall be away for about six months. It will be nice to travel for a bit.' She took a deep breath: 'I shall be back at work though,' she had added wistfully, as if she hadn't really thought about it yet.

'Can't keep away, eh?' Ant had played along.

'I don't think I can,' Lucinda had conceded, "you know what it's like, Antonia – exhausting but exhilarating in equal measure.' Lucinda had been the only person ever who had insisted calling her by her proper name. It sounded alien, but somehow nice, respectful. So she never corrected her.

'You might love it being a lady of leisure,' Ant had teased her, and they both had laughed because they knew that that was not going to happen.

'You have plenty of time to decide when you get back,' Ant had tried to reassure her erstwhile friend, who seemed now so distant, veering off into a new life.

It's time to check on the pigs again. These short days are a nuisance; everything has to be crammed into a few hours of daylight. Ant gets up, takes the cup to the sink and rinses it out.

Her memory flags up something else: there was one postcard from the Maldives. It was the last time Ant had heard from Lucinda.

CHAPTER THREE

'Miss Bell,' someone shouts from the bottom of the hill. Oh, bugger, she thinks.

'I am in the middle of feeding, Barry,' she shouts back to the postman.

She can just about hear: 'Visitor!'

She isn't expecting a delivery, or a parcel, never mind a visitor. She never has visitors, not if she can help it.

'Okay,' she shouts back, 'send the visitor up.' She has no idea whether Barry can hear her. When nothing happens, she continues - to the delight of the pigs - to empty her bowl into their long trough. She looks at Iolanthe, screwing up her eyes:

'Are you pregnant, young lady?' she asks the pig who gives her a hurried glance before sticking her snout back into the trough. That would be, well, the nearest to wonderful she can think of. Ant smiles, grabs the empty bowl and makes her way cautiously back down the hill.

The postman has disappeared, and there is no sign of a visitor either. Good! Ant is just about to unlock her door and shrug off her Wellingtons, when she hears a voice:

'Ant,' not that voice again! The voice she would recognise anywhere, and she doesn't particularly want to hear: Senior Investigating Officer Benjamin E. Cook, 'Bex' for short.

'You look glamorous,' he grins.

'Well, well, if I had known, you were coming…,' her words trail off. They are still prickly with each other.

'Nice place, you have here,' his eyes sweep over the hillside.

'Hmm,' she is non-committal. They stand there, in the light drizzle.

'Are you not going to ask me in?' He sounds keen to get to somewhere dry. 'I have come a long way.' Of course; she knows that.

She is cross that he has simply turned up, but he is right: they might as well get out of the rain to be silent together.

Once inside, she makes tea again, while he uses her bathroom. She doesn't even offer coffee; she hasn't got any. She threw the last packet out when it had become home to maggots.

'Milk; sugar?' she asks. Well, there had been a time once, when she had known. He might have changed his habits, though.

'Only milk,' he says simply and grins when he sees her ladling three spoons full of sugar into her own cup:

'You haven't changed much either,' he remarks, but she ignores his comment.

She waves him to sit down at the table, while she remains standing, holding on to the edge of the sink with one hand and grasping her cup of tea with the other, sipping occasionally and watching him, raising her eyebrows in anticipation.

He sits there, holding his cup with both hands, not drinking, deep in thought.

She waits: 'Have you come for anything specific?' she finally asks. 'I have to do the pigs again at four o'clock,' she adds, facetiously.

He wakes up from his trance: 'As I said on the phone, I am retiring at the end of the year.'

'Old age catching up?' she grins more with irony than sympathy.

'Something like that,' he mumbles.

He still looks good, she thinks; still a thick head of hair, grey now, but it suits him. He seems to keep it longer than it used to be, until she discovers that it is barely hiding a hearing aid; he had never been slim, but he looks fitter than he has ever done. Maybe a little paunch is hiding underneath that dark green Windcheater jacket?

He notices her scrutiny. Those green eyes of hers: deep, mysterious, intriguing!

'I had a heart attack a couple of years ago,' he says simply. 'I am fine now.' The obligatory exercise regime prescribed by the police surgeon has definitely improved Bex's physique.

'Okay. So what is it you want?' She cuts to the chase. The quicker this is over, the quicker she can get on with her day.

'Remember Lucinda?' As if she didn't!

'I am not likely to forget her, am I?'

'Neither can I,' his voice is rasping.

'Are you re-opening the case?'

'I wish I could, but there is not enough new evidence.'

'So you can't!' she points out.

He looks pained: 'Her husband is driving me crazy, and to be honest, so is my conscience.'

'He hasn't remarried, has he?'

'No. He is still as devastated as ever.'

Ant sighs. They both stare into their empty cups.

'More tea?' she asks. He shakes his head.

'So why did you come all the way down here?' She can have a guess, but she won't. Nothing to do with her anymore!

'She was your colleague, and I suspect, a friend, too. Don't we owe it to her, to at least have another look?'

There were times when she had thought so. It is different now. She hasn't worked for the police for a long time. She is out of practice. Things have moved on. Technology has progressed and changed. There is no way she can be of any use.

She suddenly thinks of Iolanthe and the Girls: they need her here; they might all be pregnant; they are her responsibility, her life now. She mustn't forget to read up on 'pregnancy in pigs'; or should she call the vet? That would probably be prohibitively expensive. How about a pregnancy test? Humans have it; it can't be that different for pigs.

She decides to think about it and confuses Bex with a vague smile.

'Surely, there must be better candidates to have another look at the case than me; young people, eager to make a name for themselves; ambitious to advance their careers,' she argues.

'You wouldn't recognise anybody now, Ant. The station is full of new people.' He sounds worn out. 'Nobody remembers the case, never mind her name or the circumstances. We must be the only ones left.'

She feels a little more conciliatory: 'I can't, Bex!'

The 'why?' is written all over his face.

'I have a life here. I can't just abandon everything. I am sure you will find somebody else.'

He looks at her and shakes his head. 'Pigs now, is it?' he says finally

'Yes!' She looks straight into his grey, tired eyes: 'At least they are reliable and predictable,' she flings into the gloom of the early dusk.

'Ouch!' he grins, a little embarrassed. 'You couldn't…? For old times' sake?'

'…definitely not for those!' she interrupts, 'Bex, the answer is no!'

He reaches into his jacket pocket and proffers a business card:

'My contact details; some have changed.' When she doesn't take it, he throws it onto the kitchen table.

'I thought I'd give it a try,' he says, looking at her, as if it were for the very last time. It probably was.

'Are you driving back now?'

He has booked himself into a small local hotel, he says. He won't be staying.

'Sorry you had a wasted journey,' she says lamely and closes the door behind him. The first thing she does is to throw the card into the bin. She won't need it. She doesn't intend to ever use it.

He will be on his way back to London first thing in the morning.

CHAPTER FOUR

Ant wakes up after a restless night. Usually, the physical tiredness puts paid to dreaming, but after the SIO's visit, her head was like a whirlpool of jumbled up dreams, featuring long forgotten people, the nasty feeling of impending doom and her pigs stuck in mud. The one person who seems to come to the foreground more than any other is Lucinda.

Now, that Ant is wide awake, it is the only picture that remains.

'Right, I might as well give the Girls an early breakfast;' she debates with herself. Then she will go and buy a pregnancy test at the local pharmacy in the nearest village ten miles away. Goodness knows what they are going to think if she buys three. If there is time, she will organise a delivery of straw and nourishing supplement pellet – maybe a bit premature, if she hasn't had confirmation yet, but she is pretty sure, pretty excited: there is definitely a change in movement, a sudden lack of elegance replaced by lumbering sturdiness and a certain defiant look in Iolanthe's eyes that demands pampering. A pregnant sow is entitled to being greedy!

Ant's thoughts turn back to Lucinda and her disappearance, not just from her life, but everybody's, including her new husband's. Ant doesn't exactly know when the couple had returned from honeymoon– she guesses after the planned six months. She had genuinely forgotten about them. Lucinda had a new life, a new focus and a new best friend.

There was this eerie day, when news came in, that a Mr. Turner had reported his wife missing. One disappearance among many! It only sunk in later that Mr Turner was married to Lucinda Turner, née Sheridan. It sounded more of a prank than a reason to panic. Lucinda could look after herself. Bex and his staff did all the usual checks, interviewing the husband, friends and family, establishing alibis. When Lucinda was still missing a week later, they requested mobile phone, bank and credit card statements, but it was as if the earth had swallowed her up.

Ant remembers mentioning to Bex the possibility that Lucinda might have found marriage wanting. After all, she had been a totally independent, financially secure, capable woman for most of her life:

'Unlikely. You should see their house: it is full of happy wedding and honeymoon pictures.'

'Well, that doesn't prove anything. Maybe she wanted to return to work, and he was against it?' Ant remembered the hint at the end of the reception.

It had been established that Lucinda had actually requested a reference and transfer from her previous placer of work. January the first 2016 had been mentioned, and that her husband Piers had been happy about it. He was busy running his own company. The investigators were stuck.

It was a mystery. It still is to this day, Ant muses. Why would Lucinda disappear without leaving a word, a note, any sign that she might just need a bit of breathing space? Was it a mid-life crisis? The timing would be odd: two years into a marriage to a gorgeous, successful, kind man who clearly adored her. A late romance, neither of them had expected. Every time they had asked the husband, whether they had had a row, Piers had responded tearfully and shaken his head.

Concentrate on the now! Ant drives the ten miles to the village and gets a funny look from the pharmacist's assistant who doesn't ask, but her eyes give away burning curiosity. Ant presses her lips together and rushes out.

'Right, you lot,' she announces to Iolanthe, Agatha and Persephone. 'Extra ration for you today,' she says as if to lull them into a false security. She throws a mixture of vegetables and fruit into their trough. Now to the pregnancy tests! All these strips need is a bit of urine from each of the Girls – as far as she remembers. She knows that pigs tend to pee just before eating. In theory, it should be simple, but of course, it turns out, not to be. Only Iolanthe trots according to plan into a corner to do her business by a bush. Ant sneaks up on her as fast as she can. The aim is to catch a bit of the stream, but as Ant is about to hold the strip closer to the animal, she is greeted by an outraged squeal, and a hasty retreat, which sends Ant flying into the mud. By the time she has extracted herself, wet soil clinging to her trousers, pullover, hands and hair, Iolanthe is back by her trough, munching. Ant makes one last attempt by sticking the pregnancy test into the little puddle on the ground, but of course, the sample is contaminated. Should she bother with the other two? She slips down the muddy hill and waits at a distance. Agatha is the first to tear herself away. She is, however, too quick for Ant to follow, bend down and catch the stream underneath her. They end up racing uphill with Agatha definitely winning the race. Persephone seems oblivious to the goings on and keeps licking clean the now empty trough. Ant, mud-caked, wet, cold and feeling rather foolish, decides to give up. She throws the pregnancy test into the pharmacy's carrier bag and the whole lot into the kitchen bin as soon as she has taken her Wellingtons off and thrown her clothes into the washing machine.

Minxes, she thinks. Never underestimate a pig. They have acute instincts, fast reactions in spite of their bulk, and they know their minds. There is only one thing to do, to make her forget this embarrassing episode: Ant gets up to ring the vet, who, to her relief, promises to come out that afternoon. She knows, it will cost her money and is not absolutely necessary, but her girls are precious to her, and she wants to pick the vet's brain on some other things. Next time she won't be able to afford the luxury.

'The vet is coming this afternoon,' she says to the Girls, but they are clearly not listening. They are busy scoffing the apples, carrots, pumpkin wedges and their favourite, a mushy banana each. 'I seem to be the only one excited about you being pregnant,' she tells Iolanthe, but they all keep munching noisily, with little happy grunts and ears flopping over their eyes.

Ant returns to the house for a bowl of tinned soup for an early lunch and sighs at the look of the pile of papers, she had promised herself to tackle. She might as well do it while waiting for the vet. She hates bureaucracy; it was as bad in the police.

The vet arrives halfway through her filling in of forms; a welcome break of the tedium. He needs to take blood from all three girls, but after Iolanthe lets out an outraged squeal, the others scarper and disappear among the trees. They have a hell of a job to follow and corner them. Ant bemoans the fact that the lure of an extra pumpkin ration won't work next time. They are miffed and go straight to their pens after their ordeal.

'Give me a call tomorrow. The results should be in by late afternoon,' the vet says. 'And may I suggest,' he adds in a fatherly tone, 'that you have an early night, too. You look exhausted!' It is ironic: so does he.

What now - paperwork or an early supper for the Girls to appease them? She decides on the latter and fills the bowl with pig goodies before she embarks on her routine of feeding; providing fresh straw for their sleeping hollows; checking the electric fence for damage; and renewing the water with a hosepipe connected to a spring she discovered after she had bought the house.

Afterwards, Ant pops a baking potato into the microwave. She scrutinises the headlines of the daily paper, but isn't really interested in world news. Lucinda is infiltrating her thoughts again. Why would she disappear? Where to? It wasn't necessarily a sinister disappearance. She herself had disappeared from everybody's life, hadn't she? Just because she could; she had had enough; she had wanted a new life; to start all over again. Not to be a SOCO but a pig farmer. Just for once, pleasing herself. But then she didn't have a husband or anybody else who would miss her; someone to whom she would owe an explanation.

Ant tries to picture Lucinda; the way they giggled together and the way she smiled radiantly the last time she had seen her at the wedding.

The microwave pings. She takes the baked potato out, cuts it open through the middle, smothers it with butter and grated cheese and opens a tin of baked beans. That will do.

She yawns. Her head is whirring. The vet was right. An early night will do her good. Before she goes upstairs, she bends down, peers into the kitchen bin. She can't see it at first, until she spots a corner of the black card. She pulls it out gingerly. It is splattered with remnants of tinned tomato soup and brown bean sauce. She wipes it with a damp cloth into the sink, rubs it dry and puts it on the table. Just in case.

CHAPTER FIVE

'Don't you look so smug, you lot,' Ant greets the Girls. 'You knew all along. All this fuss: chasing the vet through the trees. He'll charge me extra for this!' Ant laughs happily and they know from the tone of her voice that they are in the clear.

I wish I had trusted my hunch, she thinks. It would have been cheaper. She smiles ruefully. If she had had a pound for every hunch she had had in the past, which turned out to be the truth, she would be a rich woman. Instead, she had kept telling herself, that she was a scientist. Scientists don't deal in hunches; they only deal in facts.

She had had a hunch about Lucinda's case from the start. She never told anyone; she stuck to the forensic procedures and scientific facts. As time passed, the case dragged on, without Lucinda either returning nor any other scenario emerging, she had shrugged her shoulders and tried to forget about it. By the time the investigation was put on ice, she had retired. Nothing to do with her any longer!

And still, Bex is right: the nagging feeling never went away. It is still there, and she feels a pang of guilt whenever she thinks of Lucinda. Would Lucinda have given up or instead kept looking for her if she, Ant, had disappeared?

Ant sighs. Guilt is a strange emotion, regret, too; both useless unless they are acted upon.

Don't get sucked in, she scolds herself. You have three pregnant ladies to look after for 3 months, three weeks and three days – the gestation period. And of course, once the piglets have been born, they need special care! So forget about getting involved, forget about finding Lucinda. You are needed here.

'Don't you worry,' she tells the pigs. 'I shall be here; I won't leave you!' She feels better after the pep-talk she has given herself, and slides down the hill with renewed confidence that she has every right to resist temptation.

It surely had been a temptation, she thinks hunched over her midday soup. Bex standing there with all the memories attached to him, offering her one more chance to solve a case. Ant had loved her job, although it had taken its toll; many horrible dreams of people murdering each other and laughing into her face like Dracula, disturbing her sleep frequently. It's sometimes wearing her down, but as soon as she is with the pigs, she forgets all about past horrors. Occasionally, she has an anxiety attack, but she has learnt to talk herself out of that; only a fanatical approach to safety and security remains, and that isn't a bad thing.

And this of all unsolved cases is the one closest to her heart; and obviously to Bex's as well. Ant owes a particular debt of gratitude to Lucinda Sheridan from way back, not only when she helped out professionally by solving the case and shutting up the Press, but also on a very personal basis. Ant had confided in her, much against her nature, when she was really in a pickle of massive proportions. Her affair with Bex had just ended, when she had discovered that she was pregnant. A baby would have changed her life, if she had made the wrong decision then, but – thanks to Lucinda – she hadn't, and her life stayed on kilter.

Ant takes her soup plate to the sink, rinses it, scrubs it with a brush and lays it upside down, so that it can drain.

She can feel Lucinda's deep blue eyes upon her, serious, expectant, begging. No, I can't, Ant pleads with her invisible friend; I have a new life, my animals to look after, a farm to run; I don't want to be anywhere near police work again, and I certainly don't want to be part of a team, under Bex's direction, digging up dead bodies! Why does she think there will be a dead body? Very unscientific! Deal in facts, not assumptions! She admonishes herself. How can you ever consider accepting, if that is how your brain works now?

On the other hand, Lucinda might have settled somewhere in the world, happy with a new life - exactly like her. After all, they were one of a kind.

However, the least she can do is to find out one way or another, for Lucinda's sake and that of a good conscience. She can make sure that everything has been done that can be done to uncover the truth.

Where has she put that blasted card again? She wrinkles her forehead as if that helps to remember. A flash of inspiration: drawer! She rummages around and holds it up triumphantly.

But there will be conditions; this time; she will insist on terms and conditions, **her** terms and conditions and certainly a clause that she can pull out at any time she likes!

CHAPTER SIX

'So, when are you coming up to headquarters?' asks a happy Bex.

'Who told you I am coming up?'

'Ant, you might have been away for a bit, but you know very well that there are rules…'

'I make my own rules nowadays,' she interrupts him bluntly, but he is right: there is no way that documentation, witness and alibi statements, and exhibits relating to a previous investigation can be sent to her to be read and checked out in her own time and in the comfort of her own home. However much that would be her ideal, it can't and won't happen. However, with the state of affairs in her pig-world she is not willing either to compromise more than necessary. One day in Devizes, where the case had been handled in the past, will have to do, she tells him. 'Give me a couple of days to arrange some cover, and I give you a call the day before I come up.'

'Cover for what? You are retired.'

'And you are dense as always, Bex. Remember my pigs? You might not have taken great interest in them, but you must have noticed them.'

'Have those pigs priority over a live case nowadays?' She can hear that he is displeased and disorientated. She is not the keen, pliable Ant he used to know. He might not have changed from being grumpy and directional, but she has.

'One day in Devizes will have to do for the time being,' she repeats, steel in her voice.

He sounds uncomfortable when he gives in: 'Okay. You know best.'

'Bother,' she says to herself. Why did I agree? She is cross with herself. As a result, I have the problem of finding a house-sitter or at least someone reliable to look regularly in on the animals while I am away. One day will be a good trial period, should she need to go away for longer later on. She is not expecting to be involved right to the end. How could she possibly solve a case in her meagre spare time which the entire Wiltshire Police hasn't managed to solve in two years? She is good, but not that good…She would make her contribution, for Lucinda's sake, but then she will withdraw and leave it all behind; this time for good!

Felix, a young farmer's son, springs to mind. He is probably in his early thirties and has just finished agricultural college. He can't wait to get stuck in, he has told her last time he passed her farm gate on his quad-bike and stopped for a neighbourly chat over the fence. She goes to the old-fashioned black telephone in the hall, she had treated herself to last Christmas, and dials Felix's number. No reply. He is probably out in the field with his father checking on their sheep. She tries an hour later. Still no response… Maybe they have gone to market. It's often the highlight of the week for farmers, not only to buy or sell livestock; it is usually one of the few occasions when they meet other human beings rather than just animals.

She finally gets hold of Felix in the evening. He has to ask his father first whether he can spare him for a whole day. To her relief, he sounds delighted with her proposition.

'Can I sleep over night in your house' he asks.

She doesn't say anything yet; she is a little taken aback.

'You will probably leave at the crack of dawn,' he explains, 'and if I sleep at your house, I'll be on location early in the morning to do the pigs.' She can hear the sheepish grin in his voice as if he has said something daring. It suddenly makes sense. She wouldn't have to hurry back.

'Of course, you can, Felix!' It would suit her just fine.

'Which day is best for your father and you?' she enquires.

'Towards the end of the week, sort of, but I have to square it with him.'

'Sure,' she agrees. 'Shall we say, next week Wednesday night to Friday morning? I'll be home either very late on Thursday or with the first train back to Taunton on Friday. It's a bit of a pain that Devizes hasn't got a station, but Melksham's isn't far away.'

'Sounds complicated,' Felix mutters.

'It isn't really: bus from Devizes – or if I am lucky, a lift from a colleague – to Melksham; from there a couple of minutes to Westbury; and then a straight connection back to Taunton. Not bad at all.'

'Rather you than me,' more mutterings.

Ant looks at him: he is definitely not the adventurous type.

'Let me know when you have an answer,' Ant says. As long as he is any good looking after her precious pigs, that's all that matters!

The answer comes rather quicker than expected. Felix sounds very eager indeed. Good! The pigs deserved the best.

Now she can ring Bex; he is delighted, too!

'Steady on!' she warns. 'You won't see much of me. I shall be locked away in the archive.'

She can hear the remnants of a supressed, slightly bitter chuckle.

'How does next Thursday grab you?' she asks without formality.

'I have to shift a few things round,' he says, 'but knowing you, I have to be grateful that you come at all.'

She doesn't reply. He obviously got the message.

'See you next Thursday,' he confirms. She won't tell him that she is coming up earlier.

Felix arrives on Tuesday evening after his own work, to get instructions how to care for and deal with the pigs in various situations.

'Grandmother and sucking eggs spring to mind,' he mutters. He is a strapping young man, muscular, still lightly tanned from the summer, with curls of red hair falling over his eyebrows, and sparkling green eyes, mocking her in youthful confidence.

He doesn't really need her instructions, but Ant wants to make sure that she will not return to unpleasant surprises. The transition in care must be as seamless as possible.

'Don't worry,' he keeps saying, carefree, which does worry her. She hopes he is not cutting corners. '…and have a great time up north!' He winks at her, grinning knowingly.

'It's hardly up-north, Felix,' she corrects him. The locals in these parts of Britain tend not to be widely travelled. The West Country landscape is too beautiful and varied, and the communities are still so unfashionably strong, that most people don't feel a pull into the big, wide world.

'See you tomorrow, before dusk,' Ant reminds him. 'I intend to catch the early evening train.'

When Felix finally decides to leave, promising with an indulgent chuckle that he will follow her instructions to the letter – spoiling the pigs rotten, as he calls it -, he nods, raises a hand in greeting while already walking away. She stares at his back until he disappears round the bend in the lane, then turns round and climbs up the hill again. She sits on a tree stump for a long time watching the Girls rooting around the ground, making contented grunting noises.

'Now... from tomorrow,' she begins her little good-bye speech, 'Felix will look after you.' They take no notice. 'I shall be back quicker than you think!' she says with a hint of guilt and rising panic. She has never before left them. That's how it must feel leaving your baby with a babysitter for the first time. Ant has never had children, and wasn't ever particularly envious of other people who had. Lucinda had felt exactly the same. 'Are we weirdos?' she had once asked, and they had both laughed over their G&Ts. Why then does she feel so maternal, so protective and sentimental all of a sudden - over pigs? She hopes fervently that they won't miss her. Maybe they won't even notice her absence? They might even like Felix better. That would be best – however disappointing that would be.

She slaps Iolanthe on the rump: 'Look after yourself and the Girls,' she urges the animal, turns abruptly and stomps down the hill. All that's left now is to pack and to gather her thoughts!

Twenty-four hours later, she sits in a window seat on the train to Melksham. The seat next to her is mercifully empty. Her head is filled with apprehension and a mixture of conflicting feelings. She thinks longingly of her farm, her pigs and her own bed. There is beauty in a simple life! Felix will by now sit in her kitchen and make himself a cup of tea. She wrenches her thoughts away. No point in moping. She has a job to do. Concentrate! She jots down a few ideas, a long list of questions; she desperately tries to remember the facts of Lucinda's disappearance and puts them in order of sequence.

By the time she arrives at Devizes coach stop, she has mentally closed the door on her other life and is ready to do that very special, unique and last job for her friend.

She has morphed back into SOCO, or as it is now called, CSI Ant Bell.

CHAPTER SEVEN

The coach drops her almost outside the B&B she has chosen to stay in; in fact, she checked on the website whether it was still in business - there is so much buying, selling, refurbishing and building going on nowadays that one never knows whether the familiar haunts are still in existence She used to stay there, when she was still employed, on nights, when work just wouldn't let her go home, and it had been adequate; nothing to crow about, three stars, but all she really needs is a clean bed and a shower. It is only a stone's throw away from her old office in London Road. The tall building has seen better days. The white of the walls is illuminated by the neon lights announcing in a garish yellow that this is indeed a hotel. It looks tired; the paint on the window frames is peeling; only the entrance door seems to have had a fresh lick of glossy black. She knows it will be pristine inside. Holding her overnight bag, she rings the bell. It makes a forlorn sound which seems to disappear into the large emptiness of the place. She waits and rings again. Finally, she can hear footsteps and keys, jangling.

'Sorry, it's usually open,' says the proprietor with an Indian accent. Ant recognises her from before. The woman looks back at her in recognition: 'You have been here before, haven't you?'

Ant nods and has a guess: 'Mrs. Asif?' She remembers the previous warm welcomes; and her admiration: it must have taken guts for an Asian woman to establish a business in a typically English market town.

The lady is delighted: 'You remember,' her big smile revealing perfect white teeth.

'Didn't you work for the police?' Mrs. Asif is proud of her good memory. She is probably in her late fifties, a womanly figure, beautifully dressed in an embroidered navy blue Kaftan-type dress; a silk shawl of the same colour is draped over her thick, black hair, crossed at her throat and each end slung over a shoulder. While she rummages around on the reception desk for Ant's booking form, golden bangles tinkling around both wrists.

'Yes, here it is,' she says briskly, like the businesswoman she is. 'Will a room to the back be okay with you?'

'Fine,' says Ant with a tired smile. She will only be in the room at nights to sleep. She doesn't care about the view; being on a main road, there are bound to be other houses opposite and traffic noises which ever room you take. No, the room to the back will be fine.

Ant fills in the form and gives it back to Mrs Asif, who in return hands over two keys: 'Someone will be at the reception at all times, but I let you have a key to the main door, just in case you have to work unsociable hours.' She smiles as if they were sharing a confidence.

'Thank you,' says Ant gratefully, and then adds purely out of curtesy: 'That's very kind of you.'

'Will you need help with your luggage?' Mrs Asif asks and purses her lips in readiness to call the porter - her son, Ant seems to remember.

'No,' she shakes her head, takes the two keys and drags her rucksack to the lift. She presses the button for second floor, watches the doors closing and waits for the climb to begin with a jolt. It takes less than a minute before she walks along the beige hall carpet to her room, two-five. It's not a bad room, clean, a double bed with four plumped up pillows, an eiderdown duvet and a soft black headrest; there is a desk and a chair Ikea-style and a large wardrobe. A full-length mirror clings to the wall by the door. Thankfully, there is no air-conditioning - Ant hates those - but the central heating radiator is already warming up. Ant throws her bag into the armchair in the corner by the window and begins to undress. She needs a shower. The bathtub with associated bath oil sachets looks tempting, but she has long given up on baths – too time-consuming, lulling her to sleep rather than keeping her awake. And right now, she doesn't need any help to fall asleep.

Half an hour later, she feels better, tidier, smelling nice, refreshed. She feels peckish, but it is too late to go out, and the B&B doesn't offer late night snacks. Ah, there might be a biscuit on the tea tray. Then she remembers having bought a sandwich at Melksham station and rummages around her bag. She eats hungrily and drinks three quarters of one of the bottles of mineral water left on the tea tray. Theoretically, she would like to go out, have a little look around her old haunts, but she decides that this is not the time. Rather have an early night, so that she is ready for an early start in the morning.

She dials reception: 'Mrs Asif, what time is your breakfast?' She is given a choice and chooses the earliest time on offer: six o'clock. She climbs between the freshly laundered bedsheets and is asleep before she can form another thought

CHAPTER EIGHT

After a dreamless night, she wakes up just in time for breakfast. At home she would probably get ready to feed the pigs. She feels strangely removed. To her own surprise, she chooses a continental breakfast. She won't have much physical exertion, she debates with herself, so a full English breakfast, however tempting, would sit in her stomach for hours and make her feel queasy.

She walks the fifteen minutes to London Road and the Headquarters of the Wiltshire CID. She is quite excited to see it again, although it is not the prettiest of buildings, more functional than beautiful on the outside. However, she has read, that there are refurbishment plans afoot to turn it into one of those places to rival the New Scotland Yard building in London: three storeys of grand open-plan work space, rather than old-fashioned, dingy offices; work-stations rather than a desk for each member of staff, and rows of lockers to lock up one's belongings overnight. Ant has never experienced a work place like that nor has she ever spoken to anybody who had.

She walks round several corners and along London Road. She strides out with vigour and arrives at the heavy entrance door earlier than expected. Her heart beats fast as if it was her first day at work ever. Get a grip, she tells herself. You are only here for a day.

She reports to the desk sergeant and discovers with satisfaction that Bex has organised a pass for her, permission to be here and to go in and out – for a month? What is he playing at? At least, she won't waste time trying to explain her mission should she need to return more than once.

'Archive,' she announces, and the desk sergeant makes a call. She is picked up by the archivist, a young officer who has hardly begun to shave, and together they take the lift down into the bowels of the building. It is like a different world down there: almost like Roman Catacombs. She gives the case number, dates and Lucinda's name. He looks it up on a computer, memorises the location of the file and asks her to wait. While he is searching, she stands still, looking at the dizzying array of shelves filled with files and boxes. Eventually, he comes back, holding on to his find.

'We'll have to go to the reading room. An officer will be there to supervise.' When she raises her eyebrows at the word 'supervises', he quickly adds: '…in case you need something else.'

They take the lift up, passing the ground floor. Said supervisory officer is already waiting for her by the lift door and takes her to the reading room.

'You are an early bird,' he remarks, curious about the stranger.

'Lots to do,' she answers non-committal.

She is the only person here, except, of course, for him, who settles at a separate desk by the door and begins to consult his notebook.

Time for head down! She opens the first page of the folder labelled 'Lucinda Turner'.

She can't believe that she has sat there for three hours, when the door opens and Bex comes in. She tries to get up but feels as if she is rooted to the rather hard chair.

'Don't bother,' he says and pulls up another chair next to hers. 'Anything yet?' he asks, hopeful.

'Give me a chance!' she replies with an exaggerated sigh. She is glad that he is unsentimental and to the point.

'No inklings yet - no hunches?' he grins.

'I don't have those nowadays,' she clarifies. She knows what he means: she had always been known for her incongruous, solely instinctive opinions, which had often turned out to be closer to the truth than the contradicting, so-called established facts. 'Don't need those!' she asserts.

'More's the pity,' he laughs out loud to the annoyance of the supervising officer who looks at him disapprovingly.

'How long have you been here?'

'…about seven.'

'He whistles. The supervising officer looks up again in despair.

'How about a break? We could go for an early lunch.'

She shakes her head: 'Better get on with it. I only have today to get through the lot.'

'You are kidding!' He is seriously disappointed.

'I told you so!'

'You are not joking,' he says, his early morning ebullience deflated. He had obviously looked forward to seeing her for much longer.

'Tell you what,' she relents. 'I could do with a cup of tea. Is there a canteen in this building?'

''Are you asking seriously? You'll be in for a shock! Not like in the old days. We have gone up in the world!'

He hasn't exaggerated. Their long, silent walk through dull corridors and dimly lit staircases is followed by a gasp of admiration. The canteen looks more like a celebrity chef's restaurant. She lets him treat her to a pot of Earl Grey and a croissant, and feels instantly guilty for no reason at all. No harm in letting him pay, is there? After all, she is the one who is doing him a favour.

'Have you not got something else to do today?' she asks, which amuses him.

'No. Point one, you might have forgotten, that I am the boss, and secondly, I have seconded myself to help out with Lucinda's case.'

She nods absent-mindedly and munches silently her croissant.

'Seriously, Ant, has anything sprung to mind; anything we have missed?'

'You might not have missed anything at all,' she points out.

He shakes his head: 'There is always something…'

'Let's hope so,' she admits in a conciliatory tone. She has always thought that maybe they could have done more; that maybe they had been close; that maybe they should have carried on; for Lucinda's sake. But funds had dried up and they had to scale down the investigation until it fell asleep by itself. She shrugs her shoulders almost imperceptivity.

'Nose back to the grindstone,' she announces. 'Thanks for the tea and the croissant'. At home, she would have shared the crumbs with the pigs or the birds.

She gets up, tidies the collar, peeping out of her navy cashmere pullover – the only decent garment she could find - a birthday present to herself in a fit of profligacy – pulls the sweater over her navy blue, corduroy trousers and says: 'See you around.'

'Hang on, Ant. Can't I invite you to a dinner at least; as late as you want?'

'No time, Bex. I'll ring you when I have something to report.'

'You can't be serious, you are not …'

'Dear John McEnroe,' she interrupts him, 'the answer is NO! I have to catch a train home.'

For a moment she thinks, Bex might burst into tears. That would be a first.

'Thanks for coming up and taking a look,' he says finally deflated like a businessman whose deal has just fallen through.' I'll keep you informed of enquiries at our end.'

'That would be good,' she says, waves half-heartedly and begins to walk away, towards the lift. When it arrives, she can just squeeze in with a man in civilian clothes and a female police officer in uniform. They both smile at her as if she were a member of their clan. Ant does sometimes miss the camaraderie. It's not the same with pigs.

It's now a different supervising officer, who returns her files, notebook and Parka jacket with a fur-edged hood which she had been urged to put into one of the lockers on the wall. He notes down the time of her return and checks her permit.

By the time she finishes leafing through the files, folders and boxes and thinks she has exhausted all possibilities, her notebook is full of squiggles, names, dates and diagrams. She is famished. She remembers briefly Bex's invitation to dinner, but is glad that she resisted.

When she gets out, it is dark, but the street and advertisements lights create an artificial atmosphere of daytime. There is only one street light where she lives on Exmoor, and that's in the centre of the village - nowhere near her farm. She flags down a passing taxi at the end of the road, stops by at the hotel to settle the bill and collect her overnight bag.

'I thought you were staying two nights,' says Mrs Asif with a hint of reproach.

'So did I, Mrs Asif,' says Ant, 'I am so sorry. Maybe next time…'

'Oh, you might be coming back?' asks Mrs Asif hopefully. 'I look forward to welcoming you again.'

Ant smiles reassuringly and hurries back to the taxi.

'Parkway Station, please,' she orders. 'Can you step on it, please? I am in a hurry!' she urges the driver, who laughs out loud. 'Who isn't?' is all he adds and then does exactly what she wants him to do.

She is so relieved when she catches the earlier train and falls, with a sigh of relief, into the upholstery. The Girls will be pleased! She eats the dried out sandwich she has bought in a hurry at the station. It is hard to swallow, and she has nothing to wash it down with. Eventually, she scrunches up the packaging and pushes it into an already overflowing bin under the window. For a while Ant looks out of the window, but as it is dark, there is not much to see. She studies her notebook instead and considers each and every entry.

CHAPTER NINE

'Ant, it is Bex. I haven't heard from you for over a week.'

'I have been busy…'

'Like an ant?'

She doesn't even bother to answer with the sarcastic, long-drawn-out, staccato 'ha, ha, ha' as she used to do.

'Have y o u made any progress?' she asks.

'Not really,' he answers, taken aback.

'… and you are doing this all day? I have my farm to consider. That alone is a full-time job.'

'Can we stop this nonsense, Ant? We spend half the time fencing- back and forth, attack and counter-attack. I am sick of it. We need to concentrate on the case, not on scoring points. We need to talk, and soon!'

'Why not,' she agrees eventually.

There is silence at the other end, as if he is gulping for air with surprise.

'Where and when then?' he says quickly before she changes her mind.

She thinks about it.

'Bath,' she comes up with.

'Okay,' he draws out the syllables. He can't believe his luck. 'When?'

'This Thursday; it's the best day for Felix.'

'Who is Felix?' he asks cautiously.

'No one you know. He looks after the pigs.'

'So it worked out well last time?'

'Yes, it did.'

'And your pigs didn't complain and cry for their mummy?'

'Not that you know anything about caring.' She is quick and cutting with her remark.

'Oh come on; that's below the belt!'

She nibbles at her lower lip, a little bit ashamed of her unnecessarily strong reaction. Obviously there is still some hurt buried and festering deep inside her.

'…where in Bath?' Bex pulls them both back to the original topic.

'There is a Pizzeria near the Roman Baths. I'll book for lunchtime. It leaves me enough time to get there.'

'How long will it take you?'

'About two hours depending on traffic.'

'Right, a business lunch on Thursday, midday at the Pizzeria in Bath it is.'

They are both on time; Bex just a fraction earlier. He is already studying the long list of pizza varieties. He stands up when she arrives and pulls out a chair for her. She sits down confused by the unexpected chivalry.

'Have you ordered?' she asks impatiently.

'Not yet, but I have chosen. What do you want?'

'To make it clear, I am paying for myself.'

'No, I mean, what do you want to eat?'

'...anything.' She looks at his baffled expression and says quickly: 'Lasagne and salad.' She thinks: he doesn't even remember my favourite meal: *agnolotti* – a type of ravioli stuffed with crab meat. Not that she has ever been a gourmet, but she had really liked this whenever it was she ate it the first time; it must have been good because it had obviously lodged in her brain.

'I should have known,' he says with a smug grin. 'Always your favourite, wasn't it?' he guesses wrongly. 'No change there,' he adds proudly. He probably doesn't even know the difference.

She doesn't answer and takes her notebook and an A4 sized exercise book out of her battered rucksack.

They order briskly when the waiter arrives, a tall skinny young man with an Italian accent and studied jollity, who notices quickly that this is not a couple on a romantic date. He disappears as fast as is seemly.

'How far did you get?' is Bex's opening question.

'I don't know. I have noticed a few things; a few discrepancies; questions that should have been asked before now; some idiosyncrasies.'

'And what are you going to do about them?'

'Do you want me to do anything about them?'

'Of course, I do.' Bex sounds aghast. 'What do you think this is all about?'

She remains silent, so he continues: 'It's not because I wanted to see you again, Ant, if that's what you are afraid of.'

She feels a rush of blood to her head, turning her pale face the colour of beetroot. Great, she thinks and feels like stuffing her notebooks into her rucksack and leaving the restaurant.

'Sorry, Ant,' he says immediately with contrition. 'At least, it's out of the way now. I just want us to work this out together and make it a success - like we always did.'

She is partially placated, but still stunned: 'So do I,' she says in a whisper.

'So, tell me! What have you found?''

'Let's start with what we know - from the wedding of Lucinda Sheridan and Piers Turner to Lucinda's disappearance: it was almost a high-society wedding; plenty of money on both sides; the couple seemed eminently suited to each other, very happy; the honeymoon was long, exotic, a cruise around the world in six months with longer stays in places they wanted to explore, and a couple of flights at the end of the cruise to places they had missed out on, including an idyllic week on the beaches of Bali.'

'No reports of misunderstandings or rows?' Bex interjects.

'None at all; at least not before witnesses – fellow travellers, the travel agent and the accompanying tour guide. They came back, someone said, arms wrapped around each other and smiling from ear to ear.'

'And then?'

'They settled in their new country house for good; an old farmhouse which a team of local builders and craftsmen renovated under the supervision of an architect, while the happy couple toured the world.'

'Were they finished by the time Lucinda and Piers came back?'

'Oh yes. As far as I understand, they were under contract and would lose money daily if they hadn't.'

Grudge? Bex writes down in his notebook under the headline: *Motives.*

'And what happened after their return?'

'I had lost contact with Lucinda by then, basically waiting for her to contact me when she wanted to, but I never heard. There is nothing out of the ordinary in the witness statements for that time – friends, family, acquaintances; people from the village near where they lived.

They seemed to have settled down, him attending to his business activities, but spending a lot of time at home with Lucinda, too.'

'Lucinda didn't go back to work?'

'No. She had told me at the wedding that she would probably find it hard to keep away, but she didn't return; at least not in the months after their honeymoon. She had made enquiries at the local police station whether she could be of any use there, but nothing came of it.'

Conflict: victim returning to work? Bex writes down.

Ant reads it upside down: 'You can't call her a victim,' she points out. 'As far as we are concerned, she is still a missing person.' Bex crosses out the word *victim* and makes the correction.

'There are no indications of disagreements between the couple,' Ant continues. To the outside world they were as happy as Larry. Lucinda seemed to have found enough to occupy herself in her new home and garden, and she had also taken up painting, taking private lessons once a month.'

Bex raises his eyebrows, but Ant shakes her head: 'No chance. The artist is in his early eighties.'

'What's his name?'

'Carolus Simmner.'

'Okay. What about other witnesses?'

'They were a motley crew: several old university friends; a couple of colleagues from work; her family, particularly a younger brother she was very close to; a girl-friend…'

Bex looks up, so she hastens to add: '…not me, in case you wonder…' Bex goes back to making notes while Ant continues: There were statements from the local butcher, baker, greengrocer, actually from most people in the village in the vicinity of the farmhouse. Everybody seemed to love her. She also made quite a splash involving herself in local governance - speak parish council - and various clubs. She got especially involved in the gardening club and a little amateur dramatics group.'

Bex looks up with concern.

'I know,' Ant says. 'It will take us ages…'

'If not years…' Bex groans dramatically.

'Don't overdo it!' she says drily.

'We haven't got years,' he states the obvious.

'Correction, you haven't got years,' she states mercilessly.

'To the end of April,' he whispers as if speaking to himself.

'Well, that's a couple of weeks longer than you said the first time round,' she says, suddenly cheerful. 'We have to get our skates on, that's all. Let's find her!'

Bex nods. 'So, what's happening now?'

'First the scene where she was last seen: her home.'

'You mean I should go there?' he looks dubious and adds: 'Will you come?'

'…to hold your hand? Of course, I will. I have it already arranged with …'

'Let me guess: Felix?'

'Your memory is still intact, I see,' she mocks, and he can't help but laugh. 'Next Thursday; the battle begins!'

Bex looks a lot more cheerful than when she first saw him sitting there, peering at the menu.

The meals arrive, but neither is hungry anymore. They eat a bit. The waiter despairs: not one glass of wine to wash it down, only tap water for them. They have to drive back in opposite directions.

CHAPTER TEN

'Ready?' Bex asks over the phone on Sunday evening

'Why are you asking?'

'You might have got cold feet.'

'You should know me better than that!'

Silence while they both ponder that thought.

'Have you obtained a warrant for the farmhouse?' Ant asks finally.

'No, I thought we first pay the grieving husband a friendly visit…'

'…and ask him whether we may have a look around,' she finishes. 'That's what I will come for.'

'Yes, I know.'

'Otherwise, there is no point in me driving all the way up to the Cotswolds and accompanying you,' she drives the point home.

'Message received!'

They meet outside the ornate wrought iron gate to the Turners' farmhouse. It is one of those places which used to be a working farm, but has been brought up to city standards by people who want a greener and quieter life, but still need their comforts and proximity to London.

'You made it,' Bex welcomes her with a big smile.

'To work, Bex,' she admonishes him, 'and well done!' He looks baffled.

'You might have gone to Pusey in Oxfordshire,' she grimaces at him and opens the gate: 'We'll leave the cars here, shall we?' When Bex doesn't reply, she adds: 'I like to walk into places to get a feel.'

He shrugs his shoulders and begins to walk. It's an enormously long lane framed by a line of Lime trees, leading up to the house. They can spot between the trees a view of seemingly endless fields with a flock of sheep grazing. The air is crisp, but the milky sun is brightening and warming the land. It takes them a good fifteen minutes until they reach the house. There is a big brass knocker on the door; Bex lets it fall heavily three times onto the old oak door. It makes a satisfyingly booming sound. They wait.

Ant looks at Bex, but he only shrugs his shoulders and says: 'I have told him that we are coming.' Ant turns round and soaks up the beautiful view a moment longer. Finally they hear footsteps coming closer on the inside.

'So sorry,' Piers Turner chuckles apologetically: 'I had to lock the dog into the kitchen, and he wasn't going to have it.' They recognise the tall, almost lanky figure with the short, thinning hair and grey eyes behind a pair of tortoiseshell-rimmed glasses.

Bex introduces Ant by her surname.

They stand in a long and wide hall furnished with an umbrella stand, a hall table with a white telephone, a mirror; flagstones on the floor and huge portraits on the walls.

'All Lucinda's folks,' Piers comments when he notices Ant's gaze resting on one. She nods and smiles with appreciation. It is a naturally dark place, but an enormous chandelier, which is lit in spite of it being the middle of the day, throws its bright lights into the space.

'Beautiful location,' Bex says to Piers, to break the ice.

'Yes, we never tire of it, never take it for granted. We are very lucky!' They notice his use of the present tense.

The refurbishment must have cost a bomb, Ant thinks, but is interrupted by Piers, who seems to have read her mind: 'We couldn't afford to buy this. Luckily it was in Lucinda's family for almost a hundred years. It was the family's wedding present to us.' Bex and Ant both produce an appreciative smile, as if this was a normal thing to give.

Piers Turner opens the first door on the left to lead them into a vast sitting room. A hundred years ago, this would have been two, if not three, rooms. Now it is lavishly furnished with antique mahogany furniture and sumptuous two and three-seater sofas. Lucinda probably had the pick of the best furniture from her new husband's bespoke carpentry business. The carpet flooring is new, thick and looking as if burgundy, black and ivory threads were woven into plaits. The colour burgundy is repeated above the oak panelling which reaches three quarters up the walls

'Very nice,' Ant murmurs.

Piers doesn't move a muscle. 'It doesn't feel like home any more now that she is not here,' He says eventually.

'Do you mind?' Ant checks with Piers before picking up a framed photograph of him and Lucinda on honeymoon, beaming with happiness, the Taj Mahal, the symbol of the greatest love story ever, in the background. Ant puts it back in its place on the mantle shelf. The room has something of an exotic flavour all through. There are tassels in various primary colours, fastened onto a piece of oriental wood and hung on the wall; there is a similar arrangement with little bells. As Ant looks around her, she is dazzled by a colourful array of artefacts: a mask from the carnival in the Dominican Republic, several African giraffe and elephant statues and souvenirs of visits to American Indian reservations. Piers is very happy to explain and say a word or two about each of them.

'Lucinda wouldn't miss any of the Indian reservations if they were reasonably close to our itinerary. You should see our bed: full of dream catchers and crocheted dolls.'

One framed photograph shows the sandy-coloured ancient *City in the* Sky, home of the Acoma Indians in today's New Mexico, three thousand feet up. It takes Ant's breath away, as if she could experience the thin air under the cobalt blue sky.

'We also brought back a *Srai Wi* Indian carpet –to go with our dining room furniture; rather geometrical squares and straight lines in ivory, black and red.' He smiles wistfully to himself. 'Whenever I look at all these things, we have lovingly chosen together, I feel such pain. ...' he pauses. 'At the same time, they sustain me, too, until she returns.'

'Are you sure she will return?' Ant asks out of the blue, observing his reaction.

Piers shakes himself a little, as if he can't let go of a pleasant dream: 'That's all I live for,' he says with desperation in his voice. 'Why should she not? She had no enemies; no worries. We lived the life of Riley; we had no money troubles; we loved each other, had friends, a few hobbies and our whole lives ahead of us!' Now he really looks as if he is bursting into tears, but he recovers and pulls himself together.

'After almost two years, it is likely that she has come to harm or, if she is still alive, that she doesn't want to come home.' Bex reminds him.

Piers ponders that last remark.

'Would you mind, if we had a look round in the rest of the house?' Ant asks. 'There were a few question marks in the previous forensic report.'

'By all means, Miss Bell: anything to help, anything to find Lucinda!' He is adamant about that. 'I'll be in my study, just along the corridor.'

'He didn't even ask whether we have a warrant,' Ant whispers to Bex.

'It's our lucky day.' Ant is already climbing up the stairs and doesn't hear him. She finds the American Indian dolls sitting in a neat row along the headrest of the king-size bed. Not something, she would have suspected Lucinda of buying, but there you go: you never know people totally. The bedroom is pristine, as if no one has slept in it for ages. So are the guest rooms. He probably has a cleaner to keep it all the way he wants it. There were still various bottles of perfume in the luxurious bathroom, rows of different bath oils and shampoos on a bronze tray across the lion-clawed bathtub and a holder on the rim for a glass of whatever the bather fancied. Piers has left everything, as if his wife is going to return from a shopping trip any moment.

'Finished?' Ant asks when she meets Bex in the downstairs corridor after searching for a good half an hour.

'More or less,' he answers, 'we don't want to outstay our welcome on the first visit.'

'No,' says Ant laconically.

They knock on Piers Turner's study door.

'All done?' he asks. Bex and Ant nod in unison.

'Your colleagues were very thorough the first time round,' he states without rancour. 'I understand that it has to be done. Let me know when you need to come back,' he offers.

'Thank you for being so understanding. It can't be easy!'

He looks suddenly tired and older than his years. Ant knows from the documents that he is fifty-five.

The heavy oak door falls into its lock behind them, and once more they admire the idyllic scene, a mixture of beautiful landscape, peaceful silence apart from bird song and the occasional baaing of a sheep... Such a pity!

'Lots of out-houses, too,' Ant remarks, pointing to the left of the main house.

'Yes, a very nice property,' Bex comments.

Bex and Ant walk silently along the winding drive back to their cars outside the estate's gate.

'I'll send you a report,' she promises.

'With the horse-drawn mail coach?' he quips.

'No, by e-mail, you dinosaur.' He hasn't seen her so relaxed, well... for years.

'Now to the witnesses,' he ventures. 'Are you available on Monday?'

'I'll have to give you a call.'

The sun is slowly going down, colouring the horizon behind her in a yellow-red satin light. If she steps on the accelerator, she will be home with the Girls in about two and a half hours. Felix will have done his bit, but they will need to have their good-night cuddle.

CHAPTER ELEVEN

'So sorry, Ant,' Bex sounds rushed off his feet when he calls.

Ant nibbles at her lower lip as always when she wants time to think what to do next.

'It doesn't matter,' she says ultimately.

'Yes, it does. We haven't got time to lose. Would you be willing to have someone else coming along with you to speak to the witnesses again?'

'You mean a DS?'

'Yes, just for your protection…'

'As a second pair of eyes and ears, you mean?'

'Yeah, for general support. You know the drill.'

'So it's still going ahead? I am still visiting Lucinda's family home in Hertfordshire?'

'Yes, somewhere around Beaconsfield.' Bex sounds tired and exasperated, and doesn't notice the pun.

'Ooooh,' her voice glides from low to high with irony and feels immediately embarrassed: 'Sorry about that. That was childish'

'Yeah, I know, one of the wealthiest areas in the country.'

'Easy to get to, I imagine.'

'Yes, it's straight forward. So can I tell the sergeant to meet you there?'

'Have you got somebody in mind?'

'It will probably be someone you don't know. Most of the old team have left.'

'You make me sound like an old woman, Cheeky. But to be honest, whoever you choose will be fine.'

He is a nice young officer with a friendly face, good manners, some initiative and a talent for discretion, which, Bex knows, Ant will like.

When the detective sergeant rings her Sunday evening to find out where they would meet up, she asks him to pick her up from Beaconsfield's train station. She fancies another train ride rather than the stress of travelling by car. Anyway, there is hardly any difference in travelling time. You have become a country bumpkin, she tells herself, not frightened of local narrow country lanes, which harbour dangers of their own, but hating the rat-race on motorways and A- roads.

In the event, she has no choice: The train journey would be too complicated, leading her via Bristol, London and back with the Chiltern Railways. It will have to be the car. She is lucky, setting off very early and hitting the motorway before it clogs up with the morning rush hour traffic.

DS Weymouth is already there, waiting for her the wrong way round, staring at the outside of Beaconsfield station. He flinches when she hoots and looks relieved when she waives to him. There is something pleasant about him which gives her hope for the day.

'Morning, Ma'am. Pleasant journey?'

'Not what I had in mind, but not bad either.' She explains why she didn't come by train after all.

'In that case, I could have picked you up from somewhere along the line, Ma'am,' he comments, and she isn't quite sure whether he is joking. What an absurd suggestion, she thinks, until she sees his grin.

'Quite,' she agrees and adds: 'I am not a Ma'am, Weymouth. To you and most of your colleagues, I am Ant.'

'I know,' he says simply. 'In that case, I am Zac.'

'Nice to meet you, Zac!'

They decide to take one car, his, to the family homestead of Lucinda Turner, née Sheridan and drive through the historic High Street with its Neo-Tudor and Georgian façades to get to the other side of the town. Everywhere they look, speaks of wealth.

'Lovely area,' she hears DS Weymouth comment.

'Yes, a honeypot for celebrities. It's conveniently close to London, and yet in the countryside.'

'A bit like the Cotswolds then?'

'Yes, I imagine so, just closer to the capital.'

There is no gate, just an entrance with a sign directing them to Sheridan Hall. DS Weymouth can't help a whistle when they roll along an impressive drive through hedgerows and fields and draw up at a large country house. It isn't in any way historic, built around the 1930s for fun and entertainment. Lucky Lucinda - growing up in a gorgeous place like this!

They walk up several half-moon shaped steps and knock on the white painted door. No response.

DS Weymouth discovers a pull to a bell, and is just about to use it, when the door opens. Ant almost faints with shock as she stands opposite a slightly older version of Lucinda. The similarity is uncanny. This must be Lucinda's mother! Ant had hardly caught a glimpse of her at the wedding, or maybe she had been so tired that she didn't notice things like that.

'Mrs. Sheridan?' Ant asks, knowing the answer full well.

'Lucinda and I look very alike, don't we?' she smiles 'and you are Miss Bell?'

'Yes, and this is DS Weymouth from the Wiltshire Police Force in Devizes,' she adds in case Mrs Sheridan is not familiar with police officers' ranks. Many people get muddled; most don't care.

'Do come in,' Mrs Sheridan invites them 'it is quite nippy today. My husband is waiting in the drawing room.'

'Edward Sheridan,' the man in his early seventies gets up from the settee by the open fire and extends a hand in greeting. They take turns in shaking it. He is slightly shorter and more rotund than his wife, almost bald safe for a neatly trimmed ring of grey hair above his neck, and piercing blue eyes.

'Barbara, would you mind bringing some tea and a coffee for me?' he asks his wife who has just sat down.

'Of course,' she replies swiftly, smiles and disappears, although Ant is about to say, that tea isn't necessary: 'We don't intend to keep you long,' she assures Mr Sheridan, but he shakes his head: 'I am parched anyway,' he explains; I was shooting all morning.'

Ant and Zac don't know how to respond and remain quiet.

'So, the Wiltshire team are reviving the case? Having one more go?' Edward Sheridan states with a questioning inflection, while stuffing tobacco into his pipe.

'Yes, Mr Sheridan. We all feel terrible that we haven't found Lucinda…'

'Alive or dead, you mean?' He lights his pipe with a match. 'You don't mind, do you,' he asks belatedly, taking his pipe out of his mouth. It is a rhetorical question, not really deserving an answer.

'…alive, we hope, Mr Sheridan,' Ant says eventually.

'So, how can I help?'

'Well, we hope very much to go over the details with you and your wife once more, to make sure, we haven't overlooked anything. Sometimes people do suddenly remember tiny details which turn out to be invaluable for the investigation.'

Mrs Sheridan returns with a tea tray, puts it down on a sideboard, pours tea into porcelain cups, asks about milk and sugar – milk and three sugars for Ant; milk and two sugars for the DS; and a coffee for Mr Sheridan – and hands a plate of biscuits around, before sitting down in the same winged green armchair, she had sprung up from.

'No tea for you, dear?' her husband remarks while tipping a measure of brandy into his coffee from a flat, silver flask which he had pulled from his jacket pocket

'No, I had one before you came in.' She produces the same, slightly haughty smile Lucinda could produce stopping people mid-sentence.

'They want us to go over everything again,' says her husband with a sigh.

'Of course, we are all trying to find our daughter.'

'Tell me a little about Lucinda growing up here, Mrs Sheridan,' Ant launches into her opening gambit. 'Was she a single child?'

'Oh no,' laughs Mrs Sheridan, 'we had four boys and a girl for daddy.' It sounds ironic, almost sarcastic.

'And was she daddy's girl?'

Edward Sheridan's laugh sounds like a bitter bellow: 'No, she was a tomboy; prickly; always with her brothers, giving them ideas, egging them on, leading them astray.'

'Oh, come on, darling. It wasn't that bad. The boys were as imaginative,' and then, turning to Ant, as if speaking to another mother who would understand: 'They were so fortunate to grow up here, so nobody else knew about the mischief they caused, the scrapes they got into.' She laughs delightedly as if she had always enjoyed her children's misdeeds.'

'Is it correct that they were called Leo, Alfred, and Sebastian and ...who else?'

'Robert,' Mrs Sheridan fills in the gap. 'Robert wasn't always included because he had asthma since childhood, so he couldn't take part in most of the wild games they indulged in.'

'Did they go to school in Beaconsfield?'

'No, after the local prep the boys went to Wellington. Lucinda stayed on for a while at the local grammar, but when Marlborough became co-educational, she chose to go there,' says Mr Sheridan. 'After that, they all went to university, the boys to Oxford and Lucinda to Cambridge. She didn't want to be chaperoned by her brothers.'

'What did they study? And what are they doing now?'

'Let me see…,' says Mr Sheridan, a second before his wife takes over, counting their off-spring proudly on her fingers: 'Leo studied finance and became an accountant - he is now in New York; Alfred – we call him Freddy - studied architecture and builds churches, Sebastian studied geography and runs an antiques' shop in the High Street, and Robert studied foreign languages and works with our gardeners. He is particularly interested in growing vegetables and herbs, and he is very good with our animals, too.'

'What sort of animals do you have?'

Edward Sheridan butts in: '…the usual menagerie for a country house: horses, dogs, a couple of cats, that sort of thing,'

'Do you keep the dogs outside?'

'Oh yes! They are working dogs', he explains, 'and the horses are all hunters. I had race horses in my youth, but they are long gone.'

'Did Lucinda like animals?' Ant wants to know. She had never heard Lucinda talking lovingly about a cat or a dog nor any other animal.

'Not particularly. As I said, they weren't pets.'

'And Lucinda went to Cambridge?' DS Weymouth changes the topic.

'Yes. She first began a course in English literature, but got soon bored with it and came suddenly up with Anthropological Forensic Science,' Lucinda's father doesn't sound enamoured with her choice. 'Later she swapped it for pathology. Quite a mouthful…and for some reason, she took a job with the police force in Yorkshire. She did very well, so I am told.' It sounds more like a complaint than praise.

'Yes, she was…hmmm…is… an excellent pathologist,' Ant confirms, 'I met her first when she was seconded to help us with one of our case.'

'Oh was she?' Her mother sounds surprised and gratified. 'That's nice of you to say. When the children grow up, they never tell you quite the truth, do they?' Mrs Sheridan looks suddenly lonely and bereft.

'So when did you see your daughter last?'

'After her wedding, wasn't it dear?' Mrs Sheridan volunteers, looking at her husband for approval, 'the next morning we saw her off on her honeymoon; and when they returned about six months later, we had them here for their first Christmas together. The entire family came.'

'So you did see her for a couple of days then?'

'You know, what it's like when everybody is milling around. You haven't got time to speak to anybody properly…'

'How did Lucinda and Piers strike you as a couple?'

'Very happy! He is such a nice man. He adores her. He worships the ground she walks on...' Barbara Sheridan gushes.

'Yes, Barbara, we get the picture,' interrupts her husband. His pipe has gone out, and he doesn't seem quite so fond of his son-in-law. 'I still don't quite know where his money comes from.'

'He just inherited a lot, dear, like our children will, and he runs this exclusive furniture company. He is very good with wood. He knows all about the different kinds and their characteristics.' Mrs Sheridan won't have her son-in-law's name besmirched.

'How was he with your daughter?'

'Quite loving, quite demonstrative; it was a relationship among equals, you know: modern, consensus thinking.' She shoots an accusing glance at her husband.

Mr Sheridan shrugs his shoulders: 'I never quite warmed to him, but then I am not the one who has to live with him.'

'That's totally unfair. You don't warm to lots of people, dear; particularly when they refuse to go hunting and shooting with you.' Mrs Sheridan is clearly outraged.

'So, did Lucinda stay in touch with you during the honeymoon, during that first year of marriage?' Ant interjects quickly.

'We didn't really expect anything while they were away – we are not very good with these new things called mobile phones- but we saw their photographs that Christmas. Wonderful: a life-time's dream!' Mrs Sheridan glances at her husband again, as if to say that she had nurtured that dream for years, too.

'...and after that?'

'Well, they moved away and threw themselves into village life in Pewsey. Of course, they had also quite a bit of renovation to do, which kept them busy.'

'Were they practical?'

'Oh no, I meant to say that they were supervising it,' Mrs Sheridan corrects herself.

'And most of the renovations were done anyway while they were gallivanting around the world. It was Alfred, our son, who did the planning and supervising, adds Mr Sheridan pointedly.'

'I understand that the farm was your wedding present,' Ant says.

Embarrassed silence ensues until Mr Sheridan replies with a bitter chuckle: 'Quite. Sore point, that!'

'That's not fair!' Mrs Sheridan protests, but falls immediately back into silence and her armchair.

'So you didn't see Lucinda between Christmas 2013 and her disappearance?'

'She popped in once or twice, but only for half an hour,' Mr Sheridan volunteers.

'…and she did send us birthday and Christmas cards, and presents,' says the ever apologetic Mrs Sheridan. 'It is perfectly understandable that a young married couple wants to spend high-days alone in their own home.' She is adamant.

'Have you seen Piers Turner since Lucinda disappeared?' DS Weymouth wants to know.

'Not here. A couple of times we passed each other in the corridors of the police station, after her disappearance. I think he blames us somehow.'

'Why would he do that?'

Barbara Sheridan sends her husband a warning look: 'Rubbish!' she says, 'he just wants her back, like we all do. It is very laudable that he is not giving up. After all, it was him, wanting the case reopened, wasn't it?'

'Anything else?' asks Mr Sheridan brusquely. He obviously wants to bring the interview to a close.

'I think we have covered most of it,' says Ant to his relief. 'Would you mind, if I rang you, should I think of something else? And you can ring me any time, should you want to add something to your statements. I am working mainly from home nowadays, freelance, so just leave a message, if I am out; I shall ring you back as soon as I get in.

Ant hands over her card, she usually uses for farm business.

'Would you like to see the house quickly before you go?' asks Mrs Sheridan eager that they leave with a good impression.

They accept gratefully and make all the right noises to please their hostess as they are taken on a tour of a glamorous party mansion form the Charleston days.

'Twenty-five bedrooms,' Ant giggles as she and DS Weymouth walk back to the car. 'I don't even make my one bed every day; I would give up with twenty-five.'

'It's nice when you have lots of visitors,' comments DS Weymouth. He obviously picked up on something as well: a gulf between the grandeur of the house, and the loneliness of the two people in it. Interesting that he should do so.

'What did you think?' Ant, sitting in the passenger seat, probes further. DS Weymouth is giving Ant a lift back to the station and her car.

'To tell you the truth, I think they are two lonely people in a big house.' Same vibes I picked up, Ant thinks.

'Some of their children live nearby, at least the one with the antiques' shop.'

'It felt, as if our visit was a big event for them,' Ant muses, 'a big break in their dreary routine. As if they had nothing in common and nothing much to live for…'

'Their daughter might be dead,' remarks the DS.

'I hope you are wrong, but thank you so much for coming out all this way, Zac.'

'I didn't do very much,' he smiles wistfully.

'You were excellent moral support. I am a bit rusty, and you being there was reassuring and useful.'

Ant can see her car in the station car park.

'You are welcome, Ant. Any time!' he says. 'Get home safely.'

They don't bother driving through the picturesque High Street again, but headed straight for their motorway home, Ant for the M3, the DS back to London on the M4.

CHAPTER TWELVE

Ant informs Bex that she will return to Beaconsfield.

'Can't it wait?' Bex is still busy with a new case and his colleagues don't seem to be as attracted to Lucinda's cold case as he is.

'Send Zac! He is good.'

'Oh, it's Zac already, is it?' he teases her. She decides to ignore it.

'Look, I am going up there on Thursday. Send him if you can.'

'Otherwise you go alone? It's against…'

'I know. I shall just have to be a tourist.'

Zac can't come either, so it is just her and the tape recorder on the phone as a memory aid.

Ant parks in the station car park, which is almost full by the time she arrives.

She pays, locks up the car and heads for the High Street. She walks up on the right side and back on the left, looking for an antiques' dealer. She can't find it. Eventually she buys a paper in the newsagent's and asks. A pinched faced man thinks for a moment and then directs her to an alleyway off the High Street. She crosses the road and finds it immediately. She had overlooked the small dwelling at the end of it, the first time she passed. It is a dingy passage leading up to it - unlit and smelly –

a far cry from her last visit to the glamorous family home. You wouldn't think it's the same family. When she reaches the shop, it looks shut. She hasn't announced her visit. She discovers a small notice, stuck to the inside of the glass, just above the door handle, which asks customers to ring the bell on the house next door for attention. Ant does so. She might have to come clean about the purpose of her visit sooner than she wants to. Sher rings the bell again. Somebody seems to tumble down the stairs, and then she hears a rasping voice: 'Hold on, I'm coming!'

When the door opens, she faces a short man, barely taller than herself, bloated, looking older than his 36 years, as she has read in the police files. His clothes are unfashionable, ill-fitting and un-ironed; his expensive looking brogues are scuffed and his brown hair unwashed. He looks as if he is cutting it himself, and not very successfully: bits of it stand away from his head, while other strains fall greasily into his forehead. An uncertain smile reveals crooked, yellow stained teeth.

'Sebastian Sheridan?' Ant asks. Like the dwelling, he certainly doesn't look as if he is part of the same family.

'Yes, that's me.' He seems to be surprised himself.

'I am Antonia Bell, a friend of your sister Lucinda.'

'Ah yes. Poor old thing!' he says regretfully. After clearing his throat several times, his voice is deep and sonorous, and astonishingly attractive.

'I have also been a colleague of hers.'

'I thought that was all wrapped up?' He seems surprised. The news of Ant's visit to his parents doesn't seem to have filtered through to the High Street yet.

'Yes it was, but we can't really leave it as it is. She still hasn't been found.'

'No,' he says slowly and slightly confused. 'How can I help? I have said everything I know.'

'Can I come in and ask you a few questions?'

'Of course, do enter my humble abode, Miss Bell.'

'I am not keeping you from your business?' she asks innocently. 'I can come back another day.'

'No, no. My customers know where to find me. I don't open until the afternoon.'

'Excellent,' Ant smiles gratefully and follows him. A door on the ground floor on the left is half open; it looks like chaos behind it: newspapers, paperwork, crisp packets and chocolate wrappers on a stained carpet, a table crowded with things, hardly leaving any free space, a grimy window framed by heavy velvet curtains in a regal green, like remnants from the big house, bottles everywhere.

'Excuse the mess,' Sebastian murmurs as they pass. She follows him upstairs to his study, as he calls it. It is not quite so untidy, but far from orderly. I wonder what Lucinda made of this brother, Ant thinks; she is the total opposite of him. He takes the cat off a cushion on the chair, Ant is supposed to sit on, and puts it on his desk; it can't make any more mess than there is already.

'Off you go, Tiddles,' but the cat has its own agenda and settles on top of an overflowing laundry basket in front of a small unlit open fire grate.

'You were at the wedding?' he asks. 'I think I remember you.'

Ant thinks back with shame at her tidy trousers and buttoned-up blouse, and nods.

'Thought so! What do you want to know?'

'What was your relationship with your sister like?'

'Pretty good, I should think.' He pauses. 'She and I got on well. We both have the same sense of humour; important that, but not always appreciated. To tell you the truth, we both wanted to get out from under our parents' feet. I went to university, but didn't enjoy it, and Lucinda backed me up when I wanted to leave. My parents were furious, but she was enormously supportive.' He sighs, and adds: 'I miss her! Nobody is on my side now.'

Ant gives him time to collect himself, before she continues: 'How often did you see your sister after the wedding?'

'Not a lot. She popped in to give me a hug when she visited Mum... one Christmas and after that...once or twice?'

'You say, *visiting Mum,* surely you mean your father as well?'

'Not really. They had a stand-offish relationship. As a child, she was the only one who would stand up to him, argue with him; something we boys didn't dare. She respected him, but she wouldn't let him walk all over her, like he does with Mother. Later on, he was in awe of her, particularly after she became a police pathologist against his will. A sort of grudging respect, I would say.'

'How did he feel about her husband?'

'You have to ask him that. I keep away from Father as much as possible. But I have a feeling that he thought she had let the side down, that she could have done much better. Well, I could have told him, that Lucinda had always waited for love, not a good financial proposition. She was besotted with Piers, but he rejected Father's hunting and shooting trials which were the family yardstick to determine whether somebody was a decent chap or not. Piers is a stickler for things like orderliness, punctuality, cleanliness, and manners. His only saving grace was that he was wealthy. I think that redeemed him in father's eyes. But it was never a warm relationship between the two. They didn't really make an effort.'

'Yes, your father mentioned that he had never taken to his son-in-law.'

'Who *does* he take to? He isn't one for affectionate relationships.'

'Did Lucinda keep in touch with you apart from the couple of visits?''

'You mean, before she disappeared?'

Ant nods.

'Occasionally, she left a message on my answer phone, just making sure, I was okay. I found that always strange, because she knew the times when I was at home, and when I was in the shop with customers. I didn't like her to ring while I was working, but she seemed to make a point of ringing where she knew, I wouldn't be available - as if avoiding having to speak to me in person. I never got through to her when I phoned back.'

'Would you say that that was out of character?'

'…definitely!'

'Did you communicate with her in any other way before her disappearance?'

'There was one short letter tucked into my birthday card in March that year.'

'What was the exact date?'

'…third of March.'

'And what did she write – apart from birthday greetings?'

'At first I laughed, because she wished me love, luck and a bit more money. And underneath she wrote: Life is so transient. Grab it with both hands while you can!'

'What did you read into that?'

'…nothing much at the time. It just didn't sound like her. I thought, she might have had a bad day; maybe a row with Piers, or some other trouble; not that I knew of any.'

'Did they row a lot?'

'I don't know. I remember once when she sounded tearful over the phone. She said she had misdialled, and that she needed to ring somebody else. When I asked how she was, she said something banal like *Ah, being married is not all it's cracked up to be.* When I asked her whether she needed help, she laughed and said, it was just one of those things, and it would sort itself out.'

'Did you say anything else?'

'You mean, give her advice? No. How could I? I have never been married, and I am certainly no authority on relationships.'

'Did your parents know about that phone call and her troubles?'

'I don't know. I didn't tell them, and I don't think Lucinda would have done.'

'Was that the only time?'

'Yes.' Sebastian begins to fidget: 'Oh, I am a hopeless host. Would you like some tea or coffee or something stronger?'

Ant smiles: 'That's very kind, but no; I must go soon and let you get on with the rest of your day.'

He nods. 'Come to think of it, it really looks as if Lucinda might have wanted to disappear. Is that your line of thinking, Miss Bell?'

'Could be… one of the possibilities. I have no idea at this stage.'

Ant picks up her green rucksack which holds her mobile, purse, driving licence, notebook and pens and says her good-bye.

'Do give me a call, if you remember anything else,' she encourages him and hands him her card.

It's beginning to rain and dusk is throwing its grey mantle over the town. She can't help feeling sorry for Sebastian Sheridan. He seems as forlorn as his parents in his own way. When she reaches her car in the station carpark, she takes out her mobile and notebook and, listening to the recordings, she begins to scribble, pausing occasionally to make sure, she hasn't forgotten anything. It takes her half an hour. She closes the notebook, puts the lid on her pen, threads it into the leather loop of her notebook, and throws both back into her rucksack. Then she switches on the radio: more bad news as usual. She had enough for one day. She puts her favourite Carly Simon compilation album in the slot and begins to sing along, as she drives out of town.

CHAPTER THIRTEEN

Now to the other two brothers, as soon as possible, she thinks on the way home. The accountant, Leo Sheridan, lives and works in New York, so that will have to be a phone call for the time being, and then she has to find the whereabouts of the church architect, Alfred Sheridan. She would leave the vegetable gardener and youngest of the brothers, to last.

She grins. It is astonishing, how ever so slowly, tiny, important titbits come to the forth. She had always believed in patience. Times change, alliances break apart, loyalties end, and suddenly, people come forward with lots more information which sometimes can be turned into evidence. If they only did so at the beginning… Ant sighs.

At midnight, she puts a call through to New York, but Leo Sheridan is in a meeting, and Ant is advised to ring again the following day. On her insistence, the receptionist puts her through to the P.A., who confirms that she has just missed him. They agree that two o'clock GMT on the following day will be convenient for both parties.

'What shall I tell him it is about?' she asks

'It's about his sister,' Ant replies with caution.

'And who shall I say is asking for him?'

'Antonia Bell, CSI.' Ant can hear an excited gasp before putting down the receiver.

Ant gets finally hold of Leo Sheridan the following afternoon at the agreed time.

'I haven't got much time,' he introduces himself, 'and I have told everything I know to the police at the time of Lucinda's disappearance, so I don't know what you expect me to say.' There is a lot of impatience and annoyance in his wispy voice which either indicates that he has a sore throat or he doesn't want anyone else to hear him speak to a crime scene investigator.

'I am sorry to bother you again,' says Ant, 'but your brother-in-law has asked us to re-open the case, and I need to hear your particular side of the story.'

'There isn't one,' he says brusquely. Ant ignores the comment.

'When did you last see your sister?'

'…at her wedding.'

'And did you stay in some form of contact with her after that?'

'No.'

'…why not?'

'We have our separate lives, and I don't like her husband.'

'Why?'

'Just that: I don't like him. Some people just rub you up the wrong way. He does.'

'Did you ever have an argument with him?'

'No. I didn't stay long enough.'

'And how did you get on during the Christmas after Lucinda's return from honeymoon? You all met at your parents' house, I was told.' Ant hears Leo Sheridan splutter and then take a deep breath:

'I was only there for a few hours.'

'You came all the way from America to spend only a few hours with your family?'

'It was a duty call, dull as ever, and I wanted to visit a few friends.'

'Could you e-mail me a list of those friends and their contact details?'

'Why?' he sounds inconvenienced.

'…just to confirm that you were there.' She gives him her e-mail address, and repeats it, insisting that he write it down.

He has no idea where his sister could have gone, but repeats that he wouldn't blame her if she had left her new husband. It sounds like pure hatred. Hatred grows over time, not if you hardly ever see or speak to each other. Ant wonders what has happened between the two men and who or what keeps fuelling this hatred now.

'She hasn't come to you to hide?'

'Of course not!' He is affronted.

'Mr Sheridan, I might have to come back to you, but in the meantime, will you please, contact me if you recall anything of importance; anything that could help me to find your sister?'

He grudgingly agrees, but she hasn't much faith that he will.

Ant rings Bex who hasn't managed to contact the elusive church architect. He seems to lead him a merry dance.

'Keep at it. I need to speak to him,' she urges him. 'He is the one who organised and supervised the renovations of the Turners' mansion.'

'I'll do my best.'

'You can hand it on to Zac, if you are busy,' she suggests, but he isn't keen. Ant laughs. Male pride, she suspects.

'I'll need another day in the archives in Devizes,' she says.

'I'll organise a pass.'

'Thank you, kind Sir,' she teases him.

She is keen to re-examine the exhibits and to read the forensic reports. Maybe that will take her a step closer to the truth; maybe not. It will give her something constructive to do while she is waiting for Bex to get hold of her next interviewee.

CHAPTER FOURTEEN

A few days later, Ant sits in the same reading room at Devizes CID Headquarters pouring over exhibits and their relevant reports. The train journey had been unremarkable, even her departure from the pigs had become unemotional routine. The Girls seem to have taken well to Felix, and he is chuffed every time she asks him to stand in for her. It is remarkable how work takes over and displaces all other responsibilities. It would probably have been the same pulling at heart-strings, had she had a partner and children. She would have been a dreadful wife and mother. Working for the police is never just a job: it is a way of life, like that of doctors, nurses, firefighters, vets and other so-called caring professions: the job always manages to take over one's life, all-consuming, occupying one's thinking every waking hour and often one's dreams as well. Ant has never been good at compartmentalising, and she now admits to herself that she hasn't got any better at it. All or nothing: pigs or Lucinda's case. The only consolation is that it will all be over at the latest by April when the pigs would have her undivided attention again.

Ant goes through the procedure of registering her presence at the reception desk once more – time, name, purpose -, of signing out the exhibits relevant to the Turner case, which are carried for her in one cardboard box to the reading room. There the attending officer checks everything again, makes a note of the date of re-opening the box, time, date, Ant's details and Bex's name as having authorized it. If anything would be found to be amiss at a later date, she would be the first to be questioned and called to explain.

The meagre contents of the box is disappointing, but not unexpected. After all Lucinda had only just gone missing; there was no body to examine and she wasn't even presumed dead at all; everybody was still looking for her. No wonder, the forensic scientist had to be content with taking samples from Lucinda's car and home, with particular emphasis on her bedroom and en-suite bathroom. They examined the carpet fibres, took fingerprints from various locations like the kitchen and her painting studio. That was basically all they could do the first time round.

Ant also finds fingerprints of Piers, the husband, who, it was noted, had been most willing and cooperative in spite of being understandably distraught.

Ant is digging down carefully. This can't be it, can it? Simple routine checks producing no result due to lack of a body. There are two pairs of shoes, one high-heeled, one flat soled, size eight, rather large for a woman. There is more paperwork at the bottom and a mobile phone, Lucinda's. The paperwork consists of lists of phone calls going back a year. A comment on a separate sheet of paper remarks that all calls had been verified and were nothing out of the ordinary: calls to her husband, to her mother, a girlfriend in Yorkshire, to various people in the village, to her bank manager; none to her brothers, except for the messages to Sebastian. All in all, the list was astonishingly normal. Of course, people had speculated that Lucinda might have had a secret lover, however unlikely that sounded to those who knew her and to the protest of her doting husband, but nothing inexplicable or untoward had been recorded on her statements. Lucinda having an extra-marital affair? Of course, not! Everybody had been amazed that she had got married at all.

Right at the bottom of the cardboard box are Lucinda's bank statements. Ant takes a deep breath when she sees the figures in her friend's current account. There are several deposit account statements, too, showing equally enormous amounts; those had remained stagnant for years, fixed to achieve high yields. Ant looks at the current account again: mostly ordinary household bills like electricity, water, rates and shopping bills, all considerably higher than Ant's. There are also some large cash withdrawals, but that is to be expected from a couple who were both brought up in luxury, had embarked on a lavish wedding and honeymoon and had refurbish an entire country home. Ant scrutinises every item carefully for a second time, but she cannot detect anything out of the ordinary.

And then she stops. Something is odd. Ant's stomach lurches and her heart flutters. She tells herself to calm down, to think clearly while she recaps: Lucinda disappeared on the 1st May 2015. So why are there withdrawals from the current account listed after that date… four in all; each in a different northern town; each time a modest, but different amount?

Ant rummages around the box, but there really is nothing more. So where is the bank card?

Ant, absorbed in the mystery, turns the bank statement for the current account in her hand, automatically and unthinkingly, when she discovers at the back a small note attached to the last page, written by a previous investigating police officer. It says: bank card not found in the house or among the possessions of the husband. Mr Turner does not know the security code, and has never been to those northern parts of the country. Has Mrs Turner taken it with her and made the withdrawals?

And more to the point, Ant thinks, wide awake now, why – if so – has she stopped?

CHAPTER FIFTEEN

'Bex, are you sitting down?' Ant can hardly tame her exuberance.

'No, but what have you found. I think I can bear most news without fainting.'

'Did you know that Lucinda used her bank card after she disappeared?'

'Yes,' he says shortly.

Ant is totally deflated: 'Why didn't you tell me?'

'I thought you knew.'

'No, I didn't!' Ant is outraged. 'So why has nobody followed that up?'

'Someone has and reported sightings of a woman, tall with blond hair like Princess Diana, but people only noticed her at the cash machines. And then it stopped anyway.'

'Have you asked yourself why? And why did she bother to take out such piffling amounts?'

Bex remains silent. Finally he volunteers: 'The trail just went cold.'

'That's not good enough!' Ant roars into the receiver and slams it down.

'Typical!' Ant complains to Iolanthe, Agatha and Persephone who look up between mouthfuls of mushy bananas, carrots and swede wedges. It's not out of interest, but in hope of more treats.

'The most important bit, he doesn't tell me.' She is fuming. 'Now I can start all over again and ask everybody about the sightings.' It is not quite that bad, but she has to vent her anger somewhere. Iolanthe's pregnancy is not yet visible, but she has clearly lost interest in Jerome, the boar, who leads a solitary life two fences away, until his assistance is required again. For now, Iolanthe shrieks and grunts at him menacingly whenever he comes into view. 'Now I can sort out a totally different plan of action,' Ant rants, and the Girls, Ant believes for a moment, nod; it is more likely with the effort of chewing, but it is reassuring to have an approving audience.

'So, Lucinda has been sighted at least once. That's a fact. Another fact is that this happened after the first of May 2015, the day of her disappearance. Fact three is that the woman was spotted by strangers, not friends or members of the family displaying the wishful thinking syndrome. Four: The woman they saw looked like Lucinda, blond, short hair, tall. That's probably why they noticed and remembered her. Lucinda cuts an imposing figure. Though, at the last sighting, the witness thought that Lucinda had brown hair, but she could have been easily mistaken or Lucinda might have dyed her hair by then for whatever reason. Maybe she wanted to disguise her identity to avoid being recognised or she had just fancied a change. Those would have to be one of the first statements to be verified. Next: why would Lucinda, if she did want to disappear, leave a trail of withdrawals all around the north of England, if she could have simply gone to one branch of her bank and emptied one of her bulging bank accounts? Odd that! Lucinda was an intelligent woman and a trained scientist. Would she really have left behind such a flimsy, obvious trail?'

Ant looks at the Girls. They have now moved away from her to forage further up the hill. She hadn't noticed.

Why would Lucinda do this? Was it to teach her husband or her family and friends a lesson; to play a joke on whomever? Wanting to be found eventually? Ant shakes her head. All of these speculations sound unreal, uncharacteristic and implausible. She only knows Lucinda to be logical, sensible, reasonable, far from playful, manipulative and hurtful; she wouldn't put her new husband and her family through such pain and uncertainty. Or would she? People change. Do we ever know a person one hundred percent? Had Lucinda changed during her short marriage? And if so, why?

Ant sighs. She will have to go and speak to these witnesses up north. Just to check; to make sure nothing has been overlooked.

'Sorry, Girls,' she mumbles, as she traipses down the slippery hill, 'I shall have to leave you for a few days in Felix's capable hands again.

The sightings of Lucinda at cash-machines had been in Harrogate, Hull, Birmingham and Carlisle. Ant decides that she would like to follow the trail back to front. She is intrigued by the notion that someone saw Lucinda or a lookalike with brown hair. The witness was a woman. Ant has written down the name and contact details: Miss Alice Smith, 73 Kent Road, Harrogate; her telephone number and an e-mail address; a history teacher at the distinguished private Harrogate Ladies College for girls. Ant hopes that this Miss Smith is as level-headed as her statement looks on paper.

'Bex,' Ant announces on the phone, 'I am going up north to follow the trail of sightings.'

'…when?' Bex sounds distracted.

'…as soon as possible.' Ant narrows her eyes: she hates it when people don't listen properly.

'Ant, are you at all aware that it's nearly Christmas?' and after a pause he adds with sarcasm: 'don't you want to spend it with your pigs?'

Hmm, she really has forgotten about Christmas. Obviously, she won't bother anybody on Christmas Day, but why not go straight away. There is still a full working week left?

'People will be busy buying presents, food, preparing for family visits. Don't tell me you never do these things?'

I did; once, actually, she thinks. He should remember, but of course, he doesn't.

'All right; thanks for the reminder,' she says with a few barbs amongst her words. 'I shall see what I can do before the festivities begin.'

It doesn't deter her from ringing the witnesses, and to her surprise, she manages to get hold of Miss Smith, and the other three: Mrs Brown in Hull, Mr Mc Naughton in Carlisle and Mr Miller in Birmingham. They don't mind at all having some distractions from hectic Christmas preparations.

However, she has to rejig her plans and begin in Birmingham.

She sets off on the Monday. Christmas will begin at the weekend. The train journey is pleasant and short, two hours to Birmingham. Mr Miller will meet her at Birmingham New Street Station after work. He is a tall, athletic man in his thirties, of possibly West Indian origins. His smile is dazzling; his black, curly hair is shaven closely to his head. He is wearing a well-tailored business suit and silver cufflinks, which are peeping out of his jacket sleeves. He makes Ant feel slightly frumpy in her jeans and hooded anorak. They decide to go to a nearby café which offers a quiet corner. Ant is famished and orders a BLT-sandwich whilst Mr Miller restricts himself to an Americano. As he picks up his coffee, she notices his long, slender fingers like those of a pianist.

'Have you lived here long?' Ant drags herself away from her physical observations and opens the questioning.

'I was born and brought up in Birmingham, then studied at Sheffield, and when I saw a good job offer here just before I graduated, I took it and returned. I haven't moved around much, you could say.'

'There is something to be said for loyalty,' Ant suggests; then she comes straight to the next point: 'Tell me about your meeting with Lucinda Sheridan, the person we are looking for.'

'It wasn't so much of a meeting, more of a bumping into each other,' Leroy Miller explains with a chuckle tinged with embarrassment: 'It was a Wednesday during lunchtime. I wanted to go out that evening, so I went to the nearest cashpoint to withdraw some money. I must have stood too close because, when the lady, who was there before me, turned round all of a sudden, we bumped into each other. She was quite tall and, I thought at the time, quite athletic to give me such a jolt. Of course, I apologised profusely, she only gave me a wintery smile without saying a word, and then she left.'

'Where was that exactly?'

'Outside Lloyds Bank, in Bordesley Green, not far from the Bullring. My work is only a five minutes' walk from there.'

'Do you remember anything else - her hair, her clothes? Did she have a handbag, an umbrella?'

'She had definitely thick, blond hair, cut short, with a fringe. I didn't really look into her eyes, so no idea what colour they were. Her clothes? No handbag as far as I can remember and no umbrella. She wore an old-fashioned raincoat, beige with leather buttons. It looked a bit incongruous as it was boiling hot that day.'

'Had you seen her any time before or after that meeting at the cashpoint?'

'No, never,' replies Mr Miller looking baffled. He shakes his head to emphasize the truth of his statement.

'Can you remember the date?'

He laughs: 'Wednesday, the 13th! Not a good omen, is it?'

Ant presses on: 'Did you see how much money the woman took out - a big bundle of notes or less?'

'I didn't see it when she took it out of the machine, but she dropped two ten pound notes when we collided. I picked them up for her so that they wouldn't be blown into the street.'

'Did you notice anything peculiar, out of the ordinary?'

Not really. As I said, she didn't speak to me, but that's normal when you bump into strangers, I guess.'

Ant is not quite so sure, but it is probably negligible.

'Well, it's very kind of you to speak to me today. You must be very busy so close to Christmas.'

'Yeah,' he laughs. 'I haven't done any shopping yet,'' he admits. 'My mother will kill me, if I don't…' he stops realising that it wasn't an appropriate remark to make in the circumstances.

Ant smiles .No harm done. She shakes his hand and gives him her card with the contact details of her farm.

'Do let me know if you remember anything else. Sometimes, the smallest detail turns out to be the important one.'

'I will,' he promises.

'Would you know of a decent, but inexpensive hotel round here?'

He doesn't, but they ask the waitress in the café, and she does. It's not far, in walking distance. Leroy Miller accompanies Ant to the door, walks on, turns round and gives her a cheerful wave, before he disappears into the crowd. She spends the rest of the afternoon in her hotel room, writing a report about the interview and her impressions, apart from the last comment he made. Around eight, she goes down to have a meal of spaghetti carbonara, salads and a glass of Malbec, her favourite at the moment. She goes to bed early. She needs to catch the 7.15 train in the morning to Carlisle.

CHAPTER SIXTEEN

Ant arrives in Carlisle after an almost three hour journey. Cumbria is a beautiful county, she admits, but the proverbial rain dulls the light and throws a grey veil over the spectacular landscape.

She will meet Jim McNaughton in his office – not far from the station, he had promised. Again, she wishes she had packed something more stylish into her rucksack than a spare blouse and her overnight gear in addition to the jeans, blouse and pullover she is wearing. While she was still working, it really didn't matter what she wore underneath the CSI throw-away garb; now working with pigs, clothes matter even less. Still, there are occasions when nice clothes make you feel better. Jim McNaughton is a solicitor; people in his office are bound to be dressed smartly. Too late!

She strolls from the grade three listed station building past the cathedral towards the office's address in Lowther Street. As she approaches, she notices a branch of Lucinda's bank.

She is ushered straight through by a serious young man in a dark suit and tie. Mr McNaughton's personal office is indeed smart: white walls, a modern wooden desk, a leather swivel-chair in which he sits and a less opulent chair on the opposite side for the clients. It is neat, tidy and minimalist. The only clutter is a bundle of files bound together with string on a low table in a corner. The solicitor gets up and extends a hand in greeting:

'Welcome to Carlisle,' he says and smiles warmly. His blue eyes glint through modern frameless glasses. He looks handsome in spite of being near retirement age, as she has read in the police files. 'How can I help?'

'Do you remember the case of a lady called Lucinda Turner who disappeared on the 1st May 2015?' Ant asks.

'Yes, I remember it well.' Mr McNaughton seems eager to help.

'I know you have been interviewed at the time, after you had reported having seen her. We are reopening the case, and I hope you don't mind, if we go over the same incident once more.'

'Not at all.' he says affably. 'Go ahead,' he nods encouragingly.

'When did you know about the disappearance?'

'…when it was all over the papers and the television news.'

'That would be after her disappearance was reported,' Ant states. 'And when did you see her, Mr Mc Naughton?

'On Wednesday, the 20th May that year at precisely a quarter to four in the afternoon.' Ant likes his precision and waits for more.

'I rushed over to the bank, worried that I might not make it before they close, when I saw this lady struggling with her bank card. So I offered to help her.'

'Was the cash machine on the outside wall or in the lobby of the bank?'

'Outside, that's why passers-bye like me had to walk around her. There must have been other people who noticed her.'

'What did she look like?'

'Tall, slim, blond; short hair with highlights; light tan coloured trench coat; clumpy brown shoes; rather flustered, trembling hands.'

'Did you notice anything remarkable about them?'

'Not really. Maybe slightly bigger, longer than usual, but then she was very tall.'

'Was she wearing glasses?'

'Not that I recall. In fact, I seem to remember her blinking a lot, as if she had something in her eye. Well, it was quite a sunny day.'

'Do you remember the amount she wanted to take out?'

''No, she declined my offer of help, so I waited another minute to see whether she would manage to do it. Then I remembered that I was short of time myself, and rushed into the bank. When I came out, the lady had gone. A few days later, I put two and two together and went to the police.'

'I am sorry, I have to ask this, but it is only a routine question: Did you see that same lady ever before or after that day?'

'No never.' His smile has vanished with the allusion that he might have been involved in some way.

'Sorry,' Ant says again. 'I had to ask.'

'That's quite all right…Anything else?'

'No, I think that covers it. But please, if you can think of anything else, the tiniest detail let me know. Here are my contact details. Leave a message, if I am not in, and I shall ring you back.'

'Okay, I shall do that.' He smiles again: 'Would you like a cup of coffee before you go, Miss Bell?' She shakes her head. 'Or can I invite you for lunch?'

'That's very kind, but I better be off. I have to catch the 13.33 to Hull.'

'Oh, you poor thing!' he exclaims. 'You have to go all the way back to Manchester first.'

'I know. But thank you for the offer.'

They part with smiles and a warm handshake. What a nice man, Ant thinks, and then corrects herself: a very useful witness.

CHAPTER SEVENTEEN

Ant walks back to the locally named Citadel Station. On the way there, she buys a couple of sandwiches, just in case there will be nothing on offer on the trains. It will be a four hour journey with a change at Manchester Piccadilly. Talk about the lack of connectivity in the North! Of course, she could have done all this over the phone, but it wouldn't be the same. She needs to see their faces, their reactions, their gestures, hear the timbre of their voices when they speak to her answering her questions. It's just her way of doing things. Always has been – to Bex's annoyance.

When she sits on the train, she rings Mrs Theresa Brown, who, according to a previous interview, is a retired lady in her mid-seventies.

'Hello, Mrs Brown. It's Antonia Bell here. I am sitting on a train to Manchester, and I should arrive in Hull around half past five. Do you think we could meet tonight instead of tomorrow morning?' I don't mind if you can't,' she adds hastily.

'Oh, Miss Bell, I am so pleased you called. I have a friend coming tomorrow morning unexpectedly who wants to take me shopping. So, I couldn't see you anyway. Tonight would suit me even better.'

'Good.' Ant is relieved; it would have been infuriating to travel all the way to Hull, to turn up at Mrs Brown's doorstep and to find that she had gone out. 'Where shall we meet?'

'Do come to my house, if you don't mind. I do not go out in the evening; it gets dark at four o'clock.'

Ant reads out the address she has for Mrs Brown, to make sure that she has the correct one.

'That's it,' Mrs Brown confirms triumphantly, 'I'll have the kettle on.'

––––––––––

Four hours later, Ant sits in a sitting room that is stuck in the 1950s: doylies on the back of the flower-patterned arm chairs, a standard lamp throwing out a soft, yellow light, a well-worn settee in beige, a sideboard of polished mahogany and a glass cabinet filled with porcelain figurines of children in bucolic meadows. The kettle is already whistling on the gas stove. The ground floor flat is well heated and Ant has to strip off her pullover.

'You must be parched,' concludes Mrs. Brown and insists that Ant first have a cup of tea and a piece of home-made Victoria sponge. Ant is very partial to Victoria sponge and can't resist. When she finally dabs her mouth with a daintily embroidered napkin, Mrs Brown stops bustling and sits down in the other armchair looking expectantly at her.

Ant explains, that Lucinda still hasn't been found nor has she reappeared, and that the detectives in Devizes were hoping that, considering the progress in investigation techniques, they might have a better chance to get to the bottom of the case now; hence a re-run of all the interviews.

Mrs Brown nods in agreement. 'That poor woman,' she says finally. 'Do you think she is still alive?'

'That's what we want to find out. We have another look at everything. We won't leave any stone unturned, and with some luck we will find her.'

'Do you think she has come to any harm?' The corners of Mrs Brown's mouth are downturned in sorrow.

'It's a possibility, but we really don't know just yet. So it is important, Mrs Brown that you try to remember absolutely everything you saw on that day, when you think you met the woman who disappeared.'

'I don't think I saw her: I know!' Mrs Brown says a little piqued. 'I have a good memory!'

'Of course,' says Ant quickly to placate her.

'It was two years ago, 9th of May, a Saturday. I even wrote it in my diary. I remember it very clearly.' She looks at Ant whether she is listening. She is and writes down every word into her note book. 'Go on,' Ant looks up and smiles encouragingly.

'As I was saying,' Mrs Brown takes up the story, 'I went to the local butchers, about eleven o'clock in the morning, and as I passed Lloyds Bank, I saw this woman.' Mrs Brown stops.

'What did she look like?' Ant probes.

'Very tall…for a woman…She was wearing a brown, wide brimmed hat, a light coloured raincoat, which I thought was strange, as we hadn't had rain for days, and she was carrying a brown handbag with a shoulder strap. Something odd about that! It looked like something, my mother would have carried. She didn't look comfortable with it. In any case, as I passed her, she asked me whether I could help her to get some money out. Well, I don't like those machines - everything is machines nowadays – but she was considerably younger than me, so it was strange that she didn't know how to use it. Never mind. I helped her get out fifty pounds. She said 'thank you', turned and disappeared in the crowd. I thought I might see her later in a shop, but I didn't.' Mrs Brown remains silent for a moment.

'What was her voice like?' Ant asks knowing full well that Lucinda had a lovely voice, clear as a bell without being shrill, softly spoken with a posh southern county accent, which would surely stand out in Hull.

'I couldn't really hear her very well. She croaked as if she had laryngitis. Or maybe it was just a cold or a sore throat. To be honest, she gestured more than she spoke.'

Mrs Brown also confirms that she has neither seen Lucinda before nor after the sighting.

'If you do remember anything else, will you please ring me,' pleads Ant, handing over her card. Mrs Brown looks suspiciously at it and finally comments: 'You don't live around here then?'

'No, I work at the moment with the Wiltshire police, but I live in the West Country.'

'Lucky you,' Mrs Brown comments.

'On a slightly different tack, Mrs Brown: would you know of a hotel I can stay at for the night? I have a train to catch in the morning.'

Mrs Brown thinks for a bit, and then shakes her head.

'Not around here,' she mutters regretfully.

'Don't worry, I shall find something; maybe a bit closer to the station.'

'There is a Station Hotel,' she brightens, glad she can be of help, 'brand new!'

'Brilliant! That's where I shall go. Thank you so much for your time, and have a lovely day tomorrow with your friend.'

'We are going Christmas shopping. She has a big family.' Mrs Brown doesn't mention any family of her own.

'Would you like to take another piece of cake with you?' she asks, suddenly subdued and explains that her friend doesn't like cakes, and that they would have lunch out. The cake will be stale by Thursday.

'Well, if you don't mind. That would be lovely. Your Victoria sponge is delicious!'

Mrs Brown smiles broadly, proud at the praise, and bustles purposefully to the kitchen. When she comes back, she carries a little parcel of cake wrapped in baking paper.

'That should keep the wolf from the door,' she says and hands it over.

'You are very kind,' says Ant and regrets that she can't give her a little kiss on the cheek. Unprofessional, Bex would say.

Ant walks for a little while towards the city centre, and thinks, that actually, Hull is rather bigger and nicer than she had imagined. However, she doesn't enjoy walking in the dark in a city she has never been to before, and decides to take a bus at the next stop. She is told where to change and which bus to take to the Hull Paragon Interchange, a brand new train and bus station in the centre of the city, and the rather fabulous Station Hotel next door. People seem determined to shepherd her in the right direction. It couldn't have been easier. Ant feels rather smug, having proved Bex wrong; getting those interviews under her belt just before Christmas. She will treat herself to a slap-up meal and another piece of Victoria sponge, and then she will sink into a luxuriously soft, fresh bed. She won't think about the interviews tonight. She will have plenty of time on the train to Harrogate tomorrow morning and over the whole of Christmas at home.

CHAPTER EIGHTEEN

Ant, sitting on the train to Harrogate, is looking forward to meeting Alison Smith. She sounds a nice, level-headed person. It is convenient that the college, she is teaching at, has already broken up for Christmas holidays.

'Would you mind if we met a bit earlier than agreed?' Ant had asked her the previous evening in a hasty phone call. 'I have finished here in Hull. I could be in Harrogate by mid- morning.'

'That's fine,' Alison had agreed, 'I shall combine it with shopping. I haven't bought a single present yet.'

'Excellent!' They agreed to meet in a café on the first floor of a big department store in Montpellier Parade.

'You can't miss it,' Alison had assured her.

Indeed, she was right: it is no problem to find it. Alison is already studying the breakfast menu. 'I do fancy the full English,' she admits to Ant, as if it were something naughty.

'You treat yourself,' Ant encourages her, 'I had one this morning, too, in my swish hotel in Hull.'

'…the one by the station?'

Ant nods with a cheeky grin.

The waitress comes and says a shy: 'Hello, Miss.'

'Oh Goodness, Annie! I didn't realise you worked here.'

'Only during holidays,' the girl hastens to add, 'I need to earn a bit of money.'

'Good for you!' Alison smiles reassuringly at her pupil and then orders:

'I'll have a full English breakfast – but don't tell your friends! And...' she looks at Ant questioningly.

'...only a cup of tea and lots of sugar.'

The girl looks confused pointing hesitantly to a bowl on the table: 'Sugar is already there.'

'Don't tell her that. It's not good for her!' Alison jokes with her pupil. Annie takes notes on a pad, turns round and goes back to the counter to hand in the order to the chef.

Alison focuses her attention on Ant: 'So, you are now in charge of the case of that poor woman who disappeared, Miss Bell?'

Ant wishes she could offer Alison to call her by her first name, but it is probably better not to; for reasons of impartiality and incriminating familiarity. Who knows what flimsy reasons a court might use nowadays to dismiss a case? It's not worth the risk.

Instead she replies: 'Yes. We want to have another look at all the evidence.'

'So, you probably want to know about the time I saw her?' Alison guesses.

'Yes, that would be good. Can you remember the date, Miss Smith?' Ant decides to begin with the interview while they are waiting for Alison's breakfast.

'Oh please, you sound like one of my pupils; just call me Alison!'

'Okay then: I am Ant, short for Antonia.' Ant gives in; it is too silly otherwise.

'I have been asked this question so many times, that I know it by heart: 6th May 2015, a Wednesday. It was a study day for our GCSE and A-level students, so I finished school early that afternoon. I left at 1 p.m. and went straight to my bank - not far from here - to sort out a few things. As I approached the entrance, I had to pass the cash point machines. There was a fairly long queue, and I overheard someone shout: 'Get a move on!' So I looked who or what was holding up everybody. It was a woman who kept fiddling about with the screen and the buttons; then she dropped her card onto the pavement, getting more and more flustered. So I walked back and offered to help her. She looked at me with steely blue eyes, which I shall never forget, not very pleased about my interference, and then she shook her head. I found that very odd, not accepting help, when everybody was waiting for her to finish. The people behind her got really cross, so I quickly shouted instructions, which she followed - to my astonishment. Eventually, she managed to get something like ten pounds out of the machine; it could have been twenty, but it was only one banknote. What a fuss about nothing. And all that time, she didn't say a word, and then suddenly, she rushed off grabbing her shoulder bag.'

'...a brown leather shoulder-bag?' Mrs Brown had mentioned one.

'No. Something exotic.' Nobody had mentioned that before. 'What did it look like?' Ant asks.

At that moment, the young waitress returns with Alison's breakfast and Ant's tea in a glass with the string of a tea bag hanging out. Alison takes up her fork and knife and tucks in. Ant had hoped for a pot of tea, but she lets it go.

'Ah yes, the bag,' Alison replies when her mouth is empty. 'As I said, it was something exotic, possibly Indian; lots of pink, glossy, looked like silk, with swirls in various pastel colours printed on it, and a tassel hanging down from each corner at the bottom.

'You have a remarkable memory,' Ant states and makes notes in her book.

'That's what history does for you; trains your brain. But I remember it vividly because it looked peculiar on that tall woman in a dowdy rain coat and sturdy shoes on a dry, sunny day. She looked tired and harassed, and her hair…well, her hair was definitely dyed a strange shade of brown, and it hadn't done her any favours. She might even have been wearing a wig. Something didn't look right. But then, there are so many people nowadays who lose their hair with alopecia or through chemo-therapy, ending up with one of those turbans or wigs, poor things. In any case, she didn't look well!' Alison folds up a piece of bacon with her fork and knife, spears it with the fork and puts it in her mouth. It is nice to see somebody enjoying their food.

'Why do you think, she didn't speak?' Ant asks.

'No idea. It was odd at the time, but again, there could have been a plausible explanation. Some people lose their voice for one reason or another. One doesn't want to pry.'

'Of course not,' Ant agrees and takes a deep breath: 'You didn't know her from before, I presume?'

Still, chewing, Alison shakes her head and says after swallowing: 'No, I never saw her before or after that day; not in person anyway. Only on the news on telly, and later on *Crime Watch*.

Ant lets her finish eating, sips her tea and waits in silence, studying her discreetly: Alison looks nothing like the teachers when Ant was at school; she is petite, has a pretty face, framed by shoulder-length blond hair and a fringe; she is wearing red skinny jeans, black high-heeled boots and a black cashmere polo-neck pullover; her black leather jacket is slung over the back of her chair, red leather gloves peeping out of one pocket; but above all, she is vivacious, open-faced and smiling.

When Alison finally puts her fork and knife together on the plate, there is not one morsel left. She dabs her mouth with a paper napkin and says: 'Do you think you will find her?'

Ant shrugs her shoulders: 'I wish I knew.' She smiles wistfully.

'Will you let me know?'

'Yes, if you want me to. It will probably be all over the papers anyway.'

'I do. I have never forgotten that incident, thinking that I might have been one of the last people to have seen her alive. If I only had known...'

'She could still be alive, but we and her family need to know one way or the other.'

'Do ring if you have any more questions,' Alison offers. I will help if I can.'

'Thank you; and here is my card in case you remember anything else!' Alison reads the back and front of it and nods.

They call the waitress; Alison insists on paying for the tea. Ant notices that she leaves a big tip.

'Happy Christmas shopping,' Ant laughs, as they part outside the store.

'Thank you,' Alison Smith steels herself: 'It is fun up to a point, but at least, this year, we have broken up a bit earlier, and I can take my time. Are you heading back to the station?' Alison asks.

'Yes.'

'Cross the road down by the traffic lights and walk straight ahead along the side road. You will soon see signs to the station. Happy Christmas, Ant,' Alison says with a little giggle as if she is embarrassed to use the first name.

'Happy Christmas to you, too, Alison! And thanks for meeting me early… and the tea. It was really nice to meet you.'

'Let me know, when you plan to come to Harrogate next time.'

Ant waves briefly and follows Alison's directions. She is lucky: there is a train waiting on the platform which will take her straight back to Taunton. She will be home by six. The Girls will be pleased, having her back a bit earlier; not that they have any sense of time…or do they? But it will be nice! A Happy Christmas for all of us, she thinks and boards the train.

Felix looks a bit disappointed that she has returned early, but he is very pleased with his additional wages; farming for his father doesn't pay half as well. When he has gone, after asking her several times whether she will be all right on her own over Christmas – 'my father said it would be fine to bring you for Christmas lunch' – she changes into her farming clothes, breathes in the faint piggy smells that cling to them permanently. She is glowing and almost overflowing with pride and pleasure at what she has achieved in these past few days: crisscrossing the country; interviewing four witnesses in three days; discovering small, but vital details which hadn't been known before, and slowly edging forward to support the hunch that keeps nagging at her.

A thought crosses her mind. She has to tell somebody. She tiptoes in thick socks over the flag stones to the telephone. She dials. No answer, as she has expected. After eight rings, the message service kicks in. For a moment, she considers putting the receiver down, but then she leaves a message: 'It's Ant here. I did it, Bex! Happy Christmas!'

CHAPTER NINETEEN

'Ah, this is nice!' Ant, in jeans, thick pullover and Wellingtons, sits on the fence, muttering to no one in particular, while the Girls munch happily on today's offerings. Ant has already checked the fences, dragged armfuls of fresh nesting straw into their enclosure and filled several bowls with fresh water. 'You know, girls, it's exciting to go back to work …' she muses, brushes the thought away and continues with her speech like an orator on a podium: 'It is exciting,' she confirms to herself as much as the pigs, 'the travelling to different places, meeting new people, seeing how they conduct their lives; and I have come to the conclusion, ladies, that we all have two things in common: we all have to earn money, and we all want happiness, preferably with at least one special person.' Silence only disturbed by the greedy grunting and snorting. 'You see, I never had that, apart from one short episode; and that came to an abrupt halt.' She nibbles on her lower lip. Iolanthe looks up as if to say: 'Go on, we are listening.'

'It was probably not the right job to combine with a husband and children. I know, other people do, and I have no idea how they make it work. Working for the criminal police in whatever capacity, makes your life unpredictable, all-consuming and sometimes traumatic. You are never at home when you should be; you are working, at least in your head, when you are supposed to concentrate on your loved ones; and, in really bad cases, you take home your inner struggle with the awfulness of what has happened to the victims and their family. It's not something you can just shut away in the depth of your memory and shrug off; and if you are really unlucky, it will come back to haunt you, like rotten bananas in a fruit bowl you have refused to deal with.'

The Girls have gathered close to her by the fence, looking up at her like a bunch of mesmerised, adoring fans. Ant knows better: they expect more treats. She throws the last mushy bananas to the ground, and the Girls fall over them, fight to reach them, push each other out of the way with their fat, solid bodies, ears flapping with every movement. 'Enough philosophising for today! Do you want to hear about the interviews, or shall I keep them for later?' Ant asks and suddenly feels very silly. Talking to animals is supposed to be the first sign of madness. Well, it hasn't done me any harm so far, she thinks, hops down from the fence and gathers up the various containers she has brought with her. 'Interviews later then,' she shouts after the pigs, which are already busy rooting further up the hill.

Ant makes herself a mug of tea and nibbles on a chocolate biscuit. Ugh. Old biscuits have a strange consistency, an unpleasant softness combined with a dusty, stale taste; she swallows it quickly and washes it down with a gulp of tea. It's almost Christmas and she has not made any preparations. It's hardly worth getting a turkey for herself. She'll probably get a steak, some small potatoes and a tray of already trimmed baby vegetables plus a few portions of Tiramisu and ready-made bread and butter pudding with custard. She might even treat herself to fresh custard which is considerably more expensive than the tinned one. Who cares? It is Christmas after all. The other matter is: decorations. Will she bother? She remembers her Mum's efforts when Ant was small. Her father hadn't ever featured greatly in their lives – the odd appearance, usually ending in a row and mum bundling him out of the flat - and Ant had been quite happy that it was just the two of them. Decorations? No not this year. She needs the space for working on the case. She might need to be able to spread out the paperwork, and she certainly doesn't want to get any stains on anything important; or candles setting it alight. Moreover, she won't feel festive until she has found out what has happened to Lucinda. The stale biscuit makes her realise that she is hungry. There is some ham in the fridge and some mayonnaise. She loves the combination. She even finds a gherkin which will add bite to the sandwich. Ant takes out two slices of limp, white bread from the bread bin and puts it in the toaster. When they pops up, she puts them on a wooden board, drops a big dollop of mayonnaise on one, puts two slices of ham with a wide rim of fat on top, slices the gherkin into halves, puts them on top of the ham and closes the sandwich with the other mayonnaise slice of bread. She cuts it all in half and turns round to carry the wooden board to the table. She bites into the sandwich even before she reaches her chair. For a few moments, she is all consumed by stilling her hunger.

She hasn't even finished eating, when she begins to review the case and to consider the new insights. She always had a hunch, but now it seems to solidify, crystallise into something more tangible.

When she has finished going over the interviews again in her mind, she makes two decisions: she will approach Lucinda's local bank, and she will ask Bex to apply for a warrant. She will just be able to squeeze it in before the country shuts down before Christmas.

The bank manager of the Pewsey bank is taken aback at her request.

'I can't do that, without authorisation from higher above. You could be anybody.' It sounds logical.

'Sorry, Sir. I do understand it's bad timing so close to Christmas, but could you please, just find it for me?.'

'...and it's so far back – two years,' the unhappy man draws out the last two words like chewing gum.

'I know,' Ant acknowledges, 'but it's necessary! I shall organise the warrant and you do the same with the film. Give me a ring when you have found it, so I can come up and view it in your presence,' to which he agrees very reluctantly, pointing out that Christmas is almost upon them; as if she didn't know.

She leaves a message on Bex's phone. He might be able to help to speed things up. In the event, he calls back, in a great hurry with a lot of voices around him – he is either Christmas shopping or at a staff party: 'Ant, are you insane? Are you totally going to ignore Christmas?' She ignores his question.

'I just need to have one more look at that picture of Lucinda at her local cash point,' she says.

'I would be surprised, if the bank has kept it from two years ago.'

'Would they still be in the archives in Devizes?' she asks. 'I didn't see them among the exhibits.'

'Then maybe at the Pewsey police station? I shall give them a ring.' Bex offers reluctantly and with a heartfelt sigh, so loud that she can hear it through the line.

'Will you let me know one way or another?' She hates the thought of waiting on tender-hooks for information which might never come.

'Of course, you daft thing! Now relax and plan something nice for the festive season!' He obviously has.

'Thanks for the advice. I shall await your call.' They both put down the receivers, irritated with one another.

He does ring back within twenty minutes. 'They have got something, but they don't want you to come up and ruin their Christmas festivities. So they are going to send you an e-mail and a still photograph as an attachment. If it turns out to be something of importance, you will have to send your request the proper way later.'

'Thanks, Bex,' she says simply. 'You are a great fixer!' He chuckles with a hint of sadness. 'I wish I was as good fixing other things,' he simply says and rings off.

Ant calls off the search at the bank at Pewsey and hears a heartfelt sigh of relief through the telephone. 'Thank you for trying, and Happy Christmas,' she says, thinking that the manager might not even have started the search.

When she finally receives the e-mail from Pewsey police station the next morning, she scrutinises it thoroughly. It is without doubt Lucinda on the picture. You can just see her startling blue eyes and her short, blond fringe hanging into her forehead. At the bottom of the picture, the tip of a white blouse collar is just visible.

Ant switches on her mobile where she has stored the pictures she has taken from the Devizes archives. She scrolls through them until she finds what she is looking for: four similar pictures, taken from the CCTV cameras at the cashpoint machines in Birmingham, Carlisle, Hull and Harrogate. She looks a long time at all five photographs. And suddenly, she knows what has been bugging her all along.

There is a knock on the door. It is Felix. He finds Ant kneeling on the floor in the midst of papers she has scribbled on.

'Am I disturbing?' he grins.

'No, not really,' she smiles and offers him a cup of tea. 'No, I am in a bit of a hurry,' he replies, 'I just wanted to know whether I can help in any way.'

'You mean, whether I am going away again?'

He nods. 'Sorry not until after the holidays, and I am not sure yet where I need to go to next and for how long.'

'That's all right,' he smiles politely, and then is suddenly overcome by shyness, twisting his cap in his hands: 'And my parents are asking whether you wouldn't like to change your mind and have Christmas dinner with us. It's going to be only the three of us, and my Mum would like someone else to talk to, someone who doesn't just talk about farming.'

'So, no mentioning the pigs?'

They both burst out laughing. 'That's very nice of them both …'she looks at him with a cheeky grin, adding: '…and you. It's very kind, and I shall be delighted to come. I can't guarantee that my topics will be an improvement, but I shall give it a try.'

He is obviously relieved that he has completed his mission successfully. He puts on his cap, which sits on his curls like a hovercraft on water. As he walks away, she can hear him whistling.

Things are looking up: the investigation is progressing; she seems to follow the right instincts, and she won't spend Christmas on her own after all.

CHAPTER TWENTY

Christmas had indeed been a treat. It was the first time in weeks that she had relaxed. Felix came on the order of his parents to pick her up, 'so you can have a drink,' he said. Very thoughtful of his parents, but she had no intention of getting drunk and making a fool of herself.

It was a very nice meal, turkey with all the trimmings. Ant couldn't remember the last time someone had cooked for her. It was probably her mother, and she had died twenty years ago. Ant was determined that she would enjoy being pampered by these people, who were so kind to her.

All thoughts of work were banned!

'You are an excellent cook,' she remembers having said to Felix's mother, who had visibly grown a centimetre taller with the praise. Even the father had cracked a few jokes, mainly at the expense of his son, who cringed and then joined them all in the laughter. Before the Christmas pudding they had listened to the Queen's speech and had discussed it for a while before the homemade pudding had been served with brandy butter and cream. She had politely refused to drink home-made cider in favour of an excellent glass of wine. The meal was rounded up by a rather strong coffee and chocolates which she had brought as a contribution. They did want to know about her pig farm and discussed her hope that selling the meat would be a success. They wrinkled their foreheads, trying to think of some encouraging words and finally left it at: 'Just wait and see.' It was Felix's father who added, rather philosophically, 'that's my motto. No point in worrying before anything happens. It will all come as it must.' Ant promised them that they would be the first to sample the - it didn't bear thinking about - still unborn piglets when they had been turned into meat, and Felix's mother nodded, saying, that a pork roast would be a nice change from the eternal lamb.

As it grew dark outside, the parent's retreated, the mother into the kitchen, being adamant, that she wanted to clear up the kitchen by herself, reassuring her guest, that she did have a dishwasher. 'I'll be listening to the radio,' she said in a tone that made Ant believe that she was really looking forward to it. Felix's father went out to see to the sheep, and, Felix remarked with a grin, to have a smoke. Felix and Ant were left on their own for a while, chatting about Felix's professional past as a salesman for an agricultural business.

'I wasn't any good at it, but I stuck it out for about five years, before I realised that, what I really wanted to do, was farming. So I went back home and enrolled at agricultural college as a mature student.'

'Good for you,' Ant was always full of admiration for people who managed to turn their lives around for the better.

'And you?' he asked not sure whether it was too bold a question.

'I was working as a scientist, mainly for the police' she said, not wanting to give too much away, 'but now I am a pig farmer,' she had smiled broadly at him.

'And what about the work you are doing when you go away.' He was really interested.

'I can't say anything about it. It's still ongoing, but I hope it will finish sometime soon.' He was clearly disappointed at that statement. He had hoped for some exciting news, some spice and excitement in his otherwise peaceful, but monotonous life.

'Sorry,' she had added, smiling ruefully.

'I shouldn't have asked,' Felix had said with resignation.

It had suddenly felt strange without his parents' company, and she was briefly wondering whether there was an ulterior motive for this invitation apart from pure kindness. Stop being paranoid, she had scolded herself.

'I better be going and feed my animals,' she had ended the conversation gently. He called his mother out of the kitchen who dried her hands on her apron before accepting an impulsive, well-earned hug from Ant.

'Thank you so much for a wonderful meal. Really festive and tasty,' and when Felix's father came in, he grabbed her hand with both of his and urged her to come again to sample his home-made cider, his pride and joy.

'Of course, I will,' she promised, 'and you must come to me as soon as this wretched investigation is finished.' They nodded, not quite sure what to make of what she had said.

'Felix will take you home,' his father pronounced when he saw his son swinging car keys. Was that a wink from the old man? She beat a hasty retreat with more cheery 'Thank Yous and another 'Happy Christmas.'

Felix had noticed the wink as well: 'Sorry about my Dad. Actually, my mother isn't any better – they just want to see me married off.'

'Parents, eh?' Ant had laughed in sympathy. 'No harm done.' As flattering as it was, she thought, an attempt to match-make between her and the delectable Felix was the last thing she needed.

'I was meant to be a girl,' Felix had said wistfully into the darkness. Ant had felt uncomfortable at this piece of confidential information.

'Felicity….I was meant to be a Felicity.' Ant had been unsure what to reply. Was he trying to tell her something? Better change the topic, she had decided.

'Felix, will you be able to look after the pigs sometime this week?'

He had nodded: 'Any time.'

Shrill telephone ringing interrupts her reminiscences.

'How are you doing, Ant?' it's Bex on Boxing Day.

'Fine….and a Happy Christmas to you as well.'

'I tried to call you yesterday, but you didn't pick up. You are all right, aren't you?' Since when did Bex have a caring side?

'Of course I am. Why shouldn't I? In fact, I went to neighbours. They insisted, and it was actually good fun.' Ant wonders how he will react, just out of sheer curiosity.

'Was it Felix by any chance?'

'Yes, it was. How did you guess,' she teases him mercilessly. It shuts him up; he is probably miffed now. Not her responsibility – anymore.

'Have you started on the case again?' he asks.

'Give me a chance, Bex. It was you who told me to relax. Just because you are at a loose end…'

'I knew I shouldn't have rung. I'll ring tomorrow when you are hopefully in a better mood.'

'I am not in any kind of mood. I am quite willing to talk about the case, but remember that my private life is just that: private… nothing to do with you.' She knows he doesn't need reminding. He hangs up.

She gives him ten minutes to calm down, as she knows he will, and then she rings him. The case always comes first. That's how they both tick.

'Bex, it's me again. Let's get on. I need your advice.'

A rough 'okay' reassures her that he is listening. He must be in a panic. He has two months left to get this case off his conscience.

'Bex, whatever happens, I shall continue, until the case is solved, I promise!'

She hears him sigh. 'What did you find out; anything vastly different from the first investigation?'

'I think so. Can you remember how tall Lucinda was?'

'Let me see…' Rustling indicates that he is rummaging in a pile of papers.

'Where are you? Are you at work?'

'Yes, I am in the reading room you know so well…. Ah, here it is: five foot ten, and she weighs ten stone two. Does that make things clearer, Ant?'

'I think so, but I have to check something.'

'So what is your next step?'

'I still have to interview her two brothers, Alfred and Robert – the one who builds churches and the other who does gardening on the family estate. But, I think, I need to speak to Piers first.'

'Do you want me to come along?'

Ant is glad that he offers and says simply: 'Yes please... How well do you know him?'

'You know what it's like when you examine a case for months: you do get closer to the witnesses. Most of the time, Piers Turner was distraught, desperately willing to help, but ultimately useless. Not a bad chap, though.'

'Yeah...' Ant mutters.

'So, when shall we meet him?' Bex doesn't sound enthusiastic.

'Are you free all this week?' Ant asks in return.

'More or less...'

'I shall ring him and try to make an appointment for tomorrow or Thursday, she offers and adds hesitantly: 'And, Bex?'

'Yeah?' he sounds impatient, his mind already busy with something else. She suspects, her 'dog with a bone approach' is getting on his nerves. It always did.

'Are you listening, Bex?'

'Yeah.'

'I have a belated Christmas present for you: I have enough new evidence to warrant reopening the case.'

'Have you now?' He cheers up instantly.

'Okay, let me know when you have arranged a date with the grieving husband.'

'Mr Piers Turner?' Ant waits for confirmation through the telephone line

'Yes,' it arrives after some hesitation.

'It's Antonia Bell again. So sorry to disturb you at this time, but I need to clarify a few things, and you could be of great help. I thought of coming up either tomorrow or on Thursday. Would that suit you?'

He seems reluctant, but agrees eventually to the Thursday, which is convenient for Felix as well.

Then she leaves a message: 'Bex, we are on: Thursday, ten o'clock, at the Turner's farmhouse.'

CHAPTER TWENTY – ONE

Bex and Ant meet again at the estate's wrought-iron gate. This time, they open it wide and drive both cars up to the big house. Piers is waiting already.

'Any progress?' he asks, eagerly, grey eyes shiny with hope.

'Not yet, but I think, we are getting closer, hence our visit,' says Ant cryptically, looking serious.

'Oh, good!' Piers exclaims with relief. 'What have you found out?' He points at two armchairs for the guests to sit down. He himself takes a seat opposite in a winged black leather armchair.

'We have spoken to the family, most of them,' Ant begins and is interrupted by Piers: 'Oh dear, oh dear!'

'Why?' His mocking tone disconcerts her, and she looks at him to give him a chance to explain.

'Well, not everybody was in support of Lucinda and me to get married,' he admits.

'Why would that be?' Ant fakes surprise.

'Well,' he says again, 'to be honest, they are a rather dysfunctional family. They don't really know, never mind practise, the word *supportive*. Lucinda was really glad to get away from them.'

'Was she now,' says Bex. It is news to him. 'Why would you say that?'

'Are you interrogating me?' There is still a hint of mocking in Piers' voice and, what is new, a trace of suspicion.

Suddenly, Bex finds his subject intensely irritating: 'We did ask to question you again. Every bit of information could be immensely helpful.'

'Just joking,' Piers tries to calm the situation. 'To tell you the truth, I didn't really see very much of Lucinda's family after the wedding. I accompanied my wife once or twice, but I felt like a spare wheel, so I stopped going. Lucinda went up regularly to see her folks, but more often than not, she came back rather deflated and sometimes upset. I think, the parents tried to convince her that she had married the wrong guy, and that she should leave me,' he swallows hard as if to underline the injustice, 'but she would have none of it. We were happy, why should we listen to them!'

'Were you in contact with any of her brothers? We find it very hard to get hold of them.' Bex realises that Ant is fishing.

'No, and I think, they didn't show much interest in their sister either.' She was rather sad about that.

'So, no contact at all with any of the brothers,' Bex says out loud, while he writes it down in his police notebook. 'Why do you think, they kept away?'

'I have a vague idea: the accountant brother wanted to look after my money, but I prefer to stay with my old accountant.' It sounds reasonable.

'…and the others?'

Piers grumbles with bitterness: 'If you mean the pompous church architect, who was in charge of the disastrous renovations of our house: He was utterly incompetent, totally useless, and I told him so. I had to change most things he had supervised. He refused to speak to me after that.'

'We haven't got hold of him yet,' admits Bex.

'You probably never will. He always finds a good excuse.'

'…and what about the other two brothers?'

'You mean the drug addict and his dealer?'

Bex and Ant look at each other, alert, eyes fixed on the interviewee.

'What do you mean, Mr. Turner?' Ant asks sharply.

'Oh please, call me Piers. You were at our wedding after all!'

However much she detests it, she follows his wish to keep him talking: 'Piers, what do you mean by these accusations? They shine a different light on things. They might be crucial.'

'Don't tell me, you haven't found out!' His eyes open wide behind the glasses, his eyebrows rise above the frame in disbelief before he answers the question: 'Sebastian, the so called antiques dealer, is a drug addict. The smell wafts all over his house – you probably noticed it yourself when you interviewed him; and the youngest one, the asthmatic malingerer, grows weed in a far corner of the estate, where his father never goes…. Too busy hunting and shooting…Now you know why Lucinda and I kept our distance. It was too distressing for her, considering that she had dealt with that sort of thing almost daily while she was still working for the police…' His words of sadness and revulsion trail away.

'How do you know, Piers?' Ant asks gently.

'Lucinda told me.'

'Are you sure? It's one thing to bad-mouth others, but accusing them of crimes is another.'

Piers Turner shrugs his shoulders, distraught, looking lonely in his attempt to hold the fort without Lucinda by his side. There is an air of the tragic hero about him which makes him look vulnerable. Was that the side which had attracted Lucinda to him?

Ant can read the question in Bex's eyes and nods. Yes, she had noticed signs of drug taking in Sebastian's dishevelled home, and she hasn't got round to interviewing the sickly Robert, the youngest of Lucinda's siblings. She can't work out what their misdemeanours have to do with Lucinda's disappearance. Obviously, Piers feels strongly about it.

Ant decides on a distraction tactic and admires the exotic artefacts which cover the walls and shelves: 'Piers, can I just have another look at them?' She nods in their direction. 'They are wonderful!'

'Of course, you can; please yourself, and you, too, Sir,' he encourages Bex, who is still making notes. After a while, he joins Ant, and both make appreciative comments to Piers. He is gratified: 'We bought far too much on our honeymoon, but we chose well. Lucinda was thrilled when they all arrived and took charge herself to display them.'

'Absolutely brilliant,' Ant remarks, as she turns away from them and faces Piers: 'Just one last question: did Lucinda buy a bag in India? Made of silk, in striking colours and tassels at the bottom?'

Piers looks disconcerted, followed by a big show of concentrating and thinking back to their time in India. Finally he says: 'I remember seeing that sort of thing, but I am pretty sure,

Lucinda didn't buy one. She found them a bit garish. Why do you ask?'

'…because she was seen with one after her disappearance.'

'Are you sure it was her?'

'Yes, there is camera footage at the bank and on two street cameras.'

'So she is alive!' he exclaims. 'Why didn't you say so earlier? Marvellous!' He is beside himself with joy, eyes sparkling again behind the rimmed glasses.

Suddenly, he sees Ant shiver: 'Are you cold,' he asks chivalrously. 'If there is one thing wrong with this house, it's the heating system. I blame Freddy, the architect!'

'It's a very big house,' agrees Bex. 'How do you heat it?'

'For what it's worth, we have a big wood-burner in one of the outhouses. It does its best, but can rarely cope. There is always a freezing cold room somewhere.'

'What do you heat it with?' Ant is curious.

'Wood. We have plenty of that on the estate,' Piers declares proudly.

'You don't have to supplement it through a supplier?'

Piers shakes his head.

'That's incredible! It must be a pain to keep it going, particularly on winter days like today.'

'You are telling me? I get wood cut at the far end of the estate, where we have lots of trees, but it needs constant replanting and looking after.'

'Ever thought of moving somewhere smaller?' Bex probes.

Piers Turner laughs and then says with a heart-felt sigh: 'Maybe when Lucinda returns, but until then, I have to stay put, so that she can find me easily.'

The three of them shake hands before they leave, and Ant promises to keep Piers informed of developments.

'Not a lot of love lost between him and the family,' Ant remarks as soon as the door shuts behind them, and they are out of earshot, 'what did you think?'

'You mean, about his answers?'

'No, I mean about all of it: him; his answers; his demeanour; his opinions about the family; the house, the estate…'

'Difficult to say,' Bex hedges his bets. 'I shall let you know when I had time to think about it.'

'Oh, dear…' Ant teases him, 'the great detective has to think about it! I haven't got this luxury. I'll be off to do more sleuthing tomorrow.'

'Can I inv….' He had obviously hoped they could have dinner together, maybe in a nearby country pub, but she has read his thoughts.

'Safe journey!' she shouts, as she climbs into her car and roars off.

CHAPTER TWENTY – TWO

'Miss Bell, I rang to apologise,' Piers Turner says over the phone the following morning, and he sounds contrite.

'What for?'

'I was rather unkind about Lucinda's family. They are not bad people, just a different class altogether.'

'I must admit, I was a little stunned by the viciousness,' she is never less than candid. 'I didn't suspect you were capable of so much bile.'

'I know, and I am sorry. The months of waiting for news of Lucinda must have finally got to me…I am so sorry,' his voice is reduced to a whisper.

'Do you still stand by everything you said about them?' Ant enquires.

'I did tell the truth. You can check yourself.'

She ignores his suggestion. Instead, she takes advantage of his contrition: 'Will you help me?'

'…if I can.'

'I would like a list of all of Lucinda's friends with whom she was in contact in the two years after your wedding. Anybody, who was in contact with her, except members of her family - school friends, University friends, people she has met, old and new friends, and whatever you know about them. Can you do that for me? '

'I shall. When do you need it?'

'As soon as possible really,' Ant urges him on.

'Okay. I shall do it tonight and give myself tomorrow to check, so that I don't forget anybody.'

'That would be excellent!' Ant praises him, as if he was a naughty child who has promised to behave in future.

'Will you pick it up, or shall I bring it to you?'

'Goodness! No! We do live in the twenty-first century. Just send it as an attachment to an e-mail. You do have a computer?' she checks.

'Yes, I do. Not that I use it very often…but I know how to do e-mails.'

'So, hopefully, I'll hear from you by tomorrow night.'

'…you will,' Piers promises in a much softened tone.

'I count on you, Piers.' She can finally bring herself to say his name.'

He hesitates to put down the receiver. She waits for what else he has to say. In the end, he only repeats: 'And you have forgiven me?'

'Of course, I have. You have gone through a lot. It's understandable. Have a nice day, Piers.'

'Thank you; you too, Antonia!'

A shiver runs down her spine. Creep, she thinks. She just doesn't like him.

'Bex, I need either you or Zac to help me, she leaves her business-like message on his answer service, but before she rings off, he suddenly takes the call, breathlessly:

'Sorry, Ant; what was that?'

She tells him about Piers' phone apology, and that she has given him the task to make a list of Lucinda's friends.

'There is one already in the archive,' Bex says shortly.

'I know. It will be interesting whom he comes up two years later.'

'You haven't even interviewed some members of Lucinda's family. When are you going to fit all of her friends in?'

'Oh, and I forgot to mention that the eldest Sheridan brother sent an e-mail form America with contacts he visited during that Christmas get together in 2015.'

Bex groans: 'Is there no end?'

'You asked me to investigate, remember? You knew what you were getting!'

'I know, I know.'

'…and April is looming!' she reminds him.

He doesn't need reminding and stays silent.

'That's why I rang just now. I think I am changing my priorities. I need to dig a little deeper into the background of Piers Turner. It hasn't been done before – at least not thoroughly.'

'What do you mean- thoroughly?' He sounds outraged as if she had launched a personal attack on him.

'Hang on! Keep your hat on! Whatever has been discovered didn't leave me with a clear picture of his past,' she defends herself. Bex realises that he is not going to change her mind. Maybe she has a point? Dog and bone spring to mind again; he is too tired to think of a new metaphor. He just has to accept that nothing will deter her now. She is right: that's what he expected from her.

'I give up,' he says with resignation.

'So are you coming, or do you want to send the handsome Zac?'

'…when?'

'Well, as soon as possible: tomorrow or the day after? No time to lose. Everybody else has gone back to work, why not us'?

Bex sighs: 'I was going to take a few days off with my daughter, but I guess, I have to postpone it.'

'Bring her along. She can go shopping or to a museum while we make our enquiries.'

'Are you mad? A teenager let loose on the winter sales? She will spend a fortune!'

'Just a suggestion…' Ant isn't really bothered as long as she gets those interviews under her belt.

'And where are we going?' Bex asks. 'Whom are we going to see?'

'I thought there were lists for everything from the first investigation?'

'Not quite.'

'I can't really ask Piers to help again, particularly as it will involve his own past - however interesting that might be.'

'Ant, you are a pest!' Stunned silence ensues for several moments.

'Pardon me for doing the job, you asked me to do.' The words come out like acid.

'I shall see what I can drum up,' he concedes meekly.

'…as soon as possible. I want to make appointments.'

She isn't looking forward to working with a moody and distracted Bex, with his daughter in tow.

The weather has suddenly changed. It is sunny and the daylight hours have already lengthened by a few minutes. She can postpone feeding the pigs from mid-afternoon to early evening. When they are fed, watered and comfortable, they look smug and unperturbed by their pregnancy, like old matrons, in charge and haughty, Ant climbs on the fence and sits there watching them for a while. She needs to speak to somebody about Piers Turner. At first, she makes mental notes of points and questions which pop into her head; she looks sheepishly around herself: nobody is there, only the Girls who ignore her. No harm in vocalising her thoughts: do we know anything about the Turner family? His bank manager; his staff; his doctor; his solicitor and whoever else is on Bex's elusive list? She hopes he finds it.

She jumps down and leaves the Girls to get on with what they liked best: rooting.   Back indoors, she begins her research on the computer: first Piers' company, suitably called *Turner's Limited, Bespoke Furniture.* The website is surprisingly good, and she soon finds the names of the board members: Chairman and owner Piers Turner; Managing Director John Alsop, Director of Production Alan Sheppard, Director of Marketing and Sales: Otto Beaver; and last, but not least, the Finance Director, Benedict Crowther. She debates whether to pay them a visit first, but doesn't want to unsettle Piers unnecessarily. His colleagues are bound to report back to him. She puts the names at the bottom of the pile of 'what to do next'.

Instead, she will visit the doctors, and then the couple's solicitors. She realises, that they will both be bound by confidentiality.

The phone rings. To her surprise, it's Zac.

'Hi, Ant. Bex told me that you are both snowed under.'

'Did he?' she says provocatively.

'I am still with my parents and, to be honest, I am at a loose end here…' another way of saying *I am trying to escape*, Ant suspects, 'so I thought I ask whether I can help in any way. It doesn't matter how tedious.' Sounds, as if the Christmas atmosphere has worn off, Ant thinks and grins.

'Are you still on annual leave?'

'Yeah, well, it's not really a holiday with all the family milling around and getting under each other's feet.'

'I thought so,' Ant commiserates and says cheerfully: 'Zac, you are an angel! I have three lists of witnesses to interview and not enough time. Could you give some of the names a ring, and when you think it necessary, could you go and see them?'

'That sounds interesting, more interesting than I had expected,' he admits. 'What lists are they?'

'…the list of Lucinda's friends from the past provided by her husband. They all say that they haven't heard from her since her wedding – apart from one, that girlfriend in Yorkshire.'

'Can I take someone with me?'

That's a new twist, Ant thinks.

'Who did you think of taking?' she asks cautiously.

'DS Melanie Spooks,' he replies without hesitation.

'Are you sure, she is the right one with a name like that?'

Zac coughs with embarrassment, and Ant apologises immediately for her ridiculous remark:

'Only joking, Zac. Of course, you can take her, if she is willing to sacrifice her time.' The pigs are easier to talk to; they let most things go over their heads, and they never contradict.

Zac brightens up: '…and the second list?'

Ant is distracted by her own thoughts how to proceed. It will be such a relief, if she doesn't have to waste time travelling around the country again. Pewsey and Beaconsfield are enough to cope with.

'I am really grateful, Zac. What did you ask?'

'Who is on the second list?'

'Are you offering to do another one?'

'Why not? As I said, I am at a loose end.'

'That would be fantastic! The second list arrived this morning from Lucinda's brother Leo in New York. He made a list of people -friends of his - he visited to cut his Christmas visit in 2015 at the family home short - a bit like you'. She could hear Zac's embarrassed chuckle. 'I just need confirmation that he has been with them, when and for how long, how he behaved…you know what to ask.'

Zac sounds gratified that she entrusts him with such an important task.

'I shall make calls right now,' he promises.

'Keep me posted if anything significant turns up.'

'Will do, Ant and….'he takes a deep breath, 'Happy New Year.'

She smiles. He is a nice young man, eager and polite. He deserves a break.

Now she can concentrate on her own list.

CHAPTER TWENTY – THREE

Ant glances over the lists before attaching them to her e-mail to Zac and sending them off. It gives her a little breathing space. Trawling through lists is a little like looking for the proverbial needle in a haystack without any guarantee that she will find anything at all. She trusts Zac to be thorough.

She rings three people: Piers' bank manager, his solicitor and his doctor. She puts them all on the same day: Wednesday, the 3rd. For the afternoon she plans to visit Turner's company and speak to some of his staff, but doesn't make an appointment. She mustn't alert Piers. From now on, the less he knows – anybody knows – about her movements, the better and the more genuine the outcome of the interviews.

Felix indicated that by now, he can juggle things around on his father's farm to fit in with her plans, so Wednesday is fine, even Thursday and Friday, if necessary.

'We'll all be glad when this is over,' she says to him, smiling apologetically, but he doesn't think so.

'Take as long as you like. I have grown quite fond of PIA.'

'Who is PIA?' Had she missed something, being distracted?

Felix laughs as if she has discovered a ruse, before explaining: PIA – Persephone, Iolanthe and Agatha - see?' He watches her and is still chuckling happily, when the penny drops, as if a magic trick had worked.

She laughs now with him: 'Careful! They have a way to capture peoples' hearts.'

In the morning, before rush hour, she drives up the roads again which are becoming more familiar by each trip, singing along to *you're so vain*, a rather cheeky song by Carly Simon. For some strange reason, she is not looking forward to the day.

Her first appointment is with the bank manager of Barclays Bank in Marlborough. Strange that Piers doesn't use Lucinda's bank which has a branch in Pewsey High Street. It would surely be more convenient. Ant will meet a Mrs Fisher before they open.

Mrs Fisher is already waiting for her with keys ready to unlock the door. The manageress is a woman in her fifties with a welcoming smile. She locks the entrance door behind the two of them. They have half an hour before customers will need to be let in. There are already three employees bustling around their counters, getting ready for business.

'Coffee?' the manageress asks. Ant waits for an alternative offer like tea, but it doesn't come. They settle down in her stylish office which boasts nothing more than a desk, the two chairs they sit on, a telephone and a computer. When a member of staff brings the coffee, with three sugars for Ant and black for the boss, Ant comes straight to the point.

'Has Mr Turner always been with your bank and this branch?'

'I did some digging after you rang, and I must say, he seems a volatile customer. He seems to swap banks rather more frequently than we in our business would like.'

'Why would that be? Did he ever give a reason?'

'No. When he approached us, we assumed he had been following more competitive interest rates; after he had got married and had moved, he came to us. We found it a little strange, that he didn't chose the bank closer to where he lives, but we assumed that he had his reasons, and, ultimately, it is to our advantage.'

Ant nods and scribbles into her note book. 'Maybe he wants to keep business and private accounts separate?' Mrs Fisher speculates.

'Is his account healthy?'

'He has several. Some look better than others and he seems to be shifting his money around a lot – which some people do.'

'Why would that be?'

'To avoid over-draft charges...'

'And did Mr Turner overdraw?'

'Well, it is a business account. Things don't always go according to plan. The success of a business depends on so many other influences, the country's economy in particular, the financial health of the suppliers, customer demand...Do you want me to go on?'

Ant shakes her head.

'Did you notice any payments or withdrawals which were out of the ordinary during the last two to four years?'

'No. There were attempts to make various transfers from his wife's accounts at the Pewsey bank, but they were rejected because she, I heard, is missing, but not declared deceased. So her assets are frozen until the other bank receives different instructions.'

'Would you say that Mr Turner's financial situation is reasonably healthy?'

'To be honest, the poor man seems to be struggling lately, which is not surprising in the circumstances, but we are here to help through these difficult times. He is pleasant and trustworthy enough.' This last statement sounds like a full stop.

'I won't hold you up any longer,' Ant quickly shuts her notebook, puts it into her jacket pocket, and gets up.

'Thank you so much for seeing me before you even started work, Mrs Fisher,' she says.

'I am always early,' Mrs. Fisher corrects her.

'Let me know, if you remember anything else or if something unusual happens to those accounts. You have got my contact details?'

'Yes, I do, and I shall report back if anything happens.'

'Thanks again for your cooperation, and for the coffee.' It really is time to go. The manageress accompanies her to the main entrance, unlocks the door and leaves it open for the first customers to come in.

Now to the doctor's surgery which is also in Marlborough. Piers does seem to keep his affairs separate from his wife's.

She has to ask a passer-by to for directions to the surgery which, she is told, is home to five other doctors.

'You do realise that I have to consider patient confidentiality,' Dr Steadman announces as his welcoming greeting.

Ant nods and then adds: '…but I think you know that this is an enquiry into a missing person, a case which has been re-opened on the request of your patient. Did my superior contact you for authorisation?'

'If you mean Mr Cook, yes.'

'I won't keep you long,' she placates him. 'Just a few routine questions,' and hopes to lull him into ease of mind.

'Since when has Mr Turner been your patient?'

'About four years.'

'Did he have any major illnesses during that time?'

'Not really.'

'How often did you see him? I mean, once a year, twice…?'

'I saw his wife more frequently than him.'

Ant is stunned. Why wasn't she told that the Turners shared their doctor? The papers from the Wiltshire police archive had only listed a doctor in Pewsey.

'When did Mrs Turner switch over to your practice?'

'…about a year after her marriage to Mr Turner.'

'Did she have an on-going complaint?'

The doctor shifts uncomfortably in his seat: 'Well, let's say, they were trying…'

'Trying for a baby?' Ant can't believe it.

He nods.

'And did you encourage them?'

'It is up to them. I simply pointed out the dangers of such a late first pregnancy. After all, Mrs Turner was then already in her late thirties. She might have been on IVF for years.'

'Were they going to pay for the treatments?'

'Yes, they were private patients.'

Ant has to ask: 'And did Mrs Turner seem happy to become a mother?'

'Why are you asking?'

'Because I knew her, as a colleague, and she had never mentioned to me that she wanted children. In fact, she was adamant that she had no talent to be a mother.'

'If that was so,' the doctor rebukes her graciously, 'we must consider the possibility that she had changed her mind once she was married to Mr Turner.'

'Of course,' Ant admits. And pigs might fly she thinks and feels a stab in the heart, remembering her girls at home.

'So, did she have IVF treatment?'

'No…although Mr Turner was very keen to go ahead. Once she had contacted the clinic, I had very little contact with them. However, I was informed that something with Mrs Turner's heart wasn't quite right, a murmur, I think, so they were doing more tests. After that, I never heard again, neither from the clinic nor from the Turners.'

'Would you say, Mr Turner put his wife under pressure to have a child?'

'I can't say. From what I saw, he is quite an intense person.'

'There were no other medical complaints on either side?'

'No. As I said, I haven't seen them for years now. They didn't even bother to respond to invitations for flu jabs and annual check-up appointments.'

'Dr Steadman, you have been most helpful. I know it isn't easy.' Ant says.

He smiles his first genuine smile: 'We are trying to be helpful.'

It isn't clear, whom he includes in the 'we'.

While Ant waits for her lunchtime appointment with Piers Turner's solicitor, she rings the Fertility Clinic doctor Steadman has mentioned. They confirm what he has told her and are unable to add anything more, only to say that they have seen neither Mr Turner nor his wife since the end of 2014. If she wanted more details, someone says over the phone, she would have to come back with permission from Mr Turner or his wife for disclosure.

Ant doesn't bother to explain the situation. There is no need. Someone surely was bound to have heard of Lucinda's disappearance at the time?

Ant walks past Molly's tearoom. It looks lovely and she is hungry. Two interviews before lunch is not bad going; and the yield is higher than expected.

She enters and feels transported back to a calmer, more peaceful world than the one outside, or at least, the one she is dealing with. Just behind the entrance is a counter of cake heaven. She turns left and walks into the cosiest tearoom she has ever been to. The waitresses are wearing long, white frilly aprons which reach down over their knees, covering up most of their ankle-long dresses. Their hair is held back by a white, starched cloth tiara. Ant heads for a small table in the corner near the open fire, and one of the young waitresses rushes over to present her with a menu. For a moment, Ant listens to the animated chatter of the other clients – many of them seem to know each other: locals, meeting for morning coffee, friends meeting for a chat; a single man reading a morning newspaper. Ant orders, in spite of her best intentions to resist temptation, the substantial English breakfast, and, when it arrives, she is glad she has done so; it will last her for the day; moreover, it is delicious, probably the best she has ever eaten. Would they consider buying sausages from her farm, should she ever get that far? She is still nervous whenever she thinks about slaughtering piglets she has reared, PIA's offspring. It feels like murdering your own grandchildren.

While enjoying her breakfast, she rakes over the information of the morning. Well, well! Lucinda trying for a baby! It still doesn't sound right, but what does she know about marriage, the way it changes people and their priorities? Piers' money difficulties seem more worrying. Maybe it all culminated in a big spat over money? And Lucinda might have simply decided to leave? The other possibility doesn't bear thinking about.

Ant leans back in her upholstered chair with a soft back, wipes her mouth with a napkin and pours herself another cup of tea. She is grateful that there are plenty of sugar lumps on the table rather than the measly little paper straws with minute amounts of sugar. Ant looks out of the window onto the bustling High Street while thinking up questions for the solicitor.

CHAPTER TWENTY – FOUR

The solicitor's office is at the other end of the High Street, closer to the famous school. Mr Moss is just saying good-bye to a client, when he spots Ant in the waiting room.

'Come on in,' he says, jovially. He is about twenty years younger than Ant, probably not long out of law school. 'I hope,' he pleads, 'you don't mind me having a sandwich while we are talking. My next client has booked himself in during his lunch hour, but I think it will leave us enough time.' He doesn't wait for her answer and takes a sandwich parcel from a desk drawer.

'Fire away,' he encourages Ant, with an already full mouth.

Ant doesn't stand on ceremony and gets straight to the point: 'How long has Mr Turner been your client, and did you also take over Mrs Turner's affairs?'

The young solicitor seems to appreciate her candour and grins: 'Sharp observation. Yes, they were indeed both my clients.'

'Considering that Mrs Turner was using her family's lawyer, an old friend of her parents, why, do you think, she did change over to you?

'No idea. You know what families are like, particularly if the daughter marries.'

'No, I don't. Can you explain?'

He thinks for a moment, to choose the right words: 'You probably know that the house was given to the couple on their wedding by her parents. Mr Turner was keen to have his name on the deeds as soon as possible. He thought it wouldn't be really a wedding present for both of them if it wasn't changed.'

'And how did Mrs Turner react to that request?'

'She seemed fine with it.' He shrugs his shoulders and raises his palms as if to call upon Justitia herself as a witness.

'You do know, don't you, that Mrs Turner has disappeared?'

'Yes, sad case,' he admits.

Has anything changed since then? Have any agreements, contracts or anything else changed since Mrs Turner's disappearance?' Ant ends the jovial conversation with a stern look.

Mr Moss understands immediately. He might appear flippant a lot of the time, but when it is in his interest, he can be shrewdly serious.

'I can't really give you details…' he looks up and meets Ant's uncompromising stare.

'Well, nothing has been done yet, but Mr Turner asked recently whether he could delete his wife's name from the deeds, considering that she has still not been found. He doesn't think that she is still alive, after all this time. She must have come to harm. Why would she be hiding somewhere and not come home?'

Several reasons, Ant could think of, but she doesn't comment.

'What about his business affairs?'

'The original contracts were before my time. He just occasionally gives me something to scrutinise for the legality of a transaction and contract clauses with new partners; nothing earth-shattering. I think his business is just ticking along, nothing spectacularly successful. It's not surprising. His heart is probably not in it anymore.'

'It's hard to speculate. In my job as in yours, the only things which count are facts,' he reminds him.

'Quite,' he says drily, scrunches up his sandwich paper and throws the ball into his waste paper basket.

'Anything else?' he asks, obviously in the hope that the answer is no.

'Do let me know…'

'…if and when I have something else to report?' he interrupts, obviously keen for her to go.

'That's right,' she says without a smile, and wonders, how gullible this young man is, how vulnerable to people who are a lot more cunning than he is.

The next client is already sitting in the waiting room, fidgeting as if counting the minutes draining away from his lunch break.

That was an interesting and illuminating chat, Ant confirms to herself.

Did she really need to see Piers Turner's staff today? She might as well, now that she is up in Wiltshire. It might be opportune to catch some of them just before they go home. People are more relaxed then.

———————

The receptionist, a young woman with styled, brown hair and manicured fingernails is just packing up for the day, stuffing things into her handbag and tidying her desk.

'Can I help you?' she asks - practised, cold politeness and impatience mingling in her voice. There is also a pointed glance at Ant's Parka and rucksack.

'Yes, I wonder whether Mr John Alsop is still in his office…'

'I'll check,' the receptionist snaps, fearing that her departure might be held up.

He is, and he is willing to receive Ant after she has answered his two questions: who she is and what it is about. Ant keeps her answers intentionally vague.

'Just out of interest, are any of the other directors in?' Ant asks the receptionist, who is now drumming the desk with her fingers.

'As far as I know, they have a meeting at six, so I presume they will all turn up for that, if they aren't here yet.'

'Thank you, Miss…?'

The receptionist doesn't quite understand what Ant means; she is busy packing her handbag.

'You are…? Your name…?'

'Andrea Shriver,' she says unwillingly.

'Miss Shriver, how do I find Mr Alsop's office?'

'Oh, sorry,' Miss Shriver replies and calls out to a young man who is just passing: Tom, would you mind taking Miss Bell up to Mr Alsop.' It is less of a question than an order. The young man sighs and turns round to say: 'Come on then, Miss Bell. He takes her through the showroom of rather beautiful furniture – tables of all sizes and heights, desks, sideboards, wardrobes, bookcases hewn out of precious woods and gleaming with polish; then they reach the carpentry workshop where the machines are already standing still. Only one man in a suit is still going round checking.

'Who is that?' Ant asks.

'The production manager…' He grimaces as if in pain.

'Are you working in here?'

'Yeah, for my sins,' Tom says.

'Is he a slave driver?' she jokes.

'Not really. He is quite reasonable, until somebody upsets him, that is.'

'…and was he upset lately?' she asks innocently, 'Christmas and all that?'

Tom looks at the visitor, as if he suddenly realised that she had insider knowledge: 'Well, I don't think they were personal problems; it's the atmosphere here. We don't quite know what's going on.'

'Does that happen often?'

He shakes his head: 'No, we are quite a good team in here, the carpenters and apprentices.'

Ant smiles appreciatively. They have crossed the workshop now and climb stairs at the end of the ground floor. They arrive on the first floor where all the offices seem to be. One door is ajar, and Ant can see into a narrow galley kitchen. They stop in front of a heavy oak door at the end of the corridor. Tom knocks. Someone calls: 'Come in!' Tom opens the door and gives her a little nudge.

John Alsop gets up from his executive chair and walks from behind the desk across the room to greet her with an outstretched hand.

'Welcome, Miss Bell. Mr Turner mentioned that you might come and see us sometime. So you are now in charge of finding Mrs Turner?'

It is a bit of a shock that he has expected her.

'When were you told?'

'Only a few weeks ago; before Christmas,' he smiles.

'Coffee?' he asks, but Ant shakes her head. She doesn't want to upset the receptionist any further.

They sit down on a couch which is a cross between a low modern chair and a comfy settee – steel frame and plump cushions.

'I have come,' Ant launches into the purpose of her visit, 'to cover all angles of Mr and Mrs Turner's affairs. One of them is the company; how well it is doing; whether there are any problems; and whether you have observed anything in the past two or three years that could point to a reason for the disappearance of Mrs Turner.'

'I am not sure, I can tell you much,' he begins.

'…before my superior comes with a warrant.'

John Alsop's jaw drops slightly. He understands the seriousness of her visit: 'I have been with the company since its beginning ten years ago.'

'So, it is a fairly young company? I didn't realise.'

'Yes. It did rather well to begin with, but since the crash of the markets, it is less so. Our products are at the top end of the field, and of course, there are now fewer people who can afford them.' Ant makes notes. '…but we are ticking over,' he adds.

'Do you know of any involvement of Mrs Turner in the company?'

'Oh yes. I am not quite au fait with the exact details, but our Finance Director, is. I just know that there were several amounts transferred from her accounts. It was a great help.'

'Could I possibly speak to Mr …it is Mr Benedict Crowther, isn't it?'

'Of course, you can. Shall I call him?'

'That would be very helpful,' Ant says.

The Managing Director goes back to his desk and makes a call. 'He is on his way,' he says simply. Ant is impressed by his efficiency. Two minutes later, there is a knock on the door.

They are introduced, and Ant is baffled. She would not have associated the name of Benedict Crowther with a person of Asian descent.

'Miss Bell would like to know about the transfers from Mrs Turner's account to this company. Have you got the figures?'

He is well prepared and armed with reams of print outs: 'Have a look here,' he says in flawless English. 'We had a generous transfer in April 2013; another in November 2013, a third in April the following year and the last in November 2014.'

So, Lucinda had bailed out Turner Limited before she even got married to Piers; then again after the honeymoon, and subsequently twice more. Ticking over wasn't really the right expression.

'Did you expect another transfer in 2015?'

'Yes, indeed, Mr Turner was about to organise it, when his wife disappeared, and then, of course, he and everything else shut down.'

'How do you mean?'

'Well,' the managing director, John Alsop, takes over, 'Mr Turner wasn't himself anymore; totally distraught; he still is, understandably.' He pauses. Ant looks at him expectantly. 'He didn't come into work much; just the odd phone call to check that things were running smoothly. He wanted to devote himself to finding his wife.'

'Did he come into the office at all?'

'Sometimes, on a Monday and Tuesday; that's when we used to have meetings.'

'Yes, we moved them from the usual Wednesday to suit him,' interjects Mr Crowther. Something clicks in Ants brain.

'How much money did she transfer at any one time?'

'It depended on the state of the accounts, but it was never under a hundred thousand Pound Sterling.' Ant gasps: 'That's a lot of money,' she says eventually, and both men nod.

'Yes, she was very committed to the company,' the Finance Director confirms, and the Managing Director adds: '…and she was or is a very nice lady.' I couldn't agree more, Ant thinks.

As if he has read her thoughts, John Alsop asks: 'Did you know her?'

'Yes, she was a colleague before she married Mr Turner.'

'A very personal reason for you then to find her,' he says kindly.

'Personal reasons don't come into it in our job,' Ant says coldly and notices that the MD shrinks a little in his seat.

It's time to go. 'Gentlemen, I don't want to keep you any longer. I was told that you have a meeting at six. Thank you so much for your time and your cooperation.' And, to smooth things over she adds: 'You have been remarkably candid. It's much appreciated.'

'You are very welcome,' they chime. 'Do come back if you have more questions,' the MD offers, and Ant leaves her card for him on the glass table.

They lead her out into the corridor. Mr Crowther disappears into one of the other doors while Mr Alsop escorts her down the stairs and to the main entrance which is already locked.

'Do you think there is any chance of finding her after all this time?' he asks the obligatory question which bugs everybody.

'Sorry. I don't know at this stage.' He hasn't really expected a conclusive answer. 'Good luck. We would be so happy, if you did find her,' he says like a plea from his heart. 'Things are not the same anymore.'

He presses the buzzer, and Ant slips out into the dark.

CHAPTER TWENTY – FIVE

As soon as she gets in, the phone rings:

'Ant, I just had a visit from the church architect.' It's Bex.

'Goodness, how did that happen?'

'He is in London at the moment, and thought it better to put an end to our endless attempts to track him down.'

'So, what did he have to say?'

'Well, he is as good at ranting as our Mr Turner is.'

'What is he ranting about?' Ant has a good idea what about.

'Turner still owes him most of the renovation costs for the renovation of the farmhouse.'

'Piers said he wasn't happy with it.'

'That was probably an excuse. He lives in it now and seems to like it, doesn't he? To be honest, Alfred Sheridan is a distinguished architect. I did a bit of research on some of his projects. They are magnificent. One even won a prestigious prize; I am pretty certain that he didn't make any major mistakes. It must be about the money.'

'…which is strange, because Lucinda invested a lot of money in Turner Limited?' She proceeds to fill him in on her meetings with the Managing and Financial directors of the firm. At the end, she hears a long and loud whistle. That's exactly how she feels.

'You mean, she could have easily paid off her brother. It was probably a much reduced fee anyway,' Bex speculates.

'You are probably right, and the visit to the solicitor was pretty interesting, too.' Ant tells him about the deeds and Piers' more recent attempt at removing Lucinda's name from them.

'He is rapidly turning into our prime suspect, isn't he?' Bex states as a matter- of-fact.

Ant hesitates before she points out: 'The one thing that bothers me is, that he had primed his directors for my visit. How did he know? I didn't tell anyone, and I went there at short notice anyway.'

'It's logic! He thought you were bound to question people at his company and to ask them about the state of affairs. The best policy is always to appear to be frank and honest. People tend to get themselves much more in a muddle if they lie or try to hide things, especially when they are not used to it. He knows how to group good people around him and lets them take the blame if something goes pear-shaped.'

'You might be right,' Ant concedes, 'but it's still odd that they had permission to show me Lucinda's transfers and the staggering amounts she put into the company.'

'I get the distinct feeling that Piers is goading you. Let's face it: none of what you found out is illegal plus, we have no proof that Lucinda is either dead or unwilling to return. It could be all a big charade, maybe by both of them to fool the family, or the taxman...' he stops.

'Lucinda is simply not like that,' Ant shouts in exasperation. 'What would be the point of it? She is the wealthier of the two. She is the popular and clever woman with a successful career, a fantastic brain and a slightly dysfunctional but still caring family!'

Bex is astonished at Ant's fierce defence of her friend.

'Have you heard anything from Zac?' he changes the topic.

'No. He was busy making calls, interviewing people and now listening to your crap ideas!''

'Why has he gone to Yorkshire?'

'Who says?'

'One of his colleagues,' Bex explains.

'That must be the girlfriend Lucinda stayed in contact with after her wedding.' Ant concedes lamely.

'Do you mean an old colleague from the local police force?'

'I don't know.'

'Didn't Lucinda ring her sometime before her disappearance?' Bex persists.

'I think so.' Ant mutters.

'Shall I tell him to ring you when he gets back?' Bex offers.

'No, thank you. I shall ring him myself.'

'All right; if that's what you want…,' Bex doesn't take rejection lightly; his muffled voice indicates that he is miffed.

'Thanks for letting me know about Alfred Sheridan,' she says finally relenting. 'Now it's just the youngest brother I need to speak to, then we are done with interviews.'

'Don't forget the village folks!' Bex reminds her.

'Oh, God, I have forgotten about them.'

'It will be fun – shopkeepers, gardening enthusiasts and amateur actors.'

'I am spoiled for choice, aren't I?' she groans. She is tired and still needs to show her face at the pigs' enclosure. Iolanthe, Agatha and Persephone expect a good-night treat.

'Good night, Bex,' she says, conciliatorily.

'Good night Ant - and good work!'

It's nice of him to say that, but she is too tired to appreciate the praise.'

Zac rings dutifully the next morning, just as she comes in from giving breakfast to the animals.

'So what did you find out?' she asks. She is curious, not only about the confidences Lucinda had shared with that girlfriend.

'She was not in the Yorkshire police force, nor in any other. I don't know where that came from. She is a friend of Leo Sheridan's wife. They went to school together in New Jersey. So when he came over that one time around Christmas, he visited her and asked her to look out for his sister. Her name is Kiki Wainthrop.'

'Why does she live in Yorkshire?'

'It's a bit complicated, but the short of it is, that she got married to a Yorkshire man during her year abroad at St Mary's College in London.'

'Good work, Zac!' Ant hands on the compliment. 'What else did you find out?'

Kiki didn't hear much from Lucinda until just before her disappearance. It was never clear why she rang or what she wanted, but Kiki thought that there might have been a rift in the marriage, and that Lucinda was looking for a place to retreat to.'

'…and did she?'

'No. Kiki had offered her to stay for however long she wanted to; she had even offered to pick her up from London, but that's when Lucinda hung up.'

'Did Lucinda say what troubled her?'

Zac thinks for a moment: 'No,' he says finally. 'She thought she heard Lucinda mumble something about money and family and a baby and not knowing where to turn to without being disloyal.'

'Did Kiki have the impression that Lucinda was frightened?'

'She didn't say so. It was more that Lucinda was confused.'

'And what about the others, people on Leo's list?'

'I contacted them all, and they all confirmed the times and dates Leo had given us.'

'You are a star, Zac! You have saved me a lot of time!' Ant says and then asks him for Kiki's phone number. 'See you soon, I hope.' He is a nice chap and so easy to work with.

'Kiki Wainthrop?' Ant smiles inwardly: that is a name you end up with when you mix the USA with Yorkshire.

'Yes, speaking.' Kiki's drawl is still heavily American.

'I am Antonia Bell, one of Lucinda Sheridan's colleagues… and a friend as well,' she adds. Why not? It's the truth! She was Lucinda's friend until Piers Turner appeared.

'Kiki, you have very kindly given already a lot of time to my colleague Zac Weymouth.'

'Yes, what a nice young man,' Kiki confirms.

Ant pauses before she speaks: 'I wonder whether I may ask you one more question.'

'Of course, you can! Go ahead. I am listening.'

'In your opinion, was Lucinda frightened of anybody?'

There is a long pause. When Kiki has recovers her speech, she is cautious: 'I think you mean, was she frightened of her husband, don't you?' Another pause ensues.

'Yes.' Ant tries to stay calm.

'She didn't say in so many words, but she was certainly in turmoil. She rattled on like a machine gun about money, about deeds, about going back to work and Piers wanting her to stay at home to have a baby, about her family wanting her to have a divorce. So many demands and pulls from different sides. She was torn. Come to think of it: the state she was in, I would say that she was frightened, certainly worried – as if she was trying to find an escape route.'

'I thought so. I just needed you to confirm my suspicion. Kiki, it is a pleasure to speak to you. Do stay in touch when you come down south.' Ant doesn't know why she added the last sentence, but she sincerely hopes that Kiki will.

———

Ant is just thinking: 'That's enough phone calls for one evening,' when the phone rings again. She swears under her breath.

You are difficult to get hold of.' At first she thinks it is Bex again and is ready to tell him, to go away, but then she realises that it is somebody else.

'Yes, what is it, Piers?'

'Where are your professional manners, Antonia?' he says mockingly.

'What do you mean?'

'You visited my company today and interviewed my senior staff. It would have been nice if you had let me know beforehand.'

'They did expect me,' she says sharply.

'Well, nobody told me!' he is querulous. She doesn't reply until he says: 'Did it go well?'

'Yes, as you well know.'

'I don't know. That's why I am ringing.'

'Who told you?' That would be interesting to know.

'The receptionist,' he says triumphantly. 'I shall speak to the management tomorrow.' He waits for her reaction. There is none. 'In future,' he carries on pompously, 'anything, anything at all with relevance to my wife's disappearance, will have to be reported to me personally. I insist on it!' He is trying to put her under pressure. When she still doesn't reply, he asks: 'Have you found anything at all since we last met?' He is now mocking her.

'Not really, Piers. I am sure your managers will tell you all about my visit.' She feels sorry for them. And then she has another thought: 'As you are ringing, Piers, I might as well ask you now rather than come up again and bother you: Did you have another company before you founded Turner's Limited?'

'I can't see how that is relevant,' he says, cagey.

'It's too late to go into details, but I want to chart your career.'

'How dare you!' he is getting angry. 'What has my career to do with my wife having either run away or come to harm?' I have asked you to find her, not to write my biography.' There was a big emphasis on the word 'my'.

Ant feels like retaliating, telling him that with the state of Turner's Limited was in, his previous successes or failures were of the utmost importance; or that he has put himself into the frame by not coming to work exactly on the dates Lucinda's was seen elsewhere. Very strange coincidences indeed! However, Ant holds back. It is never a good idea to disclose anything before all the pieces of a case have fallen into place, when she can prove the validity of each clue. She will ask Zac first thing in the morning to do a bit of digging at Companies House.

'Piers, I had a busy day, as you well know. So I end this call now – not because of bad manners, but because I am tired and must go to bed.'

He seems to want to carry on talking: 'Any other developments?'

'Piers, not now.'

'Did you get hold of the famous church architect, and his little brother, the drug dealer? They should be of much more interest to you than digging around in my affairs. Lucinda used to give them money which they squandered. She used to despair of them! In case, you have forgotten, I am the person left behind, missing her, looking for her for the last two years, having sleepless nights and turning all the possibilities, where she could be, over in my head…'she expects him to sob any moment.

'I know Piers,' she says quietly, hoping she sounds compassionate, 'but I am going to end this call now. I am tired. It is very late. I shall be in touch soon.'

She puts the receiver down before he can butt in again.

CHAPTER TWENTY – SIX

'I knew it!' Ant exclaims on the following afternoon, when Zac rings and reels off a litany of names of companies Piers had been involved with in the past. At the beginning of his career as a businessman, he had partners, who rapidly seemed to resign from their co-director positions. Ant suspects, that he has always been difficult to work with.

'I even dug out information about two companies Mr Turner started when he was about twenty and twenty two,' Zac reports eagerly, 'though they were not registered at Companies House. His associate was a university friend a drop-out like Piers. They thought they could make money faster by leaving their studies and starting up a business.'

'What sort of business was it?'

'Something stupid like ever-lasting pens which they sold to their fellow students, and thought they could roll out onto other universities, but it backfired and they had to give up after eighteen months with considerable losses.'

'I can see a theme developing,' Ant says.

'It gets worse,' Zac is in full flow: 'He tried another hair-brained scheme with a different friend from university, but that fell through even quicker. I managed to speak to him personally. He is still bitter about it.'

'And what happened to all the subsequent registered companies? Did they all go bust?'

'As far as I can see, they did, whether they were simply wound up or whether they went with a spectacular bang, I can't say. They wouldn't tell me.'

'Did any of the other businesses have anything to do with carpentry or wood?' Ant wants to know.

'No. Isn't he known as a wood expert? I don't know where that came from. I half-expected him to have had a career as a master carpenter before establishing his own furniture company.'

'That's what he made everybody believe, probably including his wife, Zac.'

'But she is a clever woman. She must have seen through his lies.' Ant imagines Zac shaking his head in disbelief 'Maybe too late,' Ant fears. Love really seems to make people blind, however intelligent, and, of course, it is even more embarrassing to admit to admit to the world that one has made such a fundamental mistake at so late in life.

'This latest company, Turner's Limited, is it on the way out, too?'

'Lucinda bailed it out several times during her two years of marriage. And now he can't get at her money without either her personal signature or her being declared dead.'

Zac whistles through the phone. It has obviously become the standard expression of surprise and astonishment in Bex's team.

'Hold on,' Zac says just before they end the conversation. 'I wanted to tell you something last time we spoke and forgot: Turner and his wife once had a big spat in the office of the bank manager, because she refused to share all her accounts with him. On the advice of the manager, they compromised on a shared current account.'

'When was that?'

'…in the summer of 2014.'

The noose is tightening ever so slowly, Ant registers with satisfaction.

'By the way: can I lure you to help me some more with a couple of interviews? If I can share the burden, they will be completed much quicker. Could you ask Bex to spare you for a day or two?'

'Next Thursday?'

She laughs: 'Why Thursday?'

'Word has got round,' Zac treads carefully. 'The pigs,' he adds for clarification.

'That's very thoughtful, Zac. Thank you. Yes, next Thursday will be great.'

It's a lovely late January day, with a dusting of snow on the fields and the sun shining on it. The roads are clear, and Ant is whistling along to the tune of *Nobody does it Better*'. They will finally interview the good people of Pewsey – interest groups are always a good source of gossip - and, if there is time, she would love to finally meet the youngest brother, the sickly Robert, whom Piers has declared to be a drug dealer. It will be good to have Zac there; he can keep his eyes open while she is doing the talking.

The artistic director of the amateur dramatic society is most gratified that she has taken the trouble to come all this way.

'I didn't quite expect you so early,' he admits, 'but if you want to stay till two o'clock, I have called everybody to a rehearsal, so they will definitely be there and you can interview them.'

'There will be no need,' Ant says, but is immediately interrupted: 'They will be most disappointed,' and his look says that she can't do that to them.

'Okay,' Ant relents, 'but could you answer a few questions now, Mr Peregrine?'

He is very willing and gives the impression that Lucinda had been his most favourite leading lady in his productions and that he missed her terribly: So refined, terrific diction and such a vast register of emotions.' This is not the Lucinda she knew. Ant struggles to supress a fit of giggles, and asks quickly to avoid offense: 'Did you know of any discord in the relationship with her husband?'

'I am not one for gossip,' Mr Peregrine says with hauteur, 'and if there was, Lucinda was much too discreet to let the mask slip, so to speak.' It was a badly veiled rebuke. Ant smiles politely saying nothing and is soon rewarded by further revelations: 'There was rumour of an affair,' he whispers, 'not only amongst us actors, but even in the village. Some of our members will be able to tell you more.' He looks at Ant for appreciation of revealing a secret of such delicacy, and she manages a grateful smile.

'Any idea, who that could have been?'

'Not really. Some even indicated that it could have been a lesbian affair.'

What a feast for the gossipers! Ant can hardly contain herself with amusement.

'Do you know how this rumour came about, Mr Peregrine?' Ant likes the sound of the name. It has a certain dramatic ring to it.

'Well,' Mr Peregrine pauses, clearing his voice before imparting the next obviously important piece of knowledge: 'Mr Turner turned up in the middle of a rehearsal and began to accuse Lucinda of being unfaithful, but she bundled him out of the rehearsal room before he could say another word.' His face shows distress; whether that relates to the first or the latter part of his statement, isn't clear.

'When was that?'

'It was not long before she disappeared,' he confirms Ant's suspicion.

'That's why we weren't altogether surprised when she vanished. We thought she had gone off with her lover, whoever he or she was.' Another theatrical pause and call to attention: 'Not that I could blame her: he is a miserable old bugger!' Mr Peregrine ends with a flourish and looks startled when his visitor bursts out laughing, so she converts it straight into a violent coughing fit.

'Are you all right,' he asks when she doesn't stop. '…a glass of water?'

Ant doesn't know whether to shake her head to answer the first part of his question, or to shake her head to the second. 'Thank you, Mr Peregrine; I am fine,' she says finally with a rasping voice, hoping that he doesn't notice the tears of laughter in her eyes; '…you have been most helpful!' she says, which makes him beam with pride. 'I shall send my colleague, DS Weymouth along this afternoon, to interview your staff members.' That term seems to go down very well, and Mr Peregrine smiles, gratified, opening the exit door for her with a grand gesture, bowing graciously.

'How did you get on?' Ant asks Zac, grinning all over her face as they meet in the local café for a quick lunch.

'You look cheerful,' he remarks with a chuckle. Her good mood is infectious.

'You will have the pleasure this afternoon: twelve amateur actors with all the stories you could wish for – true or imagined – to get off their chests.' She can finally let rip and laughs hysterically until tears roll down her cheeks.

'Is that supposed to be good?' Zac comments drily.

'You'll see!' she wipes her tears away with a crumpled tissue. 'How was your gardening club?'

'Not half as funny as your thespians by the sound of it,' he says, watching her struggle to regain control.

Eventually, they compare notes and conclude that the whole of Pewsey must have been abuzz for the last two and a half years with the rumours about things not being well in the Turner household. There were variations in the speculations, various suspects, but no one knew anything concrete; nothing could be substantiated; nobody had actually seen Lucinda and her lover. Testing for everyone's sense of curiosity!

'What are you thinking,' Zac asks breaking into Ant's reflections. She has gone very quiet, her eyes seem to look inwards and she hardly seems to breathe.

'Are you all right? Is it the lunch??'

She looks at him with incomprehension, as if woken from a dream.

'What is it then?' He waits for her answer.

'Something has bothered me for the last week. It suddenly struck me: all this is meant to divert our attention to the possibility that Lucinda had a lover, and that, indeed, she might have taken off to be with another person.'

'Who would have a vested interest in making us believe that?' but before Ant can answer, it dawned on him: 'It's Piers Turner, isn't it?'

She nods: 'His way of preparing the ground.'

'...diverting attention away from himself,' he concludes.

'...exactly. And I suspect he now realises that we are getting close.'

CHAPTER TWENTY – SEVEN

Ant has a surprise for Zac: 'Would you mind if we did another interview?' He had a hilariously unreal afternoon with the amateur dramatists. His head is buzzing and he is glad about Ant's company.

She explains to him, why she wants to ambush Sheridan Hall without prior appointment.

When they arrive, the door is opened by a middle-aged woman in an apron.

'I am so sorry. Mr and Mrs Sheridan have gone to London for the day.'

'Oh what a pity,' Ant says, feigning disappointment.

'It's just that we were in the area and thought we might clear up a couple of points we had been talking about.'

'Would you like to come back tomorrow? I am pretty sure that they will be here, because they said they did require my services.'

'No, no, that's fine,' Ant says, 'I shall do it over the phone.' And then adds, like an after-thought: 'Is Robert here?'

The housekeeper is clearly pleased that she can help in some way: 'Yes, Mister Robert is in the garden…let me try to explain the way.'

'Oh, don't worry. We know the way,' says Ant quickly. 'Thank you so much, and sorry to disturb you.'

Ant and Zac wander along the main path, the housekeeper had vaguely pointed out, through meadows, climbing over a stile, penetrating deeper and deeper into the Sheridan Estate. The sun is slowly edging to the horizon and the air temperature drops with every minute. Ant draws the strings of her Parka jacket tight and looks at Zac who assures her that he is not feeling the cold.

'Youth!' she teases him, 'no sense, no feeling.'

They come to a lake of considerable size surrounded by wildflowers and a couple of stone statues covered in lichen, depicting frolicking gods.

'We could be walking for hours,' Zac mumbles. 'Do you know what we are looking for?'

'I have a vague idea,' Ant answers his question.

'Do you know how big this estate is?' he asks again, looking a bit worried.

'No, Zac, but we are nearly there.' Zac fixes her with his gaze as if to say: I believe you, though thousands wouldn't. He really is a brick!

Suddenly, they see a small figure emerging from a copse of trees.

'Hi there,' he shouts from afar. 'Can I help you?'

They wait with the answer until they are standing face to face with him: 'Rrrr-Robert Sheridan,' he introduces himself and extends his hand. They both shake it.

'Aren't you the pppp-police woman who cccc-came to see my parents the other day?' Ant nods. 'So sorry, bbbb-but they are on a rare dddd-day outing. Did you make an appppp...?'

'No,' interrupts DS Weymouth to spare him further embarrassment. 'We have come to see you.' They had no idea that the youngest Sheridan has a stammer. When he can't get the words out, he goes beetroot-red under his blond fringe. He looks anxiously around and coughs.

'Deep breathes, Mr Sheridan! We do not mind waiting.' Ant smiles empathetically.

He takes a few gulps of air and then slowly gets his breathing into a rhythm. 'That's it. Controlled breathing,' Ant encourages him. 'Now try again!'

'Where did you learn that?' Zac whispers to Ant, but she is already listening to the object of their interest who finally manages to ask: 'Hhh-how can I hhh-help?'

'To be honest, Mr Sheridan, there are two things that interest us in connection with the disappearance of your sister, so we would appreciate honest and concise answers.' He nods.

'What was your relationship with your sister like?'

'Wha-wa-ww…' 'Breathe in slowly!' Ant reminds him gently, and suddenly his speech flows: 'As a kid, I adored her. We all did. She was always suppppp-portive, even wha-whawha when…' It is painful to listen to him, but he persists: 'even after I left college.'

'Why did you leave, Mr Sheridan?'

'Hhhh-health,' he says with sadness.

'I heard you are a gardener now.' His eyes dart from Ant to Zac like those of a frightened rabbit. 'Vbbb-begetables and hhh-herbs,' he confirms. 'I learnt from our hhh-head gardener.'

'How was your relationship with Lucinda after her marriage?'

His eyes darken and he looks to the floor: 'Not thatha-that that good.'

'Why?'

'Hhhh…Hhhhh….Her hhhhusband,' he is agitated again and rushes the last word out as if in panic, 'ddd-doesn't like me.'

'Did he have any reasons?' Zac asks.

Robert Sheridan shakes his head.

'Mr Sheridan, could it be that Mr Turner didn't like you growing and dealing in cannabis?'

He begins to splutter and cough, and Ant has to hit him on the back so that he doesn't choke. Then she reminds him again of his breathing. It takes ten minutes for him to recover.

'Why did you do it?' Ant asks gently.

'Earn mmmmm-my own money.'

'But you are doing such a good job growing vegetables and herbs and fruit. That's an excellent job!' Ant exclaims with sincerity.

'So what happened? Did Lucinda find out?'

'Yes.' he says, subdued, 'She mamamama made me destroy the plants.'

'Did she now? I am not surprised. She worked for the police, like we do.'

He nods. 'She wwwwanted me to go to agricultttsch…'

'Is that the Agricultural College?' Ant helps him along.

'…yeah, to study.'

'And did you enrol?'

He shakes his head.

'Can we see the place where you burnt the plants?' He nods again and begins to lead them to the trees, through the copse until the come to a treeless inner circle where the soil has still scorching marks.

'She would be very happy to see that you have stuck to your promise!' Ant praises him. 'Did she ever see it?'

'Yes, we dddddd-did it together.'

'Just being nosey: did she reward you?'

His face darkens again with shame: 'She gggg-gave me an alllllll…, mmm-money for lllll-loss of earnings.'

'…which of course, stopped the moment she disappeared, didn't it?

He nods again, the easiest way for him to communicate.

'All the more laudable, that you have stuck to your promise. She would be doubly proud of you!'

He looks up and smiles: 'I hhhh-hope so.'

'Just out of interest: is your brother Sebastian on drugs?'

'…nnnn-not anymore.'

'Good. 'Now tell me: how did you get on with Piers, your brother in law?'

Robert scratches his hair behind his right ear before answering: 'All right, I suppose.' No stammer, interestingly.

'When was the last time you saw him?'

'...after Lucinda disapppp-peared.' Another almost complete sentence, Ant noticed.

'Did he come to your house?'

'...no, he nnn-needed wwww-wood.'

'I thought he had woods of his own?'

'He hhhh-had used his up. I ccccc-cut the last trees on his land, and he asked for more from here.'

Baffling! 'Why did he need so much wood?'

'...wwww wood-burner.'

'But that's for the heating in the house. Why did he need heating in May?'

'The hhhh house must have bbbb-been bbbb boiling,' Robert is baffled by the mystery.

'Well, that is most interesting, Robert. You have been enormously helpful.'

He beams and looks suddenly so young, innocent and vulnerable. He also has Lucinda's beautiful blue eyes.

'I'll www walk you bbbbb back to the house,' he says. '...time fff-for dddd dinner.'

They stroll all the way back along the path which is now illuminated by old street lanterns.

'You live in the most beautiful place,' Ant says, 'take care of it – for Lucinda!'

'I hhhh-hope she comes back,' he says, looking pleadingly at his visitors. The words are hopeful, but the voice tells otherwise.

'...and, Robert?'

He looks up at her inquisitively.

'You are an intelligent young man. It's never too late to do that course at agricultural college. Landscape gardening would be very useful here,' she smiles and adds: 'If not for yourself, then do it for Lucinda!'

Is that a hopeful spark in his eyes she can see?

It's time to say good-bye to her colleague as well. 'I'll be quicker home than you will,' he remarks.

'It doesn't matter. We had an excellent day. Thank you so much for all your help, Zac!'

'Any time, Ant; I mean it!'

'It's good to know.' She gives him an affectionate nudge on the arm. 'Drive carefully.'

'You too.'

Ant is so buoyed up by the outcome of the day that she sings along the entire Carly Simon compilation CD until she is hoarse

CHAPTER TWENTY – EIGHT

There is a message from a Fertility Clinic, when Ant reaches home. It's too late to respond. It's even too late to say good-night to the Girls. The traffic on the M5 had been appalling.

The message doesn't give away much, so Ant rings them first thing in the morning. Of course, they remind her of their duty to patient confidentiality, but eventually – under a veiled threat of obstructing a criminal investigation – someone confirms that Lucinda and Piers had been patients in December 2014. However, Lucinda had cancelled all further consultations the following April, a month before she disappeared.

'Did she give a reason?' Ant asks, and when it is greeted by a pregnant silence, Ant gives the answer herself: 'Don't tell me! You can't say because of patient confidentiality.'

The receiver is hastily replaced.

'Pigs, here I come!' She is determined to spend quality time with them today.

'Look at you,' she greets them, and they come - more hobbling than running. Obviously, they still consider her as their favourite treat on legs. Ant is gratified that Felix hasn't replaced her in their affections yet.

'You are bulging, aren't you, Girls? How much longer do we have to wait?' Ant calculates: three months, three weeks and three days. That takes us to the 13th of February. 'Goodness,' she exclaims, 'It is only three weeks away! No wonder, you look so… well…pregnant.' Iolanthe gives her a fed-up look, as if to say: You are telling me!

Apart from the daily feed and check on fences, straw and water, there is not much to do. Felix has done a good job.

'I wonder what the Pewsey rumour was all about,' Ant muses. Usually, there is no smoke without fire, but village gossip can be vicious and totally incorrect. How could she find out? Who would know for sure? Whom would Lucinda have entrusted with such an explosive piece it of news? Kiki would have told her, but she hadn't mentioned any dalliances. Instead, she had described a rather subdued and down-trodden Lucinda. Ant decides on trying Robert. He seems to have been closest to her when she was still around; and since he had entrusted her with his big secret, she might have done the same in return. Damn, I should have asked him yesterday, she scolds herself.

She catches him at lunchtime when he receives her call with a full mouth of something.

'Rob Shsh…'

'Mr Sheridan,' she saves him further efforts, 'I am so sorry to bother you so soon again.'

'Oh it's Ant!' How does he know her pet-name? He must have overheard Zac using it. And then Robert Sheridan really begins to stammer with a vengeance

'Sssso ssssorry!' he splutters, 'Miss Bbb-Bell.'

'Breathe in slowly!' Ant admonishes him. 'Don't worry about calling me Ant. We might as well stick to first names, Robert.'

When he has recovered, she asks her question: 'Was there any indication that Lucinda was secretly in a new relationship? Man or woman?'

He begins to laugh: 'Ddd-did Piers suggest that?'

'Hmm,' says Ant leaving it open to interpretation.

'...of ccc-course not! She loved Piers.'

'Would she have told you?'

'Yes. We www-were always sharing from childhood.' Ant is relieved that he has relaxed into their conversation.

The villagers gossip about secret trysts. Evidently, she didn't attend some rehearsals and other meetings without explanation. Where could she have gone?'

A moment of silence spreads through the telephone line. Ant waits. She hears Robert clearing his throat: 'She went to marriage counselling.' Ant is not surprised, and waits for more information, which trickled through in burst: 'She didn't want ....Piers... and... our parents to know.'

'Where did the counselling sessions take place, Robert?'

'Bbb-Bath. Nobody knew her there.'

'And she was back within a day. That figures!' Ant concludeds 'Robert, you are a star!'

Even his laughter comes out as a stutter. He sounds pleased and shy at the same time; 'Really?'

'Yes, really! If agricultural college doesn't work, let me know and I'll recruit you!' she jokes.

He laughs heartily - freed of the fear of being judged.

'Byeee!' she says, cheerfully in the knowledge that they have made each other's day.

'I shall visit Lucinda's marriage guidance counsellor next!' She leaves a message for Bex.

Then she rings the Bath number and makes an appointment for the Saturday. She is astonished that that is possible, but the counsellor reassures her that he is working sometimes round the clock. Marriages fall apart any time, day or night.

Brilliant! She can pre-empt a delivery of straw and pellets in preparation for the happy event and collect it herself on the way home. She informs the wholesaler. As long as she comes before four p.m., they will be open. Two birds with one stone, although she hates the metaphor.

It's a long way up the motorway again; for the second time this week, but it has to be done.

At least it's Bath she has to go to. She loves Bath: honey coloured buildings; a place with all the amenities of a town, but friendlier, homely, more cultured and beautiful than most. It is always a treat to visit. During her first year of retirement, before she had animals, she had driven up the motorway to see a couple of plays at the theatre with some of her favourite actors who, after a week, took the plays to London.

She won't have any spare time today, but, having left her car in a side road off Widcombe Hill she can at least walk along the golden glowing buildings on her way up to Brock Street. Even the traffic is bearable, and people seem to have a smile on their faces.

She is a little early and enjoys strolling in the sunshine, when it suddenly begins to pour with rain, at an angle which will leave her drenched in spite of the Parka hood. She begins to trot up the hill and arrives twenty minutes before her appointment. She sits down on a chair put in the landing and waits. At least, she is in the dry.

'I am a little intrigued,' admits the marriage guidance counsellor after he has introduced himself: Nathan Wise. Mr Wise is short, about Ant's age – she calls it middle-aged - wiry and about forty years old; the top button of his duck-egg-blue shirt is undone, and his jeans are tightly tailored to his slim frame. A breath of fresh air compared to the stuffy Piers Turner, Ant thinks.

'You probably know that Lucinda Turner disappeared two years ago?'

'I didn't know for a long time. I wondered why she would suddenly stay away when she had seemed so keen,' Mr Wise says. 'I only heard when it was in the news. What a pity!'

'We are re-opening the case in the hope to find her or at least to find out what happened to her. Did she ever mention that she might simply leave her husband and hide away somewhere?'

'No, not at all!' he says with emphasis. 'when she first came, she thought, their troubles were all her fault, that she was miserly, selfish, ugly, stupid – the usual things men in the wrong indoctrinate their wives with.'

'That doesn't sound like her.' Ant shakes her head. 'You probably know that she is a pathologist. I worked with her for some time. She was intelligent, self-confident, capable, and to me, the kindest and most generous colleague.'

175

'She spoke very fondly of her previous job. I think she missed not going to work.'

'She told me, she probably would return. Why didn't she?'

'I don't want to talk out of turn, but I think, her husband vetoed many of her plans.'

'You think, her husband was a domineering bully?'

Mr Wise is taken aback by her directness; he coughs a little before answering: 'I can't really say that because I never met the man, but that was my one-sided impression.'

'How many times did she come to you?'

'For quite a few weeks – ten sessions, I would say.'

No wonder there were rumours flying around Pewsey.

'…and was she going to come back after the last session?'

'Yes definitely! She was booked in for the day after her disappearance. I think it was their wedding anniversary the day before.'

'Had she come to any conclusion while she was with you?'

'She was definitely,' obviously his favourite word, 'willing to make up with her husband; she was willing to make concessions, to come to an agreement. In fact, she hoped to bring him along to the next consultation.'

'Did that mean that she was willing to give in to his demands?'

'Her ultimate aim was to save her marriage, but she needed to work out some issues like going back to work; renewing her relationship with her family; to stop fertility treatment leaving it to chance to have a baby; and she wanted him to be honest about his business interests. There seemed to have been disagreements over money, too.'

'Isn't there always…' Ant mutters, recalling the usual motives for crimes: jealousy, greed, power over somebody, opportunity or pure badness.

'So you think, it is unlikely that she was about to leave her husband?'

'As far as I can tell, she was fighting for her marriage.'

'Thank you, Mr Wise. Would you be prepared to repeat that in court?'

'Definitely!' he says again with verve.

Ant is tempted to linger in Bath, but she decides to get back and pick up the straw and pig goodies on the way home. She is happy with the outcome of today's investigation. She hasn't done too badly in the last few weeks. She is getting there; the net is tightening; soon it will be time for drastic action.

CHAPTER TWENTY – NINE

'It's showdown time, Ant!' announces Bex after she has informed him about her findings. 'Can you put it all in writing?'

'You must be joking! I am surrounded by heavily pregnant pigs, and the weather isn't helping – whenever I go outside I get drenched or frozen or both. Yesterday was absolutely awful: it hailed, and I was slithering up and down the hill on ice pellets, as if I was lost on Mount Everest!'

'Can't you wait till it stops raining?'

Ant is outraged: 'You have no idea, have you, Bex! Animals don't wait; they begin to rampage; apart from the fact, that it's cruel.'

'All right, all right! I get the picture. But you know that you will have to write a report if this goes to Court.' She knows he is right.

'One step at a time, Bex. So, tell me, for when have you planned the show-down?'

'What?' Bex sounds distracted or confuse.

'You just said that it was time for a show-down. I am asking, when?' she presses on.

'Does it have to be a Thursday?' He answers her question with one of his own.

'I shall have to ask….'

'The blessed Felix, I know,' Bex interrupts with a degree of sarcasm.

'If you are ungrateful, he might refuse to stand in altogether, and then I'll be stuck!'

Bex ignores her: 'The sooner we confront the saintly Mr Turner, the better. He gets smugger with every day that passes. I am sure he is convinced that he will get away with it!'

'If indeed he has done it... So far, it hasn't thrown up any tangible new evidence; all our evidence is circumstantial. We have no proof. We checked alibis, we interviewed most witnesses again, we know now about the state of Lucinda's marriage before she disappeared, and we mustn't forget that the re-run of this investigation has been initiated by the husband of the missing person.

'...who is now rapidly turning into our chief suspect,' finishes Bex.

'You seem very sure, Bex. Does that mean that our efforts swing from finding Lucinda to nailing her husband for her murder?'

'Admit it, Ant: you always had a hunch about him.'

'Our investigation is about facts, not hunches,' she reminds him.

She doesn't deny it, though. She knows that however much of a hunch she has, she has to back it up with hard facts; it's her task to catch out the killer if and when he or she makes a mistake. That's the game. Piers Turner is clever and will be difficult to catch out! He has already managed to survive over two years, without being officially under suspicion. No wonder he is so sure of himself! Though, that could be his un-doing. We always live in hope, she thinks.

She had better ring Felix – again. He is so accommodating, but she does feel guilty to call him away from his father's farm at all days of the week. She will have to think of something special to thank him, when all this is over.

They ring Piers the following morning, claiming that they would like to report new developments in the investigation. He sounds surprised, but of course, has to feign interest.

Ant and Bex set off early and meet at the gate of the farm outside Pewsey at ten o'clock sharp.

'We must stop meeting like that,' Bex jokes, but Ant kicks him playfully in the ankle: 'Shut up, Bex, and be serious!'

'Lucky you rang,' Piers greets them, 'I had a meeting with a new supplier this morning. I had to put him back because of your visit.'

My heart bleeds, Ant thinks, but apologises: 'Sorry, to inconvenience you.'

Bex launches straight into imparting the results of their investigation: 'Mr Turner,' Bex begins in the unsettling tone of a CIO on duty, 'we have uncovered new strands of enquiry, new leads, new witnesses and new evidence.'

Piers Turner listens attentively in silence, until Bex gives him a chance to say something: 'For a start, I am still Piers to you; I don't know why you have gone all formal on me. I am the grieving party here, I gave the order to re-open the case, I am not one of your suspects – never have been; there are plenty of those around!' He leans back into the plump cushions of the settee with a satisfied smirk on his face.

'That's not how I see it, Mr Turner,' Bex continues: 'In fact, after having interviewed everyone else, we would like to put some questions to you.'

'Ha! The cheek of it! Antonia, aren't you going to say anything, or are you just there as the pretty appendage? Will Mr Chief Investigating Officer not let you speak? Has he still that much power over you?'

It stings. It's clear that Lucinda has told him. Ant had confided in her years ago, and it was self-understood that it would remain between them. Now she finds out that her friend has broken her promise. She has told her new husband - in the flush of young love - a man, who loves having power over people. Not a good person to tell secrets to because he will use it at some point to his advantage.

Bex notices Ant's embarrassment and barely suppressed fury; he knows, too, why she reacts like that. It's his fault. He is so sorry for her.

'How is your company, Turner's Limited, doing, Mr Turner?' Bex asks icily.

'Not bad. Could be better, but then, that's always the case. It's the economic climate worldwide. I strive to keep it on track.'

'Is that the first company you ever owned?'

Piers Turner looks at Bex with hatred: 'Well,' he drags out the word, 'like all businessmen...,'

'...and women,' Ant mutters under her breath.

'...I had a few trial runs with other things, but nothing disastrous.'

'Let's call it by its name, Mr Turner: they all went bust,' Bex ploughs on: 'Would you say that your business finances are on an even keel?'

'Why are you asking? Yes! More or less,' he declares confidently and turns to where Ant is sitting. Didn't you tell him, Antonia? You have spoken to my staff recently.'

'That's true, and the bank confirmed what your employees were saying, Mr Turner.' Ant's face is frozen and her voice steely; although she hates the thought, she forces herself to look at him with unwavering professionalism without allowing him any lee-way.

'Oh, not you as well,' he sounds exasperated, takes his tortoiseshell-rimmed glasses off and wipes them clean with a handkerchief from his trouser pocket. He puts the glasses back on his nose and says, more calmly: 'All this formal bullshit! Be normal, girl!'

'...as I was saying, Mr Turner, your bank confirmed that your business affairs are indeed on an even keel, but only because your wife has put considerable amounts of her money into Turner's Limited.' They both observe his reaction to this undeniable fact. He leans back again into the upholstery to show that he is unperturbed; then he snarls, twisting his lips in contempt, his eyes narrowing warningly:

'All I can say to that is that she wanted to contribute; she was desperate to do so because she was keen to support me. It wasn't so much about the money; it was about a wife supporting her husband – but of course, you wouldn't know about that, would you, Miss Bell!'

Ant swallows hard and looks past him to a point on the wall.

'Your financial director and your bank manager,' Bex takes over, 'both men had been made to believe that there would be another big transfer to the company's account in May 2015, but it never happened.'

'Of course not! Lucinda disappeared, and I had more serious matters on my mind - like trying to find her,' he barks with indignation.

'What was the state of your marriage at the time of your wife's disappearance, Mr Turner? Would you say you were a happy couple?' Ant changes the topic.

Turner isn't easy to confuse: 'Of course, everybody can tell you so. We had a wonderful life together, and I worshipped the ground she walked on! That's why I am still looking for her!'

'So, can you please, explain: why did your wife seek help from a marriage guidance counsellor?'

'What? How do I know? She never mentioned it to me; she never asked me to join her. I had no idea! Why would she do that? I think you have made it up!' He looks mockingly at Ant and sneers: 'Women are sometimes so irrational.' A thought seems to occur to him and he adds, out of the blue: 'Was he the one she had an affair with?'

'Why are you saying that, Mr Turner? You just said that you were blissfully happy. Was that the truth?'

'I never listen to gossip, but the whole of Pewsey was full of it. It was hard to ignore it.'

'Did you ask your wife about it?'

'Yes, in fact, I did. She denied it, and I believed her.'

'In answer to your earlier question, it is unlikely that your wife had an affair with the marriage guidance counsellor. In fact, your wife seems to have genuinely looked for advice on how to save her marriage.'

'What nonsense! I don't believe a word of it!' Piers Turner spits out. 'Her parents put her up to it!'

'And why would her parents do that?'

'That's easy!' he mocks them, 'they never liked me. They always thought they were way above me. I wasn't good enough for their precious daughter. In reality, it's them being dysfunctional, petty and interfering busybodies!'

'Would you say that you were a loving, supportive husband, Mr Turner?' Now he looks confused by the quick change of subject. Is he losing control? He is red in his face, fidgeting with his hands, then clasping them tightly, his breaths coming fast and furious.

'You are insane, you two!' he retaliates. 'Of course, I was. Is that why you came out here, to tell me that I was a bad husband? Is that all you can come up with - after months of investigation? Pitiful! And I trusted you!'

'Answer the question, Mr Turner!'

'Of course, I was,' he shrieks, 'I adored her. I still do. I miss her! How many times do I have to repeat myself?'

'Would you say that you supported her in every aspect of your married life?'

Piers ignores the question, but when Bex is about to repeat the question, he screams: 'What is that supposed to mean? This is ridiculous! How dare you! You should have warned me that I am under suspicion, so I could have asked my solicitors to be present!'

'…and were you supporting Lucinda in her plans?' Ant asks gently.

'You know I was,' he turns to her with a vicious hiss.

'Did you want any children?' Ant carries on unperturbed.

'Of course we did! Is that what this is all about?'

'Why, do you think, Lucinda cancelled the Fertility Clinic treatment?'

'Did she?' he is genuinely surprised, and, when the news sinks in, he looks hurt.

'Why did she change her mind, do you think?'

He shrugs his shoulders and suggests: '…because she was too old?'

'The clinic didn't think so. But never mind. There is another question, Piers,' Ant tries to pacify him before the next ambush: 'Why did Lucinda never go back to work, although she had contacted her previous colleagues and had said that she planned to do so. I think January 2016 was the date she had set her heart on. Did you support her in that?''

Piers Turner sighs and seems to resign himself to the interrogation: 'I wasn't overjoyed, but she was a grown woman, and I wasn't going to stand in her way,' he says listlessly with a wave of one hand, as if to brush away the importance of the matter.

'What about the financial transactions? You must have been furious when your wife refused to give you any more money to bail out Turner Limited.' Bex hopes that Turner wouldn't notice that this was a guess, a stab in the dark.

Piers Turner only shrugs his shoulders in disbelief that this is happening to him.

'You see, Mr Turner, all these little bits of information add up to a picture of Lucinda being married to a controlling, manipulative and financially desperate husband. We had to ask!'

'You are saying now, that I killed my wife? That she wasn't missing at all, but dead all along, and I am the murderer?' He now shouts at the top of his voice. Are you out of your mind?'

'We didn't say that, Mr Turner. We thought more of the option that you might have driven her away. There were enough reasons.' Bex says firmly, as if to bring a mathematical problem to its logical conclusion.

'I don't accept that at all! Now, get out of my house, and start again, looking for my wife. You are an insult to her and, come to think of it, to the police!' He jumps up from the settee, comes threateningly close to them and shouts into their faces: Out! 'Do you hear me? Out!'

They get up and are ushered out of the room, along the corridor and towards the entrance: 'I shall complain to your superiors! You are a disgrace!' he repeats, opens the door and threatens to push them out physically. They quickly retreat and head for their cars.

When they hear the door slam, Bex laughs: 'That rattled him!' he says.

'I have never been thrown out before,' Ant says, bemused, and then allows herself a giggle, too.

'Bex, I could kick myself: I totally forgot something important.' Ant has stopped on the motorway service station halfway home.

'Oh great! I am just opening my front door.'

'We have to go back.'

'What, now? How do you suppose he will take this? Are you expecting a welcome with open arms? What is it?'

'I forgot to ask him about the wood-burning stove.'

'Ant, what for? Why are you worrying about his heating? And by the way, I didn't see a wood-burning stove.'

'That's just it. It's in one of the outhouses.'

'I don't think he will be willing to show you his wood burner. Not while he is seething.'

'I must have a look. Shall I go back now under the cover of darkness…?'

'Ant, what's the matter with you? Have you lost leave of your senses? No, under no circumstances! It's too dangerous. He might murder you as well! Stuff you into the wood-burner…!' There is silence. 'Oh no, you don't think…'

'I need to have a look at it. I have a…'

'…hunch?'

'Yes!' she says meekly.

'I think, so do I now, but Ant, not now! Not today! You are tired, and so am I. We'll talk soon; tomorrow morning, I promise!'

'But it's really important!' She sounds desperate like a shipwrecked sailor reaching for a life raft.

'Tell you what,' Bex relents, 'we'll find out who installed the wood-burner, so you can speak to them first. By then, Piers Turner will have calmed down. It's always better to confront the suspect with solid facts.'

'Thank you, Bex, thank you! I was going spare here trying to think…'

'That's not good, driving on the motorway and trying to solve a murder at the same time, Ant. We are both too tired to think. Now go home, go to bed, have a good night's sleep and have a fresh start tomorrow morning.'

It sounds so banal, but she knows he is right: 'Wait!' she shouts before he has a chance to switch off the mobile, 'how do I find out who installed it?'

She hears him sigh in exasperation: 'Ant, you really are exhausted. So don't try to think anymore. Give your brain a rest. And as to your question: ring Robert Sheridan or his brother, the church architect. I wouldn't be surprised if one of them knew. And after that it's easy: you ring the wood-burning stove contractor and ask your questions.'

She takes a deep breath: 'I so wanted to have a look at it.'

'You can't, not tonight, because we annoyed Piers Turner a few hours ago. However, if it helps to keep you away from doing anything silly tonight,, I think we are entitled to a warrant soon, which will give us the full run of his property, and then you can examine that wood-burner to your heart's content.'

'Are you talking about a full forensic sweep, too?'

'…if it makes you happy, yes. I'll organise it.'

'You are a star!' she blurts out. In old times, she would have kissed him. No chance now.

'Now, let's both forget all about it, and, for heaven's sake, drive carefully.'

'Shall do,' she says, more chirpily. 'Night, night, Bex.'

She keeps her promise and drives home at moderate speed. Bex had always been her protector when she got carried away – a kind of father figure to an impetuous daughter. She loved and still loves his caring side when at rare occasions it appears from underneath the hard armour of experiences of the worst kind. She had never seen him falter and crumple into a heap; he had always been there to console everybody else. She doesn't seem to be over him just yet…

You are going soft, she scolds herself. Make sure that it has worn off by the morning!

CHAPTER THIRTY

It is a piece of good fortune that the company, who had installed the heating system, including the enormous wood-burner, during the renovation of the farmhouse under the watchful eye of Alfred Sheridan - is a reputable one, still in existence and much closer to Ant's home than the Turner's.

By the morning, Ant has changed her mind and prefers a visit there to a simple phone call.

'Come out and have a look,' a friendly voice suggests. 'We are not particularly busy today.' She fears, she has raised hopes of a big sale.

When she arrives, she clarifies the purpose of her visit, and she is pleased that the nice voice's owner, an enthusiastic young man with a fierce short, back and sides haircut, doesn't stop smiling. In fact, he appears to be quite excited by the thought of helping in a murder case with his humble knowledge.

'We have wood burning stoves, multi-fuel burning stoves, boiler stoves, external air stoves, pellet stoves. What are you interested in?'

'Something that gets very hot, burns everything and copes with heating a huge farmhouse.'

'Do they have radiators?'

'Yes. I have no idea how many, but I would guess between thirty and forty.'

The young man whistles. Is that the way to communicate nowadays, she wonders?

'The output must be at least 25 kw. Is it in the house?'

No, it's in a purpose-built outhouse. You know it. Your company installed it.'

'We didn't sell one of that size last year.'

'It wasn't last year; it was in 2013.'

'Oh, I wasn't here four years ago. I only joined last May.'

'Who would know?'

'Mr Wood, the owner. He is sort of semi-retired, but he still does all the paperwork.'

'Can I speak to him?' Ant asks hopefully.

'It's his day off, but he is usually at home, not far from here. I'll give him a ring.'

'You are very helpful. Thank you. What was your name again?'

He looks at her with suspicion, and she quickly smiles at him reassuringly.

'Pete,' he says finally and with some reluctance.

'Just so I can let your boss know how helpful and knowledgeable you are.'

He trots off happily to make the call.

The aptly named Mr Wood couldn't come to the shop as he was otherwise engaged, but asks for Ant to come to the phone in the little office.

'Antonia Bell here, investigating forensic scientist for the Wiltshire Police Force. I am so sorry to disturb you on your day off, Mr Wood. Can I ask you just a couple of questions?'

'Yes, of course.'

'Do you remember installing and servicing a boiler wood-burner of enormous proportions? It was in an outhouse belonging to a big estate near Pewsey in Wiltshire.'

'When was that?' Mr Wood wants to know.

'Some four years ago?'

'I do,' says Mr Wood confidently. 'For a Mr and Mrs Turner, but the brother, an architect, was in charge.' His words are difficult to understand; he sounds as if he has a heavy cold. Then he sneezes.

'Bless you,' Ant says with sympathy before she asks the next question: 'How often did you service the burner?'

'As usual: twice a year.'

'And were there any problems?'

'Not with the stove.'

'…with anything else?'

'Yes, about two years ago, I think somebody put too much stuff into the burner - and not all wood. It was a mess, so I was called in. The owner said he was not well and needed to keep warm, so when he had run out of wood, he just burnt any old rubbish.'

'Are you talking about Mr Turner?'

'Yes, nice man. He gave us an extra bonus for clearing it all up.' He pauses and Ant waits. Will he divulge anything else? She is soon rewarded for her patience: 'Though come to think of it, he is a bit eccentric.'

'What makes you think that, Mr Wood?'

'Well, he has plenty of his own wood to burn, I would have thought, but he wanted me to recommend a reliable wood merchant.'

'And did he ever use him?'

'Ever use him?' Mr Wood scoffs, 'he almost bled him dry. That man bought it by the lorry-load. My friend had hardly any wood left for his other customers.'

'Is Mr Turner still buying up so much wood now?'

'No. It stopped only a few months after his wife disappeared. Maybe she was the one who wanted to be warm all the time?' he speculates.

'Are you sure, he used it all? He might just have wanted to stock up his log store.'

'No, when I did that horrible service two years ago, where everything was grimy and greasy and what not, I met my friend there. He was just delivering another lorry-load and moaned like stink that he could hardly keep up with Mr Turner's demand. I didn't see it, but apparently, a log store full to the brim was emptied within a month.'

'Did you see any ash heaps?'

'Nothing… Everything was pristine, at least what I saw: the yard and the outhouse the burner is in. Just the inside of the wood-burner and the flue were filthy.'

'Would you know by any chance, what he did with the enormous amount of ash, he must have produced?'

'Maybe he bagged it up and took it to the tip; or gave it to neighbouring farmers for their fields. No idea. Sorry, I can't help you there.' He sneezes again.

'I shall let you go in a minute, Mr Wood. Just one more question: When are you due to service that boiler again?'

'Ah well; that's a bit of a mystery. After being so happy with our services, Mr Turner decided to discontinue our contract, and to ask somebody more local.'

'That's a pity. I am sure it had nothing to do with the quality of your service. Mr Turner has a lot on his mind lately and one last thing before I go: your young man in the shop, Pete, is a real credit to your business; really helpful, friendly and knowledgeable.'

'That's good to know. Yeah, he is a good sort.'

'He is, indeed. Thank you so much, Mr Wood. I hope your cold gets better soon. Bye now.'

She replaces the receiver and turns to see Pete standing five foot away, beaming.

'That was worth, me coming in today. I wish, every day was that interesting.'

'I assure you, Pete, there are boring bits in every job - even mine.' He looks incredulous while holding the door open for her.

I wonder what Piers Turner has done with the mountains of ash, she thinks, as she drives back to her farm through winding country lanes.

———————

'When do you want the forensic sweep, as you call it, Ant?' she finds Bex's message when she gets home.

She returns the call immediately to tell him about her visit to the wood-burning stove merchant and her suspicions.

'What was your question again?'

'Forensic sweep, young lady?' He is so nice when he is in a good mood. 'Not keen!' Ant thinks she has misheard and asks: 'Why?'

'Why, what? Bex, we need to confirm our suspicions and underpin them with scientific proof!' She can't believe that she has to defend her request. Why is he so stroppy this time?

'I don't think I get the budget for another sweep of the house – so shortly before my retirement.' He sounds resigned.

'Bex, do you want us to solve Lucinda's case or don't you? Where is your fight? Money is the least of my worries. If necessary, I shall do it for nothing!' she shouts in exasperation into the receiver.

There is a long pause, and Ant is tempted to throw the receiver back into its cradle.

'What's the date today?' he finally asks grumpily.

'Oh Bex, pull yourself together. Has your brain gone mushy?

'I am glad you noticed; so I need to be treated with care.'

'Fat chance!' she retorts bitterly. She used to like their banter, but this is more vicious than fun. They are both on edge. She brushes her sadness away and continues her fight for this one thing she needs: another forensic sweep. She might even be closer to prove her hunch than she suspects

'Now, can I make a suggestion? My pigs are due to have their litter on the 13th of February. Let Mr Turner have a bit of time to stew. Let's make our reports water-tight until then, and prepare for the big day, so that nothing escapes us. How does 20th of February grab you?'

Bex chokes.

'That long? And there I was thinking you were ready to do it tomorrow.' She can hear the sarcasm in his tone of voice. 'Are you still on board, Ant?' He is furious.

'A moment ago, you didn't want to fight for a sweep at all,' she snaps. After a moment, she pulls herself together, calms her temper and tries to explain her preferred mode of action: 'By then, we shall be super-prepared, and nothing will escape us. I just need to be with my pigs and their little ones for a few days. I don't want any mishaps – that they squash them or lie on them or don't let them suckle, and that they are keeping them warm, should it get really cold. Big test for my fences, too: the curly-haired pigs are notorious for their escape attempts - a very naughty lot!'

'I am not happy,' she can hear it in Bex's sulky tone. 'I think we should do it earlier!'

'Once all the work in the lab starts, I have to hand over the pigs to Felix. I can't do it when the piglets have just been born!'

'Disappointing,' Bex mutters, but he seems mollified though he can't help adding: 'Time is running out,'

'You'll be busy, putting everything in place, organising a team and so on. You'll have plenty to do. It has to happen like clockwork! Don't worry; everything will turn out right. Trust me!'

'I'll have to, don't I?'

'Tell you what: 'We'll make it Monday the 21st February.'

'That's your birthday!' Bex exclaims. Goodness! He remembers.

'Correct!' Her reply is matter-of fact, in spite of experiencing a ray of pleasure; 'I will give myself a nice birthday present.'

CHAPTER THIRTY – ONE

Not that she likes doing it, but Ant decides to make use of the time at home and to get her house in order. It needs a clean; there is a lot of laundry to be done; the windows are almost blind from the winter rains, fogs, hail and winds; and her freezer is almost empty except for a packet of chips and another full of garden peas. So shopping goes on her long list of things to do.

The Girls are getting grumpier by the day. Even Jerome has decided that enough is enough; he doesn't want any more rejections nor be anywhere near them; nobody has seen him for days. He must be on top of the hill, keeping to himself. The food bowls are empty every morning, to Ant's relief. It tells her, he is around.

Ant begins with her early spring clean. It's not her favourite pastime, but she won't have much time later on in the month when the piglets are born. And shortly after that, the case will take over her every waking hour and probably some nights. She hopes that the forensic sweep and subsequent scientific tests in the lab will bring them several steps closer to a conclusion of what really happened to Lucinda. Ant has no idea how long she will have to stay in Devizes. She certainly won't be able to drive up and down the motorway every day. She will have to stay until the results are known; until she has proof one way or another. However, she is determined that she will see it through; she will solve the case. She feels she is so close. She has done all the tedious preliminary groundwork. She has checked everything over that had been done before, has collected new circumstantial

evidence; she has a suspect and an ever strengthening hunch –
now she just needs to prove it.

After three days of tidying, scrubbing stone floors, dusting and
hoovering the few carpets she owns, the house looks more
acceptable. The laundry is done, just not ironed yet (very few of
Ant's clothes need ironing, and the ones which do, might have to
wait a while), and the bedclothes are freshly laundered, too. She
likes to snuggle into a fresh bed. She could take the curtains
down, give the book shelves a wipe-down and clean out the
fridge, but she has lost impetus. She is proud with what she has
done, but can't work up any enthusiasm to carry on. She is bored
and exhausted. She turns her attention to the mail she hasn't
opened for a couple of days. Next will be the wretched
paperwork, once the piglets are born, and Bex wanted a report as
well. No rest for the wicked…

Felix comes by to check that she is okay and to find out when
his next assignment would be due. She gives him a cup of tea;
they chat amicably about the planned schedule for the next
couple of weeks.

'Will you call me when something happens?'

'Of course, I will. In fact, if you fancy and have time, you can
come and help any time you like. I am sure they will be a
handful, especially as it will be my first litter.'

He looks at her in a funny way and grins.

'Let me rephrase that: it will be my pigs' first litter.'

'And I am the honorary Dad, I presume,' he quips. Ant nods
vigorously and thinks that Felix is such a nice chap; strange that
he hasn't been snapped up yet by a good woman; he would make

someone, including his parents, very happy. Maybe he is simply the cautious type...

'Give me a call!' He leaves, chuckling to himself.

That same evening, she is having a long one-sided conversation with Iolanthe who is obviously the most patient of the Girls, at least pretending to listen, while waiting for extra titbits form Ant's bowl.

'Not long to go,' Ant says and Iolanthe grunts.

'You must be getting fed up, carrying all this extra weight. I wonder how many babies you have in there.' To the delight of Iolanthe, Ant throws down a punnet of very expensive strawberries apple and three courgettes, 'I must keep your spirits up,' Ant chuckles 'vegetables and fruit are good for you, Girl: lots of vitamin A.'

The others come to inspect what has been going on. They fight over the last two courgettes.

'Persephone, you look terrible,' Ant exclaims. Persephone isn't quite sure, how to take this. 'You look like a potbellied pig not a Mangalica!' Persephone takes that as a compliment and tucks into grapes, more strawberries and half a cucumber. '...and Agatha!' she exclaims, 'my goodness! I am astonished that you can still waddle. Your teats are like balloons.'

She shudders at the thought of pregnancy happening to her. It won't happen now, thankfully. It is not something she has ever aspired to; pregnant women looked always so uncomfortable. No, truly: she has no regrets. Luckily, the pigs seem to take it in their stride. They don't want sympathy, just food.

'Give me a squeal, when you need me,' she says, grabs the empty containers and marches down the hill. It hasn't rained quite so heavily today; the soil is drying in places along the way down. As she turns round to give them one last look, she sees them stuffing their nesting hollows with fresh straw.

Ant wakes up in the middle of the night and has a bad feeling. She opens the bedroom curtains and can hear the howling of the wind immediately through the glass panes. It drives something white horizontally through the night air. Sleet, she thinks, listening to the sound it makes as if someone throws handfuls of pebbles at the window. Can she hear squealing? Maybe her instincts and imagination are working overtime? No harm in checking, though, now that she is up anyway. She pulls her washed-out thick pullover over her head and pulls on her jeans. By the door, she clamps an old battered rain hat over her unruly hair and steps into her Wellingtons. She shudders, when bits of sleet hit her in the face. Still, she trudges up the hill, bent forward, leaning into the squalls. As she gets closer to the pigs' enclosure, she can indeed make out squealing and grunting and groaning. They can't hear her above the howling wind. She climbs over the fence and almost treads on something soft, like a cow pad. She bends down and can feel a warm, smooth little body still sticky and slimy to the touch. 'Oh no! Not the piglets tonight!' Ant shouts into the wind and hears more groaning in reply. It's Persephone who is giving birth. 'What a night to choose,' Ant commiserates. Persephone lies in the straw hollow, the gales sweeping over her shuddering body, oblivious to the world, just groaning, contracting and pushing, until another piglet pops out. Ant picks it up and puts it with its sibling, away from the sow's enormous body. Mum could easily squash one of her new-borns.

'You are doing so well, girl' Ant cheers her on, drenched to the skin; her pony-tail-elastic has broken and wet strains of hair are falling over her eyes; her hands are slippery from a mixture of rain, sleet and birthing goo. The other two mothers-to-be are sitting in their hollows, looking languidly at their sister.

'Don't look too closely,' Ant suggests, 'you might be next.' After an eternity, and the birth of eleven piglets, the straining, groaning and grunting stops. Ant, covered in a sticky mess and wet through, grabs some of the piglets, as their mother sighs and makes an effort to drag herself up and, walking away, almost steps on one of her off-spring. 'Don't worry,' Ant picks it up and cradles it, 'she'll be back in a minute. She is just thirsty.' So it is. When mum comes back, she lets herself fall heavily into the hollow and each piglet finds a teat to suck. Iolanthe and Agatha have got up and now stand like matronly guards over the scene. The gusts of wind are still blowing over the hillside, and Ant is loath to leave them to it.

'Are you going to have your litter tonight, too?' she shouts across the whistling and howling. Half an hour later, Ant tells herself, that she will catch her death if she spends all night out here. Mum, aunties and piglets have gone to sleep, unaware of the gravity of what has happened. Ant checks one more time to make sure that Persephone is comfortable. It is a picture to behold: a mother pig exhaustedly resting, ears still pricking up occasionally in her half-sleep, and eleven miniature copies of her snuggling up. 'Night-night,' whispers Ant as if tucking them in.

When she gets back to the house, she takes all her clothes off, takes a hot shower, rubs herself dry and climbs back into bed with a contented smile on her lips. Two more to go now!

She rings Felix as early as she can, and asks him to do the morning round.

'Last night?' He is aghast. 'Isn't that a bit early?'

'I know. I must have missed the moment when they got pregnant. I did make a note on the wall calendar, but obviously on the wrong day. Anyway, who wants to be born on the 13th of February?'

'Why?' Felix's brain is obviously not in gear yet either.

'The thirteenth, get it?!

'I didn't know you were superstitious…'

'Forget I said that.' She is too tired to explain.

'So, when are the others due?'

'No idea,' Ant grins. 'They have totally thrown me. Your guess is as good as mine; I would say, any time now.'

'Oh great! Well, I don't mind staying overnight to help.'

'I know, Felix, that's very sweet of you, but I think, we girls don't want a male observer while we are at it. But if you could help after a sleepless night, that would be great!'

He knocks on the door twenty minutes later. 'I'll go straight up to see to them,' he says, and with a nod towards Ant he adds: '… and you better go back to bed for a couple of hours. You look as if you need it.'

It is nerve-wrecking, waiting for the other two litters. Ant would like it to happen rather sooner than later, but on the other hand, the 13th is still the official date. She is not in favour of premature litters just so she can get back to the case. With a bit of luck for all concerned, she might have miscalculated.

In the end, one litter arrives three days later; the last surprises her the morning after that.

'You have given birth all by yourself, you good girl,' Ant is thrilled, but Agatha ignores her. She is far too busy rounding up her babies to keep them together. They mustn't wander off and get cold. Every so often she guides them to the cosy nest hollow, lies down and lets them suckle; luckily, the number of teats and piglets tally, so there is no need for fighting.

'Persephone eleven, Iolanthe nine and Agatha twelve: thirty-two! My goodness! You will eat me out of house and home!' Ant couldn't be happier.

'You are old hands at this,' Ant turns to Iolanthe and Persephone who look on, *blasées* with their day old advantage of experience in mothering.

The only problem now is that it is freezing cold, even during daytime. Ant fears for the little energetic, squealing bundles that they wander off and get separated from the rest. Their safety lies in their togetherness, the warmth and shelter their mothers provide. Ant checks on everybody hourly. The next day the weather isn't any better: morning thick fog, low sky heavy with snow, freezing; early afternoon: the odd ray of milky sunshine, its warmth not penetrating the icy air, and later, before dusk: rain turning into hard, painful sleet. It is pitiful! Poor little things! Even Ant doesn't want to leave the house, never mind stay outdoors all night. When she finds them, they are huddled under trees, shielding the little ones in their midst to keep them warm.

Luckily, the weather forecast promises more clement weather for the following days, and they are mercifully right. The nights are not quite so bitingly cold, and the warmer days raise hopes of an early spring.

By the thirteenth of February, everybody is doing well; the pig pen has turned into a noisy playground. The boar is nowhere to be seen, and the Girls carry on with their old life of rooting and sleeping between impatient feeds of their broods.

Ant is amazed that they have already begun to be boisterous youngsters, rather than cute babies one can cradle. She is satisfied that Felix can take over.

She leaves a message on Bex's telephone: 'Piglets arrived; doing well; ready for the last push!'

CHAPTER THIRTY – TWO

Bex is delighted and has organised the obligatory warrant. Every day counts. When he rings Piers Turner on Sunday evening, the nineteenth of February that a whole team of police officers and forensic scientists would be on their way to his address the following morning, he senses annoyance rather than panicked. Either that man has a clear conscience or nerves of steel. Bex isn't sure which.

When they all arrive at seven in the morning, Piers comes just out of the shower, a black silk dressing gown hastily slung around his tall frame and secured by a gold coloured belt.

'Do I have a choice?' Piers asks pointedly, as Bex shows him the warrant. Silence confirms that he hasn't.

'Do you want me to be out of the house?' he wants to know.

'That might be a good idea, to begin with, just so that the officers can get on with the rudimentary work, but we would like to know where you will be in case we need to ask you questions.'

'Does that mean that I am now officially a suspect?'

'Why are you asking?'

'Because that's what it feels like,' Piers looks crestfallen and rather disappointed. 'I have trusted you! This is totally unfair!' He stands around undecidedly for a while, before saying to no-one in particular: 'I shall go into the office and be back here at lunchtime,' 'I need to do something; I can't just stand around all day and watch you taking my house apart.'

'That's probably a good idea, Mr Turner,' Bex tries to sound conciliatory, but Piers rolls his eyes finding the comment obviously patronising.

'We shall be as quick as we can, but you will understand, Mr Turner, that we must be thorough – for Lucinda's sake!'

'Is young Miss Bell not talking to me today?' Piers changes tactic, smirking.

Ant has heard it and smiles at him with all her charm: 'I am concentrating on work, Mr Turner. We do want to find your wife, don't we?'

He looks at her with suspicion: 'Well, I can assure you, she isn't here! And on another point: why is everybody suddenly calling me Mr Turner? I used to be a friend of yours. You came to my wedding,' he seems at a loss to understand.

'This is a professional visit; and we do want to maintain the highest professional standards, don't we?' Ant points out and adds as a kind of consolation: 'I shall save all my questions for this afternoon, and I promise you a long chat.'

Piers bursts into a dry laugh: 'Is that a threat or a promise? I wish you good luck, Miss Bell! I shall get ready now and make myself scarce.' With these words, he storms back along the hall and disappears upstairs, the gold coloured belt ends swinging.

'Leave the upstairs for when he is gone,' Ant whispers to her colleagues. 'Let's get started down here: carpets first!'

By the time, Piers comes downstairs again, freshly showered and beautifully suited, they have taken up the sitting room carpet. He is outraged:

'This is a brand new carpet. Your last lot ruined the one we had initially. What the hell are you hoping to find? Everything has already been several times under the microscope.' He sounds genuinely upset.

'I promise, we shall put everything back as it was,' Ant says apologetically and nods to everyone to carry on.

'You better go now, Mr Turner,' she whispers in sympathy, takes him gently by the elbow, leads him through the entrance door and promises: 'We shall put everything back the way it was.'

'Bex, can I have a word?' she calls when she hears the furious roaring of Piers' car driving off. They stand in the middle of the vast bare-floored sitting room. 'We are now assuming that he has killed her. First question: Where?'

'It could be anywhere.'

'Right, let's be systematic: room by room. Somehow this sitting room seems to play a big role. He keeps leading us into here as if to goad us. Don't ask me why, but most of the other rooms simply don't make much impression on me.'

'…another hunch?' Bex grins.

'Possibly… Now…Let's have a look at the photographs from two years ago.' She is searching for it on her mobile screen, letting her index finger scroll it up and down.

'Where did you get that from?' Bex asks.

'I photographed a lot of the evidence collected two years ago. So, let's compare.'

'Are we playing *spot the difference*?'

'Clever boy!' Ant teases him.

'Well, to start with, he has changed the carpet.'

'Quite!' Ant agrees, 'he changed the carpet only in this one room; not in any of the others.'

'Is it possible that any traces have survived any heavy cleaning efforts and the first forensic sweep two years ago?'

'You never know. When you think, how blood spurts out from wounds, like a sneeze or a fountain, and sticks to any surface, there could still be a chance that we find some blood droplet in a crevice. We only have to find it!' Ant is really warming to her theme.

Bex doesn't look quite so enthusiastic.

'We also,' Ant continues, 'have to find the murder weapon which, of course, he might have cleaned or discarded or both.'

'Surely he has got rid of whatever he used to kill Lucinda by now.' Put into words for the first time sounds so awful, so final. 'If he has,' Bex reminds her.

'I have known murderers, who actually used the murder weapon as a tease for the investigating officers. It was literally staring them in the face, until the penny dropped. Murderers always think that they are cleverer than the police; and if they realise that the investigation has hit a dead-end, they like to taunt them.'

'We also need to think about the entry and exit path of the victim,' Bex takes up the train of thought. 'Where did she come in, where was she murdered. Was her body stored anywhere before it was bundled out of the house; how? Was the body wrapped and if so, in what? Did the murderer carry the bundle outside? If Lucinda was dead, she would be heavy, heavier than if she was alive or unconscious. There must be traces!'

'My guess is,' Ant elaborates, that Lucinda was killed somewhere on the ground-floor, and dragged out through either the front or the back door.'

'…which means, the corridor on the ground-floor would be our path of exit and entry,' Ant deducts.

'Most likely,' Bex agrees and calls one of the forensic team to cordon off the space spanning from the entrance of the house to the sitting room door.

'Is there a back door?' Bex shouts to no one in particular, turning round to locate it.

'Yes, but it leads directly into brambles,' a young police officer replies quickly. Bex is impressed by his initiative. 'No harm in combing them as well,' he orders.

'Right,' Ant announces, 'I shall wander around the house, take photographs before the team move everything, and then we can play our game of *Spot the differences*.'

'Meet you in half an hour,' Bex suggests.

'At the latest… I'll start at the top.'

Only ten minutes later, she hears Bex calling her name up the stairs. She comes out of the main bedroom and sticks her head over the banister:

'Yeah? This better be good!'

'It is, Ant! They found something in a groove between the floor boards.'

'What?'

'Come down and have a look yourself. They think it might be blood.'

'Coming!' she shouts down. As she arrives on the ground floor, she sees the 'path' having been cordoned off with tape to indicate the places where not to tread. She squeezes past.

'Where?' she asks Bex who points to a group of crouching colleagues. One young woman gets up, as Ant approaches to make room for her. They look at each other and the white clad SOCO (Ant still thinks of them as SOCOs rather than the Americanized term of CSI) called Jo Morello, nicknamed Cherry, , nods in confirmation: It is blood, as far as we can determine without looking at it under the microscope.'

'Great! Where did you find it?'

'In a groove on the parquet flooring, close by the window.'

'Bag it up and send it to the lab as soon as possible.' Bex was glad that he had warned the laboratory staff that there might be a lot of work coming their way.

'Shall do, Ma'am', the eager young woman assures her. 'I am not…' Ant begins to explain, but then thinks the better of it. How they address her, isn't relevant, and a bit of respect never hurts. Instead she says: 'Good work, Cherry! Carry on!' Praise is much more important.

'I wonder why this trace of blood was missed the last time.'

'Let's face it, there is always something that is missed the first time round,' Ant comments. After some time has passed, things are rarely in the same place; things appear which were hidden before; and of course, there is a lot more haste and pressure in new investigating; two years later we have all the time in the world.' She sees Bex's facial expression change from triumphant at the find to unease. '…unless somebody is in a hurry to retire.' She laughs at his horrified face. 'We'll get there, Bex,' she whispers and winks at him.

She finishes taking pictures and then they compare what has changed in each room since they were called in the first time round.

'The carpet is definitely new.'

'Talk of stating the obvious,' Bex says, 'Mr Turner told us so himself.' Nothing much seems to have changed in the dining room, nor in the bedrooms, as if he is keeping it all in aspic. There is only one difference: Piers seems to sleep in a guest bedroom rather than the marital bed. Not too unusual if your partner is missing.

'The pictures on the sitting room walls have been swapped around,' Ant points out. 'Look at the displays before and after.'

'To be honest, that is not unusual either. Obviously, Piers likes it better the way it is now,' Bex comments.

'Ah, I just remembered something,' Ant rushes back to the team in the sitting room, addressing the leader, a burly male SOCO called Robert Pegg, known as Lofty because of his height.:

'Could you split up your team?' she asks him.

'Okay. Shall we start at the other rooms?' he pre-empts her instructions.

'I have taken photographs already, but could you search and swab upstairs thoroughly. Look out for a tassel like the ones hanging on the wall in the sitting room and a brown shoulder bag with a brass buckle.'

'Shall do,' Lofty replies cheerily and delegates a group of three, calling after them: 'I'll follow you in a minute. I just tidy up here,'

'Ant, you keep looking at that mask,' Bex notices, 'Is something wrong with it?'

Ant doesn't reply, but approaches Lofty again pointing to it: 'Can you, please take that down?'

Lofty does so and hands her the enormous and unexpectedly heavy face of a devil.

'From the carnival in the Dominican Republic,' Ant repeats what she has been told by Piers, when they were still on better terms. Bex raises his eyebrows, not quite sure what to make of this comment.

'It's the *Limping Devil*, something to do with a local legend and a devil of curiosity. Piers and Lucinda took part in the procession during their honeymoon.'

Bex looks at it, not half as fascinated as Ant is. 'The colours are striking, aren't they?' she remarks. 'Quite scarily garish, but then that's what masks are supposed to do: frighten you.'

'If you say so…' Bex is not the philosophical type.

'Shall I carry on?' asks Lofty.

'Lofty, have you taken a photograph of the mask on its own yet, and one in context with the room?'

'Cherry did that earlier.'

The mask is getting heavy for even Lofty to hold, so Ant helps him to put it gently in a large cardboard box: 'Ouch!' she exclaims, grips it with her other hand and begins to suck on the freed palm. Then she has a closer look at where she has injured herself.

'Oh look!' she beams all over her face. The mask is damaged at the back of the devils forehead and clumsy attempts at repair have been made.

'If there is blood on it, Ant, it will be yours, won't it?' Bex comments drily.

'My DNA has been recorded and can easily be eliminated!' she corrects him and turns: 'Lofty, that mask needs close examination. Leave it in the box and secure it with string through the holes at the bottom as usual, you know what to do…cellotape it all up and send it to the lab with the other exhibits as soon as they go off.'

As she leaves Lofty and his team to get on with it, Ant turns to Bex who is standing there, grinning.

'What?' she asks sharply with irritation.

'Wasn't that a bit patronising?' he whispers. Lofty has probably as many years of experience as you…'

'Why didn't you ask him in the first place then?' She didn't mean it to come out quite as cutting.

Did she hear someone giggling? She looks at Lofty's team, but they are busily manoeuvring the mask into the box, careful not to wipe or contaminate any traces: a guy called Pettigrew, whom everybody calls Petticoat; Detective Sergeant Karl Otter, who was nicknamed Tarka; and Detective Constable Ken Furlong, whom everybody calls Shergar. She is keen to know the names of the people she works with and the nicknames make it easier.

'It gives me the creeps,' mutters Cherry who has just walked in, as the sneering face disappears under the box lid.

Ant sucks again at her wound and pulls out a splinter, she hasn't noticed before: 'Take that with you,' she says to Cherry, who lets it fall into an exhibit bag, labels it and puts next to all the others on the dining room table..

They hear footsteps from the top of the stairs. Ant and Bex rush out into the corridor, gingerly tiptoeing round the cordoned-off path.

One of the upstairs team removes his white mouth guard. Something dangles between his fore and middle fingers and his thumb.

CHAPTER THIRTY – THREE

'Where did you find this?' Ant asks with a big grin of satisfaction.

'...in the back of an empty wardrobe, in the room where Mr Turner sleeps. We almost overlooked it because the wardrobe is so deep and dark.'

So did the murderer, Ant muses.

'Any sign of the brown shoulder bag yet?

The young DCI Pippa Constable, who has hung on to her name and is called simply Pippa, shakes her head.

'Don't forget the attic space,' Ant reminds her. 'You can be the loft monkey; you are small enough.'

'Oh thanks!' Pippa says sarcastically. 'I'm looking forward to getting a leg up from those good-looking hunks...' She nods in the direction of Petticoat, Tarka and Shergar.

Ant sees Bex grin, too. Obviously he remembers that that role had always fallen to her in the past because she had been invariably the shortest, lightest, slimmest and most agile member of any investigation crew. Embarrassing at times! Particularly for the poor sod, usually a strong officer, who had to heave her up through a trap door?

'The tassel could, of course, come from the display on the wall in the sitting room,' Bex remarks.

'You are a cheery soul today, aren't you,' Ant sends Bex one of her ironic side glances, while Cherry goes to check. To everybody's relief, the set on the wall is complete.

'...maybe a spare?' Bex ventures. Ant raises her eyebrows as if he has told a questionable joke. 'In any case, I doubt that the fibres match.'

'Bag it up!' Ant orders and young Jo does so.

'Ma'am, shall we take the curtains down?'

'Good thinking! It's worth checking the creases.'

'I'll check all the books on the shelves,' Lofty says.

'Quite right, Lofty,' Ant agrees, 'Murderers tend to think of wiping down the shelves and forget that something flying through the air might have landed on a book.'

The team proceeds in silence, each member with his or her own task, while Ant and Bex pour again over the two sets of photographs. There is nothing more, they can pinpoint. Ant sighs and decides to go on another round through the house.

When she returns she says two things to all assembled: 'Has anybody got the key to the back door?'

Everybody shakes their head. 'Shall I walk round the house and have a look?' offers DC Shergar. Ant and Bex nod in unison.

'Secondly, where does the door underneath the stairs lead to? It is locked as well.'

'...the cellar?' Lofty guesses. 'Shall I break the door down?'

'No need,' says Ant, 'Mr Turner promised that he would be back by lunch time. He should be here any minute.'

'Oh good, you have returned,' Ant greets Piers Turner. 'We need the key to the cupboard under the stairs.

His face has turned from pale to ashen: 'That's my wine cellar,' he replies huffily.

'Is it now? How nice! Can we have a look at it?'

'I can't imagine what you are looking for down there. There are only wine bottles. But if you must...'

'Yes, please,' Ant confirms smilingly, lips pressed together.

He pulls a bundle of keys out of his trouser pocket, which he should have left behind in the first place. He obviously wanted to be present when they examine beyond usually locked doors.

'Now?'

Ant nods and smiles again her crooked smile. She feels his unwillingness. He is tense. So is she – in anticipation.

He takes a while to unlock the cellar door, clumsily as if he had never done it before. He switches on a neon strip light on the ceiling which throws just enough light on the steep concrete steps to make them out. They climb down. Ant notices a dark, strangely coloured stain on one of the steps and makes a mental note to mention it to Cherry. When they have reached the bottom, Ant's eyes widen: each wall is covered in wine-racks and very few slots are empty.

'That's a lovely collection you have here.'

Piers sneers sarcastically: 'Thank you, Miss Bell. I appreciate your opinion.'

Please yourself, she thinks and walks around the cellar, past each rack before returning to the stairs and Piers.

'How many bottles do you think you have here?' he looks at her in in-comprehension and doesn't grace her with an answer. Instead he asks: 'How many do you think there are? Have a guess!'

She doesn't give an answer either apart from another faint, polite smile. Touché, she thinks, but she is not willing to play games. He fills the ensuing silence by walking to the rack nearest to them and straightens up a bottle out of line with the others. Ant observes him with veiled interest, and goes on another round of the cellar. This time, Piers follows her. As she brushes a couple of bottle necks and displaces them by an inch, she hears an irritated sigh behind her. By the time, they have both returned to the concrete staircase, he has straightened the displaced bottles up to lie parallel with all the others. Ant narrows her eyes. This is not the reaction of a relaxed person she thinks and wonders whether Piers Turner suffers from a touch of OCD. Was he obsessive - compulsively so? She remembers the pristinely kept bedrooms where each doll has its place. They haven't varied, as she had noticed on the photographs. A dead body would be the ultimate nightmare for a man with OCD, wouldn't it? Messy; disturbing the usual order; not being able to control things flying through the air right up to the ceiling; dropping on the floor or on racks and bottles. And the ultimate horrible task of having to clean it all up: blood, bodily fluids; the mess a dead person leaves behind. After that, he would have had to discard the body, leaving a mess in another place. Not to mention having to remember to wipe off his own fingerprints where ever he had left them, most likely bloody ones. Enough to send anybody into a frenzy; and finally, after discarding the body once and for all, he would have had to travel the country and stage sightings, to give himself time and to obscure why he hadn't reported Lucinda's disappearance earlier.

Would Piers Turner really be able to cope with all this? Was he callous, calculating and misogynistic enough?

Come to think of it, his entire behaviour towards Lucinda points to obsessional possessiveness. He managed to restrict her contact with her family to next to nothing within two years of marriage; he cut her off from her old friends and colleagues; he wasn't keen on her getting involved and being popular in the village; he wanted to take over her finances and add his name to the deeds of the house; and he, by all accounts, was adamant that she should not go back to work, but have a baby instead. Where was the self-confident, intelligent and determined Lucinda she had known? Blinded by love and loyalty to a man who deserved neither?

Ant knows very well that her thoughts are based on speculation. However plausible her reasoning, she will have to prove each and every detail.

'Bex, tell the team to move into the cellar. I want every bottle examined!'

'You are joking!' he exclaims. 'We are running out of time,' he adds feebly.

'There is always a tomorrow,' she reminds him.

'The contents as well?' he asks provocatively, pursing his lips in displeasure.

After a moment of reflection, she understands: 'Not the wine, silly! The outsides of the bottles will do, particularly the necks. I have...'

'Spare me the details,' Bex moans and slopes off to tell the team who are still examining each and every volume on the bookshelves. They found another blood droplet on a spine and one at the top on the pages between the covers. Amazing how they spatter across a room and survive such a long time.

'Found also three on the inside rim of the window between the glass and the frame,' whispers DC Coltrane.

'The more the merrier,' Ant gives her the thumbs up in praise.

'Am I going down to the cellar now?' Cherry asks.

'Yes, we need your sharp eyes.'

The young woman packs up her utensils into her personal tool bag, zips it up and carries it to the cellar. The team from upstairs haven't found anything more apart from a handful of something undistinguishable: a thick brown dust cloud from the top of the same wardrobe where they had found the tassel. Clouds of dust on top of wardrobes: nothing remarkable, really. Ant thinks of the state of her own at home. Though, this stuff is different: stringy, tough.

'Bag it up!' she orders. 'The lab will find out what it is. At this moment in time, everything is of importance… By the way, where is Mr Turner?' she asks Pippa who is passing.

'In his office, I think,' she whispers, pointing to the back of the landing with her thumb.

Ant tells the team from upstairs to put the sitting room back to how it was when they arrived and then to join her outside as soon as they can. They take fifteen minutes to get everything back to normal apart, of course, for the items they have removed. The carpet flooring is rolled back onto the floorboards and expertly secured at the edges. As Ant is on her way out, she hears somebody mutter: 'I could always get a job as a carpet fitter.'

Piers is furious about his wine collection being removed. He stands by the front door waiting impatiently, jangling keys. Ant has asked him to provide access to the outhouses.

'Soon everything will be back to normal,' she says in a soothing tone of voice. He shrugs his shoulders as if he couldn't care less.

As they wait, he hisses: 'My patience is running thin! This is harassment!' His eyes are blazing with hostility. Ant takes that as a veiled threat.

'We won't be much longer. We can always come back another day.' she suggests. She doesn't mean it – it would be far too time-consuming to organise another warrant and to bring back the entire team another day – but she guesses that he won't accept anyway. In fact, he looks horrified.

'Please, understand that we need to be thorough,' she tries to be nice. No point in riling him.

It doesn't work: 'I have no idea why you should be thorough in my and Lucinda's home. After all, she is not here and hasn't been for two years!

'I know,' says Ant in a conciliatory tone, 'we are just doing our duty.' He can't object to that. He has asked for the review.

Piers strides ahead, while Ant walks flanked by three of her colleagues across the yard, until they get to the imposing barn conversion which, she knows, houses the wood-burner. When Piers opens the door, they are amazed at the size of it. They knew from the merchant that it was big, but nobody has seen a wood-burning stove that size before. No wonder, Piers burnt wood by the lorry load.

'We'll be alright by ourselves, Mr Turner,' says Ant. 'I think CI Cook, has a few questions to ask you. He is waiting in the house for you.' Piers Turner seems to have expected to stay with them.

The wood-burner is cold. It was the first thing they had requested in the morning: that he switch off the burner and heating system. It had been met with resistance, citing the icy rain and dropping temperature outside. Regretfully, they had to insist on it being switched off. The team from the CID would be far too busy to notice the cold. Now they are raring to begin their investigation.

'I thought you were doing the interview,' Turner protests like a grizzling child.

'No, I better supervise here, but I gave my questions to CI Cook.

He now turns around himself twice as if disoriented, and finally veers off as if having come to a decision where he wanted to head -only to reject his destination and turn around his own axis again, torn between remaining and going back. In the end, he shuffles back obediently across the yard, as he was told.

'Here we go,' Ant is jubilant having got rid of her suspect. They all gape at the size of the installation and the task.

'Now remember: look out for fatty residues, anything that is not wood; look particularly in corners, creases and up into the folds of the flue.'

They look bored with instructions.

'Go on then,' she gives the order, like giving an official starter at a race.

They set to work in a coordinated routine, practised and perfected in many cases. She can leave them to it; they know what they are doing; they will do an excellent job.

'I'll be next door, in the other barn,' she says. 'Call me if you need me!' but she suspects they don't, and they won't need to.

Ant strides quickly across the yard, past the wood storage hut which is open. She has a little peek inside, but it is loaded with logs to the roof and along each wall. She can hardly enter. Once she has the results from the exhibits collected today, she might order an inspection of this log store. It's too late today to do it, and it's not likely that something untoward is hidden behind there –like a body. The wood-merchant would have been the first to notice the stink of a decaying body, and by now, there would just be bits left covered in flies and maggots. The smells of a dead body or body remnants have a way of penetrating everything, like cheese gone off. She pushes that unpleasant thought away. Her lunchtime cheese sandwich, eaten on the hoof, might take revenge. Back to the log store: there is nothing that flies, buzzes or wriggles. Yes, it is a locked space, but the doors are being opened whenever logs are needed or delivered, and creepy crawlies have a way of squeezing through the tiniest gaps or clinging to logs.

She enters the next barn, in which all the agricultural tools and machines are kept. Everything is neatly hung up, stacked or parked alongside a wall, almost as if in some sort of alphabetical or arithmetical order. The floor is neat as well; not the bare concrete floor that she has found in the other outhouses, but this one is covered by a mixture of clean sawdust and something else. She bends down, scoops some of it up in her hand, smells it, looks at it and wonders. She goes to another corner and does the same. The consistency of the covering is slightly different, but not by much: again the dull yellow of saw dust with bits of grey mixed in. Nothing spectacularly out of the ordinary, but something bothers her. Her mind has put the words of the wood-burner merchant, of the chap delivering the logs and the Sheridan son Robert together. After Lucinda's disappearance, Piers Turner burnt a hell of a lot of wood; there was no obvious need because it was summer; and he used such quantities of wood that even the experts had been astonished. All these fires must have created an awful lot of ash. What did Piers Turner do with it?

Ant walks across to the main house. It's getting dark and the temperature has dropped to freezing. She finds Bex in conversation with Piers on the sitting room sofa.

'All done?' he asks.

She looks at him sternly, so he gets up and follows her out into the corridor. She coughs to clear her voice and then tells him, what she wants to happen.

CHAPTER THIRTY – FOUR

'Give it a couple of days,' Bex advises. He understands Ant's impatience, but they are all tired. They need a break; they need to go home, have a good night's sleep and a day or two to think things over. Moreover, it might be advantageous to wait for the analyses results from the various corners of the house and the wood-burning stove. They might find something to confront Piers Turner with.

'And what about the barn with the peculiar mixture of floor covering?' she pesters him. 'It didn't just smell of sawdust; there was something else mixed in and there were various textures trickling through my fingers.

'It will have to wait! Turner is not going to change it. I'll remind him not to make any changes until we return...if we do. I want him to feel safe; as if the ordeal is over, and then, if possible, catch him out.''

Ant is unhappy and Bex sees it in her eyes: 'We can't do anything more tonight; you surely can see that...'he argues, 'and the lab has enough to get on with what we have collected already.

'When then?'

'Does the dishy Felix need to know?' he jokes, but Ant doesn't feel like laughing. She only pulls a disgusted face. Nothing is further from her mind at the moment than the piglets. Pity, he has to bring it up; now she feels guilty again.

'Day after tomorrow ... as a favour,' Bex relents. 'We should have at least some results by then.

'Wednesday it is.' She grabs the opportunity. They won't tell the irate Mr Turner just yet.

———————

'Guess what?' Bex rings her at the farm the following afternoon. He sounds elated.

'Results?' she guesses.

'Yes, and it's a positive identification of Lucinda's blood.'

'Did they have anything to compare it with?'

'As I said, she had given a sample when she was employed by the Yorkshire police, but her mother and young Robert volunteered straight away when I rang them to report about our progress.'

'That was quick.' Ant is pleasantly surprised.

'Yes, they went to the surgeon, I mean at the police station, the local one, and he rushed it to Devizes.' Bex sounds really excited, muddling up his words.

'Is there any news about the tassel?'

'It is not the same as the ones hanging on the sitting room wall; totally different fibres. So, it could easily be one from the bag she has been seen with. But it would be better if we could find the bag.'

'Good work! Any results from the wood-burner yet?'

'No, that's far too involved. I think, they said that they found fatty deposits, but it's not confirmed.'

'That fits.'

'Fit with what?' Bex asks.

She grins to herself at the other end of the phone: '...call it what you want....oh, one more thing, Bex,' she has just remembered: 'Have they found anything on the mask?'

'No, they have put it on the back burner, and have called in a dendrochronologist.'

'To read the tree rings? I don't quite understand, Bex.'

'Neither do I,' Bex admits, 'but I am sure they have a good reason and they know what they are doing.'

'There is something about that mask...'

'*Creepy* is the word you are looking for,' Bex comments helpfully.

'It's pretty heavy,' she muses. 'It's terribly hard, the wood it is carved from.'

'Yes, certainly not something you want to be hit with,' Bex agrees.

'And there was a bit missing,' she reminds him.

'Repairs, too' he adds.

'...some at the back.'

'He will probably say that it was damaged in transit; lugging it all the way home.'

'They must have used a shipping company to get all their souvenirs back - easy to check. And they would make sure that nothing was damaged...'

'You never know.'

'Ah well, it will all be revealed...'

'Right, see you tomorrow then. It will be a busy day! I'll give the gallant Mr Turner a call.'

'Is that wise?'

'I mean, from the car, when I am five minutes away from his house. Just in case, he plans to make alterations to his farm in the last minute.'

'Or he might be packing a suitcase,' she adds. 'Okay, see you tomorrow morning after dawn. Will you bring an arrest warrant?'

'Hold your horses. I want to have more concrete proof, not just little incoherent and unfounded accusations.

He can't see the face she pulls, almost as horrible as the mask.

———————

'This is totally out of order,' stutters Piers Turner, not quite as impeccably dressed as usual. Bex seems to have truly surprised him in bed with his early call.

'I don't understand,' he begins to shout. 'I thought you had finished on Monday.'

'So did all of us, Mr Turner,' Bex replies laconically.

They send the forensic team in a beeline to the barn with the strange floor covering: 'Bag it all up,' Ant orders.

'All of it?' All three of them, Cherry, Lofty and Shergar look aghast.

'All of it!' Ant says with determination. 'I'll come and help.'

'Are you insane?' protests Piers Turner. 'What do you hope to find in a covering of sawdust? There is only a cement floor underneath.'

'We'll see,' says Ant, vaguely looking at him, but her thoughts are elsewhere. She now finds it hard to look him straight in the eye. If she is right, he is a despicable man! If her hunch is correct, he has murdered his wife whom most in the team have known and admired. What does she hope to find indeed? You tell us!' she would like to say, but doesn't.

'When do I get my artefacts back?' Piers enquires petulantly. 'The walls look terribly bare without them. Lucinda would be so upset…'

'…as soon as they have been through the analysis.'

'I really miss them! They remind me of happy times with my wife,' he tries to pull on Ant's heartstrings. Of course, it backfires, and she stomps off to the barn to follow her colleagues.

The three of them crouch already on the floor, sieving every ounce of sawdust and whatever else is in it, into huge bin-liner type paper bags. When one is full they secure the opening at the top with string and label it in sequence: name, place, date, their initials, case number and batch. Whatever is left in the sieves will get bagged up separately, first in plastic bags, securely labelled in the same way and put delicately into a lidded box.

Those pieces are precious. Goodness knows what they are, but Ant is determined to find out. She has already told Felix that he will have to stand in, because she expects to be in the laboratory in Devizes for an unspecified number of days. Ant joins her colleagues. The work is painstaking and takes them all day. The cement flooring has reappeared in its functional blandness.

In the late afternoon, in time for the evening news on radio and television and morning editions of the newspapers, Bex calls the local and national media to the Pewsey police station for an appeal. He wants people to come forward to help clear up several more niggling points in the investigation. He takes Piers with him for support, as he tells him, but it is really, so that possible witnesses can recognise him. Bex rattles off his script matter-of-factly, while the monosyllabic Turner needs prompting to plead for his wife to return and for witnesses to come forward. He is tired and worn out, and certainly not enjoying the attention.

'Are you coming to Devizes with us tonight?' Bex asks.

The moment, Ant opens her mouth to answer, her phone rings. Her face darkens. It's only a short call.

'Sorry, Bex,' she says. 'I have to go home.'

'Problems? Felix being miserable?' he asks, but she is already running to her car.

'I'll ring,' he hears her shout without turning.

CHAPTER THIRTY – FIVE

'They are so naughty,' Felix had said in panic on the phone, 'I didn't know what else to do. Sorry Ant. I usually can cope with most things.'

'Don't worry. I am on my way.'

It is long dark, when she arrives at home, and the piglets have been missing for four hours.

'Sorry, if I interrupted your work,' Felix apologises for the umpteenth time. I checked every two hours, and the last time I went to check they were gone. How far can they go in one hour? I looked everywhere. They are simply vanished.' He looks terribly unhappy and upset.

'Don't worry, Felix; they would have done the same to me. Let's search for them,' she tries to sooth him. It's sweet the way he feels responsible; deep down she is pleased about his concern – proof that her Girls are in good hands.

Ant slings on her 'piggy' clothes and Wellingtons, Felix hasn't got out of his all day. They each grab a big torch and then trudge up the hill. The enclosure is empty except for the mother sows that seem totally unperturbed by the absence of their off-spring.

'Let's go round the perimeter fence,' Ant suggests. They examine every inch including the electric wire, meant to keep them in, but of course, it is set to the lowest dosage, not to harm them - obviously not strong enough for that little lot.

'Oh look!' Felix shouts into the wind and points to a part of the fence.

'I can't see anything?' replies Ant when she reaches him. 'Where are they?'

'I don't know yet, but look at the ground!' And there was the explanation: the little blighters had found the tiniest gap in the fencing, had dug underneath it and escaped.

'Now we just need to scour the fields around it. With some luck, they are still together. Do you know whether they would make a bid for freedom each on their own, Felix?'

'No idea. Only ever had lambs, and they don't leave their mothers; they make a terrible din when they get separated.'

Ant grins proudly: 'Pigs are obviously more adventurous!'

'Well, right now, we could do without that,' Felix states.

They climb over the fence, walk through the enclosure in darkness, only their two torches shedding light on their path. They can hear the snuffling noises of Iolanthe, Agatha and Persephone, who seem oblivious to the fact that their brood has gone astray hours ago.

Ant and Felix climb over another fence that leads into the top field where the boar, father of the piglets, lives.

'Oh, my Goodness: Do you think he would harm them?'

Felix remains silent, hoping fervently that he had not.

'I can see them!' Ant stands still in pure rapture. Her outstretched harm points to a little group of piglets under a tree: all together, imitating their father who, only a stone's throw away, is absorbed in supplementing his diet.

'Aren't they cute?' Ant is totally besotted with the shadowy bucolic scene. Felix feels a little aggrieved that they had made of fool of him.

'Come on then,' Ant nudges him in the side with her elbow: 'Let's get them home.' They grab two piglets each and the rest simply follow them. When they reach their escape gap in the fence, the piglets just scamper through as they have come out and rush to their mothers' teats, remembering suddenly that they are hungry. The sows sniff at them - one at a time - and then carry on with their own business unperturbed.

'Unbelievable! Only a couple of weeks old and they do already exactly as they please!' Felix sounds put out. His sheep are obviously obedient.

Ant quite likes unruly animals… As for unruly people: some of them - not many.

Mission accomplished, they go in, make tea until Felix stutters that he better get back, now that she had taken over again.

Ant wrinkles her forehead: 'I'll be off to Devizes tomorrow morning first thing. Don't you want to do it anymore?'

'Oh, I thought I had blotted my copybook,' he states simply.

'Don't be silly, Felix, I can't do without you.' Both blush, drink up their tea and quickly go each to their own bedroom to sleep.

CHAPTER THIRTY – SIX

Ant is installed in Mrs Aziz's hotel by 9 a.m. and at work in the laboratory somewhere in the bowels of Wiltshire Police Headquarters by ten. She meets the dendrochronology expert at the entrance door. He is a jolly man with rosy cheeks, a round, bald head and small brown eyes surrounded by blond lashes, a slightly hooked nose in a round face, about 5 foot 8 tall, and considering that he is portly, he is astonishingly sprightly; Ant guesses that he might be in his early sixties.

'George Morris,' he introduces himself and they shake hands. Are you the SOCO in charge?' She nods. 'We are not called SOCOs anymore; its CSI now,' she points out shrugging her shoulders to indicated that she has no idea why.

'Following in American footsteps, are we?' he acknowledges with resignation. Never mind, I was called in to identify and date some wood pieces.'

'Yes, we have a mask.' She doesn't want to give anything away he is supposed to find. His conclusions have to be genuine to be accepted as part of the Prosecution's arguments.

'Garish?' he guesses.

'Quite intimidating,' she chuckles.

'Where from?'

'I think, Dominican Republic.'

'Interesting,' he says slowly as if little wheels in his brain are already ratchetting away.

As soon as they enter, the Head of Laboratory takes charge and leads Mr Morris away, through another door.

'See you later,' she hears, but then he is gone.

Ant turns to the staff who are already working hard to put each drop of blood or bodily fluid recovered through its paces to reveal its secret. There is already a report of the first tests on a desk reserved for her: all blood droplets from the sitting room are from Lucinda; there was even one on the mask where it is damaged, where a bit of wood is missing. They are now working on the cloud of dust-like material found in the empty, dark wardrobe.

The phone on her desk rings. She looks around whether anybody else feels authorised to take a call. When no one rushes towards it, she picks ups the receiver.

'Ant, it's Bex,' he says excitedly.

'How did you know I was here?'

He doesn't understand. 'What?'

'Forget it, Bex. I just wondered…'

'If you mean how do I know you are there, well, you might wish to know that I set it all up! And knowing your habits, I knew you would set off early.' He sounds proud and a little annoyed that she doesn't think him capable of it.

'Well done!' she says quickly, and even she feels his reply is justified:

'Don't be patronising, Ant!'

'So did you just want to know whether I have arrived?'

'No, no! Good news!' He keeps her in suspense.

'Come on, spit it out!'

'The media appeal! Two people came forward.'

'Great,' says Ant, 'who are they?'

He sneezes three times, and then it sounds as if he is blowing his nose rather thoroughly.

'Oh Bex, don't keep me in suspense. I need to get on with my work,' she pleads.

'Can't I even sneeze without you bullying me?' she knows he is joking.

'You can, but now that you have stopped, tell me: who came forward?'

'Sorry about that. Two people called into Pewsey police station.' He stops.

'Yes, and?' she is getting impatient before she realises that he is struggling to supress more sneezes which finally overwhelm him and burst out in one big explosion.

'I hope you are nowhere near an exhibit!' she giggles and adds a heartfelt: 'Bless you!'

He is now really struggling with a blocked nose.

'Tell you what: Blow your nose again and maybe put a decongestant up your nostrils, and ring me in ten minutes again. She can just hear a very stuffy voice croaking a 'thank you'.

While she is waiting, she flicks through the papers on her desk. One has photographs attached, blurry pictures of a face. The report mentions that these were taken by the cameras at the cash machines in the north of England where Lucinda had been sighted and had taken out small sums of money.

'Well, I never…,' Ant murmurs.

The phone rings. It's Bex again.

'I just discovered something, Bex,' she says. 'Did you see the pictures from the cashpoints up north?'

'Not yet,' he says with a restored voice.

'I saw the ones from her Pewsey branch…'

'And what did you discover?'

'They are not the same!'

'Of course, they are not the same. What do you mean?'

'Let's say, all cashpoint cameras are set to catch the face of each customer or those who have criminal intent, right?'

'Right,' Bex confirms.

The ones in Pewsey show almost all of Lucinda's face.'

'Good.'

'The ones from Birmingham, Carlisle, Hull and Harrogate show only the lower half of a face.'

'So what do you deduct from that?'

'What do you think? What's your conclusion?' she teases him.

'That there is a difference in height of the persons photographed?'

'Exactly! To all intents and purposes, the two customers were not the same. The one in Pewsey was quite clearly Lucinda, the other ones was not. She or he was taller!'

'Wow!' For once, Bex is speechless. When he recovers, he repeats Ant's thinking: 'So, somebody impersonated Lucinda.

And why should anybody want to do that?' Ant is now in full flow, 'because she is dead and someone wants to make us believe that she is still alive.'

'In whose interest would that be?' Bex drives her on in her reasoning.

'The person's, who knows that she is dead and is most probably the murderer. Moreover,' Ant continues, 'the photographs up north were all taken on a Wednesday or Saturday, the days, he was not in the office.'

'Who is *he*?

'What do you think?'

'You mean Piers Turner?'

'Of course, I do!'

'But the witnesses did clearly recognise the impersonator as a woman.'

'It was summer. Whoever it was had him- or herself wrapped up in a raincoat and a scarf or hat which every time half covered his or her face or threw a shadow over it.'

'Okay…what else points to him?'

'He or she didn't speak, or only once and then it sounded as if the person had a terrible cold.'

'…Or was trying to hide his real voice.'

'Quite.'

'What else?' Bex pursues the argument: 'He or she was always nervous and clumsy, dropping things, not being able to work the machines; and none of the witnesses have ever seen him or her again.'

'That could all have been an act to make sure, the clumsy woman would be remembered.'

'The witnesses described more or less someone who let's face it, resembled Lucinda: tall, blond, slim…'

'Yes, but the machines revealed that there was a difference between her height and that of her impersonator, and the way they described her, the person at the sightings moved and behaved differently. We knew Lucinda fairly well: she was graceful; the person at the cash machines was awkward and clumsy; Lucinda always dressed stylishly; that one was frumpy; Lucinda was a people's person, always friendly, cheerful and at least courteous; the one described was grumpy, secretive and brusque even when people tried to help her.'

'Now, I have something to add to that…' Bex sounds delighted. 'An optician from Bristol came forward to say, that he remembers clearly that two years ago, Piers Turner insisted on having contact lenses fitted.'

'He is wearing glasses, isn't he?'

'Yes, but the peculiar thing was that he wanted to change his eye colour to blue.'

'Did he explain what?'

'He didn't. He ordered them, paid for them and never returned.'

'That fits! Now I understand why the witnesses thought he kept blinking uncomfortably. He wasn't used to wearing contact lenses.'

'His own optician in Pewsey had no idea, until he met his colleague from Bristol, a university pal, at some conference.' Bex is very pleased with the success of the appeal.

'He obviously wanted an optician as far away as possible, but near enough, so he could return home in one day.'

'And the hair the witnesses saw?' A shadow crosses Bex's face: 'The witnesses said that she was definitely blond.'

'No, they didn't,' Ant contradicts: 'her hair was either covered up or brown.'

'Yes, and his is grey.'

'I have my thoughts on that…' Ant says mysteriously.

'Have you? Out with it!' He looks funny when he is impatient, a bit like an excited schoolboy.

'I have great hopes for examinations which are taking place at this moment.

'Which one? Everybody is working on finding Lucinda's killer. Don't make me guess!'

'The one with the stringy dust cloud from the top of a wardrobe. It looked like dust, but when I handled it, it didn't feel like it.'

'Tell me when you know more.' Bex seems happy with that compromise and asks another question: 'Any ideas on the murder weapon?'

'The mask, of course!'

'A simple wooden mask?'

'This one is ancient, made out of a very hard, heavy wood. Hitting somebody with this is like hitting them with a rock.'

'And a bit had fallen off…'

'Exactly!' Ant says, glad that Bex seems to come round to her way of thinking: 'With some luck, we can find it among the ashes, because that sort of wood doesn't disintegrate easily; it would probably take a lot longer to burn a piece of it to a pulp.'

Another phone rings behind the door which leads to a second lab. After three rings, a colleague comes through to ask Ant whether she could come through to take the call. Ant tells Bex that she would ring back in a minute and follows the young woman called Carina.

'I am listening,' Ant says briskly and then does so intently. She puts the receiver down, walks back to her place and dials Bex's number: 'I was right. He used wigs. The stringy dust cloud is the remnant of two strands of dead hair, one brown, one blond, covered in two years of dust. He has probably burnt them with everything else, but has forgotten to clean out the wardrobe.'

'So he burnt the original wigs together with Lucinda?'

'I think so. We might find remnants of them in the ashes, too. Good that we have already identified that he used wigs.'

'Why would these hair fibres be in a wardrobe, when he burnt the rest of the wigs?'

'I guess they were cheap; they fell out; or they might have got stuck on something like a nail or a hanger, fell to the bottom and stayed there, while he took the wigs and burnt them. He probably didn't spend a lot of money on them, knowing that he would have to destroy them. He is probably mean. Does he strike you as particularly generous?'

'No,' Bex says. There is a pause. She can hear a deep sigh at the other end, followed by Bex clearing his voice: 'I knew it, Ant! I knew you would do it!' He sounds uncharacteristically emotional, but before she can thank him for the rare compliment, he has put the phone down.

CHAPTER THIRTY – SEVEN

Ant pins her hair up, which keeps falling over her eyes. She makes an effort to create a stylish rather than orderly hairdo. After all, she is not on her farm; and everybody else looks reasonably groomed. When she is with the pigs, anything will do: just keep the hair out of the face and protect yourself against wind and rain or burning sun. Ant likes the white coat; she hasn't worn one in months. She has always liked them: they give her an air of authority.

She wonders who the second person was who had come forward. Somehow, she and Bex had forgotten to talk about it. She must remember to ask next time she speaks to him.

The examination results on the wood-burner flutter onto her desk. She had been right: in spite of Piers' protestations of innocence, the test results point conclusively to the fact that a body, alive or dead has been burnt in there. The report clearly states that the possibility of the body having been that of an animal has been eliminated by the science lab technicians. They had also found that not only wood, but diesel had been used to fuel the fire, which indicates that somebody wanted more than heat for the house. That somebody wanted to burn, obliterate things in more than the usual temperature. Masses of wood doused in diesel would produce temperature of possibly one thousand degrees centigrade, enough to burn most parts of a body to ashes. A wave of pure disgust and hatred rises up in Ant: this monster has not only killed Lucinda, he has quite likely dismembered her, once she was dead, to make it fit into the wood-burner, and then he let her disintegrate in an inferno. Only a monster can do such a thing! Ant's brain screams with outrage, imagining the pain, dear, poor Lucinda must have endured. Why hadn't she stopped him? Why hadn't she ask somebody for help Her colleagues would have understood; they were most familiar with *gas-lighting*, when your partner, or someone else you are close to, uses emotional blackmail to undermine another's self-confidence, slowly turns the light down and separates her or him from family, friends and the outside world. It begins subtly and is dressed up as love and concern; to keep the victim safe from others and his or her own follies and mistakes. Some people end up totally brain-washed and lose all self-respect and drive to communicate with anybody except with their torturer. Did Lucinda really succumb to *gas*-lighting? Has Piers Turner fooled them all by playing the caring, distraught husband, grateful for a chance of love late in life; keeping his murderous tendencies well hidden? You won't get away with this, Mr Turner, she promises herself silently.

The forensic team had also found a button flung into one of the folds of the flue lining by the enormous heat, and have assigned it to the type and model of a rain coat, Lucinda's impersonator had been seen in. The coat itself has not been found.

The dendrochronologist approaches to her desk.

'How are you getting on?' Ant asks him.

'Nearly finished and then I shall write my report.' Before she can express her gratitude, he adds: 'I am going down to the canteen for lunch. Would you care to join me? I could tell you about some preliminary results.'

Would she indeed fancy lunch? Of course she would!

They climb down the stairs and end up in the canteen, where she had sat before with Bex. They queue at the counter, and when it is their turn, they both choose ham, egg and chips: 'Shush! Don't tell the wife!' He jokes. That's when Ant remembers that she doesn't even know his name yet. He seems to read the question in her face:

'Allow me to introduce myself: Thomas Butterfield….' And just as Ant is about to reciprocate, he says: 'your fame has proceeded you: You are Antonia Bell; Ant for short.'

She grins with embarrassment. 'So, tell me more! What have you found out about our mask?'

'Well, it's an interesting piece. Not many of those around nowadays. They originate from the Dominican Republic, which is near enough the only place on earth, where these trees still grow.'

'Which trees?'

'*Guaiacum vitae.* Those trees used to produce the hardest wood in the world; it is also known as Ironwood or Pockenholz, and was mainly used for carving, like our mask.'

'That explains why it is so heavy.'

'Yes, it wouldn't be any good for building boats; it is so heavy that it sinks in water.'

'How old do you think the mask is?'

'Let me think…. maybe a hundred and fifty to two hundred years old… maybe even older. This wood was used for centuries to carve carnival masks, sculptures, household items and souvenirs, but now, those trees are quite rare.'

'What are they made of nowadays?' Ant asks.

'If they find it, mahogany, but that is actually illegal; or blends of different woods.'

'Fascinating!' Ant is riveted. 'Pity, it was the weapon that killed my friend.'

Thomas Butterfield looks at her in shock, and says, after a short silence: 'I am so sorry. I didn't know.' Ant stares past him, trying to suppress a sudden wave of tearfulness.

'I have something you might like to know,' he remarks.

'Have you?' Ant is eager to hear it. She hates it when she gets weepy.

'They found a piece of the same Guayacan wood in the ashes. It looks a bit charred, but quite easily distinguishable from the wood-burner logs. This wood is almost indestructible. Luckily, the murderer didn't know that.'

'Thank you,' she grabs both of the older man's hands, which had just finished putting the cutlery on his empty plate. 'I didn't quite know, what to expect from your expertise, but this is magnificent!' A bond between the two scientists has been established, giving them a boost to get to the bottom of the tragedy.

They take the lift back up to the laboratories, both determined to carry on with their individual investigations. 'Good luck!' they shout to each other as they disappear behind different doors.

She makes a note of what she has just heard and concludes that this most recent news and the damaged rim with Lucinda's blood on it should suffice to crucify Piers Turner.

It would soon be time to confront him with all the evidence they have collected.

CHAPTER THIRTY – EIGHT

Bex and Ant meet for a drink in a pub near the police HQ and exchange news of results and findings up to this point.

'Any news of the wine bottles yet?' Bex enquires.

'No, but they will tackle them tomorrow first thing.' And then she remembers what she wanted to ask him all day: 'you didn't tell me, who else came forward after the appeal, apart from the optician.'

'…a volunteer from a local charity shop. She remembered that Piers had handed in a colourful Indian bag, but that there had been something odd about it.'

Ant listens up: What was odd?'

'On closer inspection, a colleague of hers pointed out that there should have been tassels hanging from the bottom of the bag; there were marks that something had been attached, but whatever it was, had been cut off.'

'…another little nail in the coffin of Mr Turner?'

'Looks like it. But it still doesn't prove that he was the one who has done away with his wife. We need a link between him and her being battered and killed.'

'It's early days yet,' Bex says brightly until he realises that Ant is mocking him: 'You are the one who is in a hurry!' she reminds him and finishes her drink.

'My bed at Mrs Aziz's is calling. Thanks for the drink. See you tomorrow.'

'Good work!' he says again, but she is already putting on her anorak and weaving her way through the pub crowd.

The night is balmier than it should be in February, and she suddenly doesn't feel sleepy any more. Her feet have automatically taken her in the wrong direction, back to the laboratories. People rush past her, home, she presumes, to attend to more responsibilities and duties. She has no such duties tonight. Furthermore, she loves working in silence, on her own, without interruption. Now, that she is nearly there, she might as well report back and do some work.

Her pass allows her access at any time; it comes in handy now. She rings a bell, and when the door opens, she flashes the pass at the young policeman and a skeleton reception team and is allowed to go to the lift, which takes her up in seconds. Nobody is around anymore – just as she likes it. She unlocks the door. Everything is covered up, locked in and secured from any contamination. It had been an eventful and satisfyingly productive day. She goes to the drying cupboard and takes out her cardboard box with a see-through strip. She carries it to her desk and opens it carefully: it contains all the finds from sieving the ash in the barn. There should be many more to come from the sacks of sawdust and ash which would be put through the sieving process a second and possibly a third time.

Ant thinks nostalgically about a machine at university which archaeology students used to separate their finds from the dug up soil. It was a simple contraption of tubes of decreasing diameters slid into each other to form one long tube. Between each section, cloths with holes of decreasing size were tightly fitted between the tube sections to act as sieves; each section would catch fragments of varying sizes. It would be so useful now! Once the loose layer of barn floor were sent through the tubes by a jet of water from the very top of the machine, any solid pieces would be caught in the cloth sieves. Simple, but effective, catching even the tiniest of fragments at the very end. Well, she hasn't got that machine, that's all there is to it. The forensic team will just have to do it painstakingly in the lab.

She puts on protective gloves and opens her precious box of sieved finds. Most of them are hardly visible. Ah, there was a tooth fragment, not looking like a tooth at all. Teeth are hard to burn, so there might be more in one of the bags of ash, but even her section will probably be enough to establish - in cooperation with Lucinda's dentist - that the tooth had once belonged to the victim.

Ant takes an exhibit bag from the drying cupboard, puts the tooth fragment into it, seals and labels it, and puts it back in the cupboard.

Next, she picks up a bone fragment, tiny, but she recognises the creamy colour of a bone. It wouldn't belong to a long bone, like shins or arms. Long bones have the structure of hollow tubes, like a honeycomb; they are therefore less strong than others and the reason why people tend to break their arms and legs before anything else. In a fire of the intensity of the one Lucinda was cremated in, the long bones would simply collapse and be totally destroyed.

She spies several more tiny hard bony pieces, which look promising: one she recognises immediately as a metatarsal, the bone in the foot, footballers easily break. To her delight, she discovers a tiny fragment of a mandible, a lower jawbone, much finer and more delicate than a man's; it's clearly that of a female (which deflates the joke of strong jaws in females because they talk so much); the mandible might be delicate, but its density points to an adult. DNA will show whether it was Lucinda's. Next, she uses her tweezers to pick out the rounded shape of a knuckle and puts it gingerly into an evidence bag.

'Great!' she exclaims to the empty office and admires a little bone with a bump. She identifies it as a temporal bone. She turns it between her gloved fingers and feels for something specific. There it is: a little bump. The tiny bone with the bump could easily be Piers Turner's downfall. Ant whoops with joy. Somebody knocks on the door and shouts without opening: 'Are you all right in there?'

She goes to the door and opens it, beaming: 'I am perfectly all right, Sergeant. I just found something important.'

He looks bemused and she offers to show him, but he is on his round through the building: 'No, no. I believe you. You get on with the good work!'

Ant shuts the door and whoops again: the temporal bone with the bump, she has found, must be that of Lucinda. Men don't have that bump on that bone.

'I found you, girl,' Ant whispers welling up with tears, 'I found you, Lucinda!' Then she allows her tears flow.

CHAPTER THIRTY – NINE

Suddenly the lab feels lonely, Ant sitting there with the remains of her friend Lucinda spread out on a velvet cloth. She wants to spend some time with them, before she will hand them over in the morning for forensic and DNA tests plus other examinations which should confirm her conclusion that Lucida has been murdered by her husband. Ant sits motionless for a while, remembering Lucinda, the way she had appreciated her most: as a confidante and advisor. No one, apart from Lucinda and Bex know about young Ant's dark times, when she had fallen in love with a married man, Bex, her boss in many investigations, and had fallen pregnant with his child which was most inconvenient at the beginning of her career. Lucinda was the one who had sensed it straight away, had sat her down, commiserated and helped her to come to a decision. Not that she had pressed Ant on the issue; she made it absolutely clear that this was Ant's decision and hers alone. The two women were cut from the same cloth; they understood each other; they thought like each other, they were soulmates. Unsurprisingly, they came to the same conclusion, independent from each other: you do not shirk responsibility and you certainly do not kill your child. Once the uncertainty had been removed, Ant had looked forward to having her baby. She had already begun to organise her new life as a single mother with a demanding job, when destiny had intervened and inflicted the physical and mental pain of a miscarriage on her. There she was, her life had been turned upside down, she had made every effort to adjust and re-organise, and then it was all taken away; all for nothing. She wasn't even sure anymore whether to be devastated or relieved.

Lucinda had rung her almost daily to make sure she wasn't sliding down the slippery slope of depression, and had come down from Yorkshire to visit her in her chaotic one-bedroom flat in Devizes. 'It's my punishment for not wanting the child in the first place,' Ant had moaned in agony in front of her friend, and Lucinda had simply hugged and held her close, until the tears had stopped. Eventually, she told Bex, the married man, who had looked rather relieved. Their relationship never recovered, and they broke up. Unfortunately, there had been no escape from professional contact, but Ant kept it to a minimum. It was a lesson she had never forgotten. Lucinda had commiserated and confided in her that she had learnt a similar lesson long before her. It helped to speak to someone who understood.

Another picture of Lucinda emerges in Ant's memories: She used to love Lucinda's throaty laughter; she bellowed and hooted until everybody else fell about laughing, too. Ant can hear it now, sitting in the deserted lab all by herself, only in the company of Lucinda's bones. Who would have thought, when they had all attended her wedding that this happy bride would come to such a terrible end. Strangely enough, Ant, when she thinks back to it, cannot remember much of the groom; somehow he only floats around like a shadow in her reminiscences. What Ant does remember of that day, was Lucinda's radiant smile, as if she had found the pot of gold at the end of a rainbow. So sad!

'I'll make sure, you get home to the people who really loved you,' Ant promises, puts each piece of bone and tooth gently back into the box, closes it with the lid and puts it back into the drying cupboard for safekeeping.

Then she dials. A very sleepy Bex grunts something.

'It's me, Ant.'

'I know, only crazy you would ring at such an ungodly hour.'

'Sorry,' she murmurs.

'Go on then,' he sounds suddenly wide awake.

'I found her Bex. I found Lucinda. She is here with me.' He listens attentively while she explains.

'Shall I come and get you?' he offers.

She thinks for a moment and then declines: 'A walk in the fresh night air will do me the world of good. Just do me a favour tomorrow morning: give the box to the scientists as soon as you can, so that I can back up my theory.'

'Shall do,' Bex promises. 'And I shall organise an arrest warrant.'

'Yes, it is show-down time – finally!'

'Yes, it is! We have enough to nail him, and we haven't even got all the results back yet. Some of those might prove to be helpful, too.'

'My work is nearly done,' she mumbles wistfully.

'Ant, you might be sometimes a pain in the proverbial, but you are a damn good scientist.'

She smiles to herself, but doesn't reply.

'Be careful on your way to the hotel! I presume a taxi will be out of the question?' Ant always has her own ideas and won't listen anyway – admirable in one sense, occasionally foolish, and certainly damn hard to live with. Maybe the pigs might tame her? She seems to love them more than she has ever loved anybody else. Maybe it was Lucinda, who got closest to her…

'I will be careful, Bex. See you tomorrow.'

She locks up the laboratory, takes the lift down, hands in the keys to the desk sergeant on night duty, who presses a button to let her out into the night. The air is crisp with February frost, almost cutting her face under the anorak hood; the air she is breathing in hits her lips and teeth with the sharpness of below zero temperatures. The streets are almost deserted. A couple of taxis rush past her. It is past midnight, and there are very few people out walking. The ones she meets seem to be rushing past her in a hurry, towards their homes; she suspects they are night-workers, maybe hospital staff, people from clubs, bars and restaurants What would it be like to have one of those jobs? She has never considered any other profession. Forensic Science had always been her first love and passion: to right wrongs; to find out as much as possible for the bereaved, and to bring perpetrators to justice. It had always been important to her to sooth the families' inexplicable and unfounded feelings of guilt, blaming themselves for not having been there when their loved one needed the most. They needed to be certain that at least after the victim's death, everything humanly possible had been done to get at the truth and to punish the person who has done this. How else could they carry on with their lives?

Lucinda's family had not been terribly close, but they had loved her each in their own way: her caring mother, the brusque but secretly proud father and the brothers, who owed her a debt of gratitude and tried to shield her from a possessive, greedy and cruel husband. It might not have looked like it to outsiders, but they did love her and will miss her for the rest of their lives.

Ant reaches the hotel, puts the key into the lock, greets the night porter, Mrs Aziz's son, finds her room and falls into bed.

She sleeps without the heavy weight of Lucinda's case playing havoc with her sleep.

CHAPTER FORTY

'I am beginning to get fed up with you two,' Piers Turner welcomes them two days later. He speaks in this posh way with an underlying, ice-cold viciousness.

'There won't be many more meetings, M. Turner. We came to tell you about the findings of the forensic sweep,' Bex explains.

'I don't want to know the ins and outs, do I?' he complains, 'it's for you to deal with it!'

'Not entirely, Mr Turner,' Ant buts in, 'we found remains of a female body of approximately the age of your wife plus a possible murder weapon.'

'Oh, have you?' he chuckles. 'So, who is the murderer, and what was the weapon?' Piers Turner barks provocatively.

'Let us tell you our theory,' Ant begins.

'Ah, it's still a theory, is it?' their suspect mocks. 'Go on then, amuse me!'

'On the first of May 2015, you had a row with your wife Lucinda. We think, it began here in your sitting room. For whatever reason, it escalated into violence: you hit your wife on the head with that devil's mask and injured or killed her. While she was lying there, you were disturbed by someone, panicked and dragged her body out into the corridor, and down the cellar steps. You dealt with whoever or whatever had disturbed you outside your front door, and dismembered your wife at a later time in the cellar, using a sharp tool. Soon afterwards, you had worked out a plan, how to dispose of her body: you threw her in the fire of your huge wood-burning stove when you were sure that nobody would be around. You stoked the fire to enormous temperatures and discarded not only the body, but also everything that could incriminate you.'

Bex and Ant look at Piers Turner who has taken a seat in an armchair. He smirks: 'Carry on!' he goads them, 'I am listening.' He sounds devious and dangerous.

'Ash heaps would have been too obvious,' Bex continues unperturbed, 'so you decided to cover the cement floor in the tool barn with a mixture of sawdust and the ash from Lucinda's cremation.'

'Bravo! Bravo!' Piers Turner shouts as if he had gone mad. 'So you can prove all this?'

'Yes, most of it.'

'Well done, you two! The magic bond still seems to work.' He knows it is a stab to both their hearts, but they pretend they haven't heard him.

'There will be more evidence forthcoming within the next few days,' Ant mentions, but he only glares at her with a devilish grin.

'Oh dear! Needle and haystack spring to mind, don't they!' he cheers. 'Let's face it: you are defeated! I shall embark on my own search for my wife. You are both useless!' Turner snipes.

'Why didn't you do so two years ago, instead of going round pretending to be her?' Bex remarks calmly.

'Well, at that time, I still trusted in the police and in their capabilities! Little did I know that you were such imbeciles!' Turner has totally ignored the hint at the sightings. Maybe he hasn't heard them, or maybe they are too close to the truth. He is beside himself. 'So how do you explain the sightings; my wife traipsing round the country, withdrawing money from cashpoints?'

'I just told you so: it was you impersonating her,' Ant retaliates.

Piers Turner's laughter turns into the hysterical salvos of a pantomime dame.

'Me, impersonating my wife?' he shouts, 'that is pathetic! They all saw a woman with blue eyes, tall, slim and blond hair.'

'Not quite, but close enough,' Ant agrees to his astonishment, 'but a witness came forward who can certify that you bought blue contact lenses around that time.'

For a moment, Piers looks confused, but recovers quickly: 'They were for Lucinda. It was before she disappeared. He must have got his dates wrong...'

'Who is *he*? Ant casts a hook, and Piers notices it straight away.

'I meant, he or she, whoever came forward,' he corrects himself quickly.'

'Are you talking about the optician in Bristol, Mr Turner? Why should he give you contact lenses for your wife who is not his patient, and who had blue eyes anyway? You see, it doesn't make any sense.''

'How do *I* know,' he stutters, disconcerted for the first time. 'So where is the credit card then?' he shouts.

'You tell us!' Bex replies, steel in his voice.

'I promise you, I never had it, and I have no idea about her security number.' He is desperately trying to calm down, by concentrating on a different point.

'We find it hard to believe you, Mr Turner,' Ant replies stoically.

'So, are you going to arrest me then?' the suspect ridicules them.

'Yes, I have brought an arrest warrant along with your name on it, and I am taking you in for further questioning.'

Piers Turner is fighting for breath: 'You can't do that! You will never be able to prove anything! I am a widower; an upright citizen. I have contacts. I won't be treated by you like this. I shall call my lawyer right now. You will regret this! Instead of bringing my wife back to me, you accuse me of murdering her! Would I have made such a fuss to get her back, and asked you to re-open the case, if I was in fear of being discovered as a murderer? You two are out of you minds!'

'Get your coat,' Bex replies coldly, 'and then come with us to the station. And by the way: Piers Turner, I am arresting you on suspicion of the murder of your wife, Lucinda Turner, born Sheridan; you do not have to say anyth…' He is interrupted.

'Yeah, yeah, I know the words by heart. You can save them,' the suspect mimics him, 'I have seen enough murder mysteries to remember…'but Bex carries on: 'but it may harm your defence if you do not mention, when questioned, something which you later rely on in court. Anything you do say may be given in evidence. Did you understand that?'

Bex can be sufficiently intimidating if he chooses to be, Ant thinks. She is glad that he is here. She would hate having to supervise the suspect gathering a few clothes for a few days at the station, or driving him to Devizes Police Station.

'I will not go anywhere without my solicitor,' Turner screams, pushing his way past them to the telephone in his study. Ant and Bex follow him.

'I don't need minders!' Piers Turner shouts and shuts the door in their face, locking the door.

'I'll go to the back,' Ant reacts instantaneously and runs out of the front door, round the house and to the brambles and scrubs at the back. She can't see anyone climbing out of the window or running away, so she simply stays, until Bex appears inside at the study window. He waves her back in.

'Only ringing my solicitor, Miss Bell,' Turner says in that irritating , patronising voice of his. 'I keep my promises; you don't!' he sneers.

The wait for the solicitor from Marlborough seems endless. In fact, Piers told them, that the young man lived somewhere halfway between his office and the Turner's house. Still, it seems an eternity.

When the solicitor finally arrives, Piers gets up, without offering the poor man a drink in reward for rushing to his aid, and demands: 'Let's get this over with. Let's go!' and quickly heads out to Bex's car, the three following him.

'I'll ring you,' Bex says quietly to Ant who will drive home to the farm. Piers Turner must have overheard them because he looks at them mockingly with the most evil grin.

'Can I ring you, too?' he says hoarsely.

Bex snaps: 'Shut up! If you try to intimidate us, you have another think coming! Get in the car!' For a moment he is tempted to withdraw his hand from the car door frame which is there to protect the suspects head.

Ant turns and goes to her car. She suddenly thinks of Iolanthe, Agatha and Persephone and her heart leaps with joy. What a blessing to have this other life!

She waits till the men have roared off, puts on her Carly Simon CD and starts the car, singing along.

CHAPTER FORTY – ONE

'You know, animals are much nicer to each other than humans,' she talks to them. She has given them courgette, pumpkins, apples and bananas, and they are busily munching away.

'Look at your babies!' she says full of admiration, 'so energetic … and so unruly!' There they are, chasing each other on the hill side pushing each other around and inspecting various places along the fence for a weak spot to play the game *Escape* again. Some of them were already imitating their mothers, rooting for grass and little insects. Soon there would be the first flowers, too and berries later on in the year. Whatever berries are left over from autumn, are on the floor, dried up and unpalatable. The piglets try to eat them once and then decide to play with them instead.

It is lovely, to be physically active again, stretching and straining her body, rather than sitting glued to a desk chair; not to worry about being dressed, not only tidily but as smartly as possible. She will totally let herself go for a few days, until she is fed up with looking a mess, and ready to scrub up and tidy herself again.

She sees Felix coming up the hill, waving.

'Just thought I check whether you have arrived last night,' he shouts cheerily before he reaches her.

'You would have heard about that,' she says, straight away regretting it. She is unfortunately still in the mode of arguing about the smallest point, for and against with a perpetrator over the traces he left. It is unfair and patronising to correct nice and well-meaning people like Felix on unimportant and small matters.

'Sorry,' she apologises straight away; luckily, Felix doesn't seem to have heard it all and looks baffled. As he advances, she hops down from the fence and walks towards him.

'Nice to see you!' she says; he only grins cheerfully in reply. He doesn't mind if occasionally she is impatient with him. She has all these fascinating problems to solve; how could he be cross with her?

'I reckon this will be it now? I mean, me standing in for you, looking after the Girls.' He has adopted her habit of calling them that. He points at them: 'They look happy to have their Mum back.' He laughs at himself.

'You have become soppy with them like me,' Ant remarks. They just have a way of doing this to you, haven't they?' He nods.

'Tell you what: Let's go and have a cup of tea, or if you need something stronger, I have a great bottle of cider in the larder.

They end up sharing it and nibble on the last two muffins, Ant had bought at a little tearoom off the motorway.

'Ant, I might over-react and I don't want to worry you...' he stutters.

'...which is the surest way of having me worried!' she interrupts.

'I am not even sure I should mention it...'

Ant looks at him with interest and amusement.

'Is it about your parents' intentions of getting you married off?

Now he looks baffled: 'I don't know what you mean.'

'Remember, Christmas? When you told me about their hopes for your personal life?'

'Ah, that!' he laughs, 'no, and there is no girlfriend on the horizon.'

'It doesn't matter to me, Felix. As long as my Girl's like you, I shall be happy with you coming here!'

'No, something totally different…'he tries to steer the conversation back to its original topic, the one he wanted to talk about.

'Sorry, we got a bit side-tracked…' Ant giggles disingenuously apologetic. She enjoys Felix's company. No strings, just sympathy, banter and laughter. That was all that was needed. I wonder whether he is…

'Just after you left for Devizes, I caught someone sneaking around the farm.'

It is as if a bomb has exploded in her head.

'Who?' Felix shrugs his shoulders, 'I have never seen him before.'

'Definitely a man?' He nods.

'What did he look like?' She is back in interrogation mode.

'Tall, lanky, older than you,' he says, throwing her a cautious glance, 'about my father's age,' he adds quickly to smooth offence if he has caused any.

'Anything else?'

'He wore glasses, grey trousers, black shoes and a black duffle coat.'

'Excellent description! You could go far in the police!' she praises him.

Felix clears his throat in embarrassment: 'No thank you! I only remember because he looked totally out of place on a pig farm in his smart outfit.'

'What car did he drive?'

'I was at the top when I saw him arriving. He came in a taxi.'

'So, what did he want?'

'It looked to me, as if he hadn't expected anybody to be here. When the taxi had left, he made a straight beeline for the pigs' enclosure as if he knew his way around.'

Ant holds her breath.

'He didn't notice me at first, but when he made a move to climb over the fence, I appeared from behind my tree and challenged him.'

'Oh my God!' Ant exclaims.

'To be honest, his duffle-coat was bulging at the front, and I thought that he might have hidden something there to harm the pigs. That's what it looked like to me.'

'That was very brave, Felix; this was not included in your brief. I am so sorry!'

'This is the third time you are apologising. Can you stop it?'

Ant nods. 'What happened next?'

'I remained calm. I didn't see what he had under the coat because he buttoned it up as soon as he heard my voice.'

'You didn't want to know, I assure you, Felix!'

'Do you know who it was?' Felix sounds more curious than perturbed.

'I might be wrong, but he sounds to me like the man I was trying to catch out during the last few months.'

It was Felix's turn to look horrified.

'Is he a murderer?' he whispers

'Could be,' is all, Ant can say.

'Is he going to come back?' he looks worried.

'Possibly…' She bites on her lower lip.

'Does that mean that you are in danger?' His eyes widen in disbelief and shock.

'I could be…and the Girls,' she admits, 'but not at the moment. He has been arrested. However, there might be a chance that they release him if there isn't enough evidence.'

'You are joking?!' he can't believe it. Suddenly, playing cops and robbers doesn't seem quite so fascinating any more. He looks at the floor, folds appearing between his eyebrows. 'You can move in with us, Girls and all,' he offers, out of the blue. He has such a good heart.

'That is the sweetest thing anybody has said to me in years!' she smiles broadly. 'I hope that won't be necessary, but thank you. I shall make a phone call to my colleague in Devizes which should sort it out.'

As soon as Felix has left – reassured, she hopes that she is not in danger - Ant rings Bex.

'Holy Cow!' he exclaims. 'He doesn't give up. He obviously tried to intimidate you by trespassing upon your property and possibly dispatching your pigs with whatever he held under his coat.'

'My thinking entirely.'

'I shall send somebody down. How about Zac? I'll try him first. You two were getting on, weren't you?'

'Yes, but what for?' Ant doesn't feel quite so shaken anymore.

'What do you think? Security, of course!'

'There is no need.'

'There might be. Things aren't going too well at the station. If we haven't found new evidence by the end of tomorrow, we might have to release him.'

CHAPTER FORTY – TWO

When Zac rings the following afternoon, he sounds anxious:

'The CI says you needed protection,' he sounds worried, too.

'I told him, I didn't need protection,' Ant contradicts, exasperated about the fuss she has caused.

'He seems sure you do,' Zac argues weakly.

'Tell you what, Zac. How about, I ring you, if I feel I really need your protection?'

'He will not be pleased,' he groans.

'Don't worry about that. He knows how stubborn I can be. He won't blame you.'

'I wish I was as sure.'

'Why?'

'He was already angry, because I mentioned that it was bad timing. My girlfriend bought us a City break holiday for this weekend - a Valentine's present.'

'You got it together with Melanie then?' Ant laughs. She can just imagine how he blushes at this moment.

'Sort of,' he admits. 'It's difficult, us both being in the same Force.'

'I know.' She feels with him. She has experienced the same.

His dispirited voice calls her back: '…but then, I never meet anybody else, or if I do, I never have time for them,' he laments.

'Well, Zac. You go on your weekend break, and don't you worry about me. I have friends down here. They will keep me safe.'

'That's a relief!' he says and hangs up a lot happier than when he started. No sooner has she heard the click, the phone rings again:

'We had to let him go, Ant. His solicitor got bail for him.' A distraught Bex gives her the news. She can't believe it!

Ant spends a restless night, as if she were expecting Piers Turner to hammer on her door any moment. When she has a second sleepless night, she asks whether Felix could sleep over a couple of times:

'My parents will be pleased,' he laughs out loud.

'I can see the complications…' She doesn't feel like laughing.

'Don't worry. We let them be happy in the hope of a daughter-in-law for a few days, and then I shall put the picture straight.

'Thank you. See you for supper then.'

Felix moves in, but after a week nothing has happened: they have had neither a nasty surprise from an unwanted visitor, nor has the friendship developed into something more than they have already. Most days, Felix commutes the short distance to his father's farm when he is needed, but as soon as he finishes, he returns to Ant's farm to sort out the animals and to sleep in the guest bedroom. Ant uses her free time, to assemble her report for the courts.

One evening, after a nice dinner of a spicy corned beef hash, which Felix has produced, and still sharing a bottle of red wine, Ant's curiosity takes the better of her, and she asks him straight out: 'I hope you don't mind me asking, Felix…' She narrows her eyes to discover any sort of hesitance in his face.

'No, no, go ask…anything,' he says innocently.

'Are you gay?' Typical Ant, Bex would call it; straight out with it; no embellishments.

Felix chuckles, unashamedly and not a little relieved. 'You knew all along, didn't you?'

She nods: 'Not that it matters,' she adds and means it.

'Do your parents know?'

'I haven't told them, if that is what you mean.'

'It might dash their hopes,' Ant speculates, 'but there are other advantages. Maybe tell them sooner rather than later? Then you can all get on with your lives.'

'Yes, I have begun to think so as well. It simplifies things, doesn't it? I am just afraid that they will be angry and upset.'

'They might regret not having grandchildren, but otherwise, it shouldn't really make a difference to them. You are still their son, and you look better after them than others would. So courage, young man!'

After that chat, Ant was even happier in Felix's company. Clarification had simplified their relationship - carefree, like brother and sister or best of friends.

And then, one evening, the phone rings. Ant listens and hears a familiar voice: 'Hi, it's Lucinda. I am having a whale of a time. Don't worry about me: I am perfectly fine. Must go,' is followed by a click.

CHAPTER FORTY – THREE

Ant would have fallen to the floor with shock, had not Felix pulled a chair quickly under her.

'That was a call from Lucinda, who is supposed to be dead for two years,' she explains.

'That doesn't sound logical,' he states the obvious. 'Tea?' is the only remedy he can think of to offer. When Ant nods languidly, he goes to the kettle, fills it with water and switches it on for a strong, sugary cup of tea to ward off the shock.

'I must ring Bex,' she says and already dials his number. Only the message service takes her call. She leaves only a few words, hoping to hide her dismay.

Bex rings back within minutes.

'I'm in a late meeting right now, but I just sent everybody for a cup of coffee. Tell me, what happened?'

'Lucinda rang. Or at least, it sounded very much like her.'

'And what did she say?'

'It was a bit stilted. Terribly cheery, that she was having the time of her life, and not to worry.'

'What did you say to her?'

'Nothing; I was so stunned, and before I could think of something to say, she hung up; or we were interrupted, or the phone went dead.'

Bex stays silent. Finally he clears his throat and comments: 'I'll get the techies onto it. I think this is a diversion tactic coming from Piers, to put you off his scent; or even to frighten you. I don't know how it works, but the experts can explain it to us.'

'It was such a shock - in a nice way,' Ant mutters tearfully.

'Ant, you know as much as I do, that Lucinda is dead. You have found her bones. We have found clues that her husband has murdered her. This could well be an old message he has stored somewhere and is using now to confuse us.'

'It would be so wonderful…'

'I know, Ant, but that's a miracle that won't happen.'

'I'll send the Pewsey force again to have another search; maybe they find the phone. It's probably an easy thing to do, to re-use an old message.'

Ant feels deflated and sad, but reassured. Strange that she had deep down still hoped that she might find Lucinda alive, in spite of all the signs to the contrary.

'Thanks, Bex. I should have known; I shouldn't have fallen for it.'

'He is probably trying to scare you, now that you have rumbled him. He is one of those evil people who can't bear to lose, to be caught out, particularly not by a woman.'

'That will teach him…' she tries to joke weakly.

'People like him never learn. We all know that. If we let him get away this time, he will do it again, just to prove how clever he is. Don't worry too much. I am only a phone call away. You'll feel better after a strong, sugary cup of tea.'

'Felix is...' she blurts out and then stops herself. Bex has been so nice and understanding; she shouldn't play with his emotions.

'Ah,' he says in recognition, 'Felix is with you, I see. I shall leave you in his capable hands then,' he ends the call curtly and hangs up.

'Wait,' she says into the silence but he is already gone.

Ant is pleased when Bex rings back in the morning: 'Sorry about yesterday,' he mutters absent-mindedly. It really is none of his business, but she tells him anyway that he has nothing to fear from Felix. He doesn't seem greatly relieved. Good because she has no intention of installing him in her life either.

'You will be pleased to hear that it is quite simple to take a recorded message and play it back through another phone. You just need two phones.'

'Good!' Ant feels slightly foolish having crumbled under the initial shock.

'And there is some more good news: the chaps from Pewsey Police found a new mobile in Turners car, which he didn't have last time they looked.'

'Even better!' Ant is pleased: everything is coming together - slowly but surely.

'And of course, he gave them an earful that he is totally innocent, and how he is feeling hard-done by, and how devastated he is at her loss - all that bullshit. Does he really still think he can get away with murder?' She can imagine Bex shaking his head at the brazenness of their suspect.

'He does,' she says quietly, 'he knows from his solicitor that we have collected a lot of circumstantial evidence, but he can deduce as well as we can, that we haven't established the vital link between him and Lucinda's death.'

'Whatever happens, we are going ahead with the court case,' Bex is adamant.

'I expect no less, Bex! By the way, have the results from the wine bottles come through?'

'No,' he draws out the word, realising that this particular point has escaped his attention: 'I shall give them a reminder.'

'Let me know!' She says unnecessarily; she knows he will. There can only be two results. The entire case could swing in one direction or another. If her hunch in that cellar was correct…

It is a bright and sunny spring day on the farm, when the front of one's body grows gradually colder and colder in the still wintery air, and the back is warmed by already remarkably strong sunshine. She has sent Felix home. She doesn't want to give in to the taunts of an evil person like Piers Turner. He will get his come-uppance soon, she hopes. Still, she feels jittery, nervous and on tender-hooks. Why? The case is almost closed; her work is certainly finished and with some luck, Piers Turner will be tried and found guilty. It was so unsettling, hearing Lucinda's voice – stirring up hopeful joy in one sense, but horror in another. It was a vile thing to do; Piers Turner obviously stops at nothing to unsettle and upset people. A psychopath, that's what he is; a nasty, obsessive man who strikes people down if he doesn't get his way. Pity he isn't behind bars yet!

The piglets have grown enormously, she can see, and are bullying their mothers into giving them a drink. It's funny to watch, when they push their offspring away, now more often than not. The mothers prepare their young early on to become self-sufficient, so that they, the sows, can get read to come into season again, to mate once more with the boar and to give birth to another lot of bothersome piglets.

There has been a message from a local restaurateur who has heard about her special breed of pigs. He wants to know whether she would sell them for pig roasts. Ant is not ready yet. They are still her surrogate children. Admittedly, she can't keep them all, but right now, she refuses to make a decision. She might hand them on for breeding, a much more palatable option. Iolanthe appreciates the bananas Ant has thrown to her. They will be gone by the time Persephone and Agatha get wind of the extra ration.

It's so much nicer now to be out with the pigs. The soil on the hill is slowly drying out and has stopped being slippery. Soon the tender buds on the trees will emerge and unfurl into fresh, light green leaves to form a shady canopy. Ant loves spring, the time of renewal and new beginnings; time to close past chapters.

She makes her way slowly down the hill; the Wellington boots remain almost clean and she is sweating in her thick pullover in faded blue. As she enters the house, she takes the two combs out of her hair which have held it up on her head until now. It has grown long and tumbles to her shoulders. She might treat herself to a haircut. She laughs out loud thinking that it won't make the slightest difference to the pigs; she doesn't really see many other people. Now she laughs even more uproariously: pigs have become people to her... She hears the phone ring, quickly shrugs off her boots and rushes in on socks.

'Bell,' she says in a clipped voice. Not another fake message, she hopes. At least, she is better prepared for it this time.

'You sound happy.' It's Bex's voice.

'Hi,' she says with relief. 'Any news yet?'

'Nothing so far.' He sounds dispirited.

'Are you asking me for a brain storming session?'

'Do you mind?'

'No, of course not.' Ant really would like to have her dinner.

'We know the mask is the murder weapon.'

'Have you found the tool with which he dismembered her body?'

'No.'

Ant has an inspiration: 'It could be an axe, and where do you need an axe?'

'In the log store,' Bex picks up her train of thought immediately.

'It was full up to the gunnels with logs last time I saw it. Come to think of it, I remember the log merchant mentioning that he had seen an axe leaning against the back wall, and had been told to leave it there and just stack the logs in front of it. He thought it most peculiar; but then the whole business of so many log deliveries was odd. My advice: Have a look in the log store!'

'Great,' Bex says in mock-desperation. 'The team will be delighted to clear out the entire log store'

'It's worth a look. I'll let you get on then.' She really is going to faint if she doesn't eat soon. At least he is happy because there is something more to do.

'Oh, just before I go: Did you get it?'

'Did I get what?' Ant is impatient.

'I sent you a parcel!' He sounds exasperated.

Now she remembers: she did receive a parcel two days ago which she hasn't even opened yet.

'Oh yes. That. Thank you.'

He laughs at the other end: 'You haven't unpacked it, have you? Use it!

He has replaced the receiver, before she can get out a 'thank you.

CHAPTER FORTY – FOUR

Ant is awoken by a noise. She listens, straining her ears. It's quiet again. Maybe the wind blew a loose bit of ivy against the window? Or maybe an early bird has shrieked? Or she had dreamt it? That talk with Bex had brought it all back: the ins and outs of the case and the horrible death Lucinda had suffered. No wonder she has nightmares! However, she is grateful for the top-quality mobile phone he has sent her. She turns over and snuggles into her duvet. A moment later, she hears a similar sound, metal on metal, a clinking noise. She tiptoes to the window, barefooted. A little gap between the two curtains reveals only pitch darkness like black ink. It must still be the middle of the night. None of the birds would have left their roosts just yet. Maybe a fox was rooting around her flower pots by the entrance? But why are there clinking and scratching noises? The geranium pots are too heavy to move, never mind to topple over. Ant listens at the door, then opens it and listens again. Nothing! Nothing at all! Total silence! She waits, tiptoes back to bed. Silly girl, she scolds herself. You are being neurotic!

Just as she drifts off again, she hears a faint engine noise… someone needing to be somewhere early. Lots of people on Exmoor have long commutes, unless they are farmers.

She hears something else, and sits suddenly bolt upright in bed. Now she can even smell it. Had the range cooker overheated and exploded? Did she forget to blow out a candle? Quick as a flash, she jumps out of bed, grabs automatically the new emergency mobile phone from the bedside table and runs out into the corridor. Thick smoke is drifting up the stairs, making her choke.

It will shortly envelope her. She runs into her little bathroom, holds a towel under the cold water tap; when it is soaked, dripping with water, she holds it tightly over her face and tries to fight her way down the stairs. The black, toxic smoke catches in her throat. Something made of plastic must have melted at an enormous temperature.

She rushes back up the stairs. She can't climb from her bedroom window, because there is nothing to catch her on the outside; there is only a sheer drop onto concrete. She flies into the guest bedroom like a bullet and slams the door shut. A draft would only whip the smoke and fire after her. Ant opens the only window. At first she can't see anything, except the glow of the fire downstairs, licking at the outside wall through the blown out kitchen window. She still can't imagine what could have caused the fire. She can just make out the trellis fastened on the wall for her climbing roses. Will it hold her? She would just have to try and hope for the best. She climbs onto the window sill, steps on the outside ledge and tests the trellis by rattling it a bit. It seems sturdy enough, only the old rose stems, covered in spikey thorns would scratch her to pieces. Better that than being burnt alive, she decides. She steps onto the outside ledge, grabs the trellis with determination and swings herself off. For a moment she hangs in mid-air, feeling the heat drifting up. She hears the wooden frame cracks under her weight, and makes a hasty descent. Her feet can hardly take hold of the narrow wooden slats and her legs and hands feel as if they are being shredded. She is panicking now. Her hands and legs are shaking, and her mobile reaches the muddy floor before she does. At that moment, the moon appears from behind a cloud; she can see the emergency button on the mobile and presses it. A faint thought makes her feel sick: has she sent all her findings in the Turner case off to Bex? What if her laptop melts, together with her investigation reports and research results?

She inspects the scene of the fire, while it destroys her home and she waits for help.. The kitchen window is totally shattered, but something catches her attention. She is too dazed to make sense of it. Eventually, she tears herself away and walks through her wrought iron gate into the country lane. There is nothing she can do on her own. She sits on a bolder which looks as if it has been there for centuries.

Ten minutes later, the voluntary fire brigade arrives, first one fire engine, than another from a neighbouring village. In all there are now fifteen men trying to extinguish the fire. A police car drives up for good measure. She rings Bex and tells him what has happened. He answers drowsily, but awakes with a bang after her first words.

'Let me speak to the policemen, he urges her'

'There is only one. This is Exmoor. He was probably only passing by chance.'

'No. He might have been in the vicinity, but the fire brigade must have informed him, too.'

'You are right. I am not thinking straight.'

'I am not surprised, Ant. Keep me informed! And if you want me to…'

'Any excuse for you to try!'

They both giggle. It is the nicest thought she had all night.

———————

The emergency services stay until late morning. Once the fire is under control, they inspect the damage and any fire pockets remaining. The kitchen is ruined, the staircase charred and treads have in places disintegrated into black kindling. Only the bedrooms were largely spared, blackened, but undamaged, with nothing that couldn't be sorted out with a lick of paint. The police finally put into words the strange creepy feeling she had experienced looking at the original scene of the fire: the kitchen window had not been blown out by the fire; it had been smashed in by something somebody had thrown with great force against it; thousands of glass shards lay in the inside on the charred kitchen floor, amongst them a strange container.

'Looks like a firebomb to me,' says the fire officer, looking at Ant with concern. 'A Molotov Cocktail, if you ask me. Would you know of anybody who wants to harm you?'

'Oh yes,' Ant says, and tells him that she is involved in a nasty murder case.

'You better move out, in case they are coming back tonight…. And it's a mess anyway. Have you got somewhere to go?'

She nods, although she has no intention to go anywhere. She will clean up the top floor rooms as soon as everybody has left, and will make it habitable. Just now, they are waiting for the forensics team. Ironic, really when she could do the investigation herself.

When she rings Bex and tells him the latest, he springs into action:

'I thought so. Damned, we should have kept him locked up! My initial investigation uncovered, that Turner might have left his house last night. There are very fresh tyre tracks on his drive and somebody saw him parking at the station. Officers are with him now and in the village to make enquiries. It looks as if he took the train down to Taunton from where he took either a taxi or hired a car. I just don't think, hire car companies would be open that late in your area.'

'I have no idea. I wouldn't have thought so, but I mean that the attack on me was definitely premeditated.'

'Exactly!'

'Thanks, Bex.'

'What for?'

'For….for…,' she has suddenly a frog in her throat and feels overwhelmed with tiredness and emotion.

He gives her time to recover: 'Where are you going to stay tonight?' he asks eventually.

'I'll find somewhere…'

'Tell me, you are not sleeping in that burnt-out shell!'

'It's not that bad. The upstairs needs a bit of cleaning, but I can sleep there, no problem.'

'How can you sleep with that smell? Promise me, that you will go to a hotel or at least the divine Felix, however much it hurts me to suggest that…'

Ant can't help chuckling: 'I will, promise! I can't enter the crime scene anyway until the forensics give me the all clear.'

'Good!'

Bex rings her again at lunch time. She lies slumped in a garden chair, smoke smudges still on her face and her mat hair tumbling over her shoulders.

'Good news. I was right: he took the last train to Taunton and the first one back at the crack of dawn. He also hired a car the day before to pick up at an agreed spot outside the premises. This morning Turner rang them to say, that he hadn't needed it after all, but they could keep the money. They only checked the mileage when the police contacted them, and discovered that there were a few miles more on the tachometer. It fits perfectly with the distance to you and back.'

'To cover his tracks he pretends now that he hasn't been out at all,' Ant suggests.

'Yes. He is losing it – thankfully. He just made his case so much worse. He told the officers that he had been tucked up in bed all night, feeling a bit chesty.' Bex imitates a sickly man, his voice spiked with irony.

'Brilliant!' At least he won't come back tonight, Ant is grateful for small mercies. Hopefully, they keep him under surveillance from now on.

'Oh, and I almost forgot: we re-arrested him, and he will only get out before the court case over my dead body!'

'Don't tempt fate!' she says, shuddering at the thought, 'and by the way, you left that neatly to last, you…you…!'

Bex burst out laughing: 'Don't try. You won't find the word. Just say thank you.'

Whatever their story, she couldn't bear the thought of Bex coming to harm. 'Thank you,' she whispers gratefully and with relief. She would now indeed ask Felix for shelter.

CHAPTER FORTY – FIVE

From her temporary abode at Felix's farm, she keeps track of the investigation and the repair of the cottage. A lot of locals have volunteered to help with the clean-up, and after the insurance assessor has been, they set to task: somebody repairs the window; someone else rips out the kitchen cupboards and replaces them with some handmade ones; the carpenter and the decorator work hand in hand and seem to have a lot of fun whenever she comes over to bring them tea and coffee in a flask and cakes which Felix's mother so kindly has busied herself with. This daily totally self-imposed task of baking for an army of workmen and women seems to give her a new lease of life.

As to the Turner case, the results of the various forensic investigations flood in thick and fast: Zac has located a computer at Turner's Limited which shows the purchase of two wigs - one blond, the other brown – a few days after Lucinda's disappearance.

'That cleared up that mystery,' Zac says happily to Ant over the phone. 'Although, the marketing director was very upset that he was implicated.'

'Did Bex ask you to inform me?'

'He doesn't need to tell us. Anything that happens has to be run past you.'

Ant smirks with glee. It was nice to be valued.

'How was the weekend break?'

'Fabulous! Rome was wonderful.'

'Good for you. And how is…?

'Oh,' he stops as if embarrassed.

'Never mind,' she apologises quickly, 'I am too nosey for my own good.'

'No, no, Ant. I don't mind telling you: we got engaged.'

'Congratulations!' she exclaims, genuinely delighted for him.

'And you will be our guest of honour at the wedding,' he announces.

'I don't know, Zac,' she says, overcome with awkwardness.

'We insist! We shall send you the invitation in due course, and we won't accept any excuses!' He sounds a new man, confident, in charge of his life.

'All right then; and give my best wishes to your future wife. It was Melanie, wasn't it?

'Yes. She can't wait to get rid of her surname. Weymouth is not a posh name either, but at least it's not creepy.' He laughs heartily.

Yes, Spooks is not a good name in a crime squad; too many possibilities for nasty nicknames, Ant agrees inwardly.

'Nice to hear from you, Zac,' she says; 'Stay in touch.'

When she puts the phone down, she has an inexplicable feeling of dëjà vu. She is beginning to dread weddings.

'You were right, Ant,' Bex sounds triumphant. 'The axe was there, all the logs stacked in front of it.'

'And was there anything on it?'

'Not on the axe itself. That was as clean as a whistle, but they found a couple of smears on the floor after everything had been removed.'

'How did Mr Turner take it?'

'He was almost apoplectic! But we put it all nicely back for him, minus the axe. If that's Lucinda's blood it will be a great help!'

'And the wigs will help, too,' she reminds him.

'Have I told you that the lab found a splinter of exotic wood from that wretched mask imbedded in a fragment of Lucinda's skull bone?'

'Well done them! That's fantastic! He surely can't escape this time?' Ant hovers between wishful thinking and doubt.

'I hope not. I think it is time to re-arrest him and tell him about our good fortune in finding his mistakes.'

They half expected that Piers Turner is not willing to come with them, and Bex is glad that he has brought along DS Weymouth and DS Otter, in short Zac and Otter, with him. Mr Turner has obviously not ever imagined that he would find himself in handcuffs. The following interview in the Devizes office is a farce, because all he ever says is either 'no comment' or 'I deny any knowledge of this.' Or 'How often do I have to tell you that I have not murdered my wife. I want her back.'

'Difficult,' says Bex sarcastically, 'because these things on the photographs are her bones. Each and every one shows her DNA.' Turner's eyes begin to well up.

'It's too late for tears, Mr Turner! You should have thought of that before you hit her with that mask.'

'I have done no such thing!' he struggles to speak between sobs. 'Somebody else must have got hold of her.'

'I doubt that,' Bex contradicts, 'Lucinda was a well-respected, well-loved woman and colleague. There can't have been many people who would have wanted to harm her. Furthermore, she knew how to handle herself, but, of course, she didn't imagine that the danger would come from the man she loved.'

Turner composes himself and remains stubbornly silent and uncooperative for the rest of the interview. Even the solicitor is at a loss and calls finally an end to it, pleading emotional exhaustion of his client.

'You must admit,' was the solicitor's parting shot, 'that you have no concrete evidence that Mr Turner has murdered his wife. All you have is evidence that a murder has been committed on their farm, but you have no evidence that my client is the murderer. It could have easily been somebody else; an intruder, a burglar, that sort of thing.'

'You keep on believing that,' Bex grins, 'and we might just surprise you!' He hopes fervently that he will.

He doesn't have long to wait. In the afternoon two most important results come through: the reddish smears on the log store floor stem from Lucinda's blood- Turner had obviously paid more attention to cleaning the axe than the smears it left behind. The second result has very much to do with one of Ant's hunches: The wine bottles.

'Ant?' he just catches her before she goes to feed the pigs.

'Did you arrest him?

'We did! And he tried everything from denial, contradicting, mockery and finally sobbing.'

'Poor lamb,' she remarks unenthusiastically, 'Is there anything else interesting?'

'Brace yourself, Ant!'

'Why? Is it bad news?' Her heart hammers in her throat and her mouth goes dry.

'The wine bottle result came back...'

'And?' she interrupts hardly able to breath.

'You are a genius, Ant. You are an absolute marvel!'

'Tell me!' she screams into the phone desperate to be released from the tension of all that waiting.

'First of all, Zac found out, that these bottles were bought a couple of days before and delivered on the day of Lucinda's murder. He saw it on a credit card statement and rang the wine merchant.'

'Which means...'Ant's brain is working it out fast, 'that her fingerprints wouldn't be on the bottles, because she was already dead.'

'According to the delivery driver, it was a rather strange encounter with Mr Turner that day,' Bex continues. 'He said, that usually, he was meant to carry the bottles into the house and down into the wine cellar. However that day, Mr Turner was quite flustered and insisted that he would carry the boxes down himself. Something about workmen doing repairs down there, but he couldn't see anybody around or their van.'

'By then,' Ant concludes, 'he had dragged the body already into the cellar to dismember it. He probably had forgotten about the delivery and was taken by surprise when it came. ..What a shock being disturbed while cutting up your wife! Serves him right!'

'There was one bottle he must have straightened up when he still had blood on his hands in that cellar.'

'And can it be proven?'

'Yes! No doubts anymore: on one of the bottle necks was Piers Turners fingerprint with smears of Lucinda's blood.'

'Oh Bex,' Ant stammers and bursts into tears.

'It was all worth it. Congratulations!' She can hear the delight in Bex's voice.

'And you. Thanks for letting me know.'

We are still a good team he thinks but hesitates to say it.

'It will stick, won't it? I mean, it will be enough for a judge to convict him, won't it?

'Of course it will, in spite of Turners denials and assurances.'

'I might make a courtesy visit to her family,' Ant suggests.

'You'll have to appear in Court to give evidence.'

'I know. I leave it until he is safely put away. On a different tack: You are retiring soon,' she teases him.

'Don't remind me!'

'I might have a few ideas how to keep you occupied…'

'Ideas are fine, but no more hunches, please!' he groans. 'See you at court! I'll ring you with the dates…and…give my love to the Girls!'

'Since when are you interested in animals? 'she is about to say, but he has already hung up.

CHAPTER FORTY – SIX

The result of the court case is a forgone conclusion, but they all do their best to communicate their evidence in a clear, dispassionate and logical way. They have worked hard, and being precise in presenting their evidence, is all they can do now.

Piers Turner is still pleading 'not guilty'.

The case has been referred to the Crown Court in Winchester. Strange, Ant thinks. Winchester is in Hampshire, as far as I know? However, her summons states clearly that that is where she is supposed to present herself. Ant takes a train and spends a nerve-wracking wait in a kind of ante-room. She can't even be bothered to go to the canteen for lunch and nibbles on half a sandwich Bex shares with her. She recites her long list of proven clues in her head over and over again, like a pupil before a school examination; nervous, as if she had never given evidence; jittery as if she were going for her first job interview! Pull yourself together, she tells herself. She hadn't been out of the business for that long.

'It's not that you have never done it before,' Bex tries to calm her.

She nods nervously. She has to get it right – for Lucinda.

'It's like riding a bike; you never forget how to do it,' he keeps encouraging her.

To Ant, it doesn't ring true right now.

When she is called in for cross-examination, it is much easier than she has feared: she simply answers the questions put to her by the prosecutor and the defence lawyer, who go over each and every disputed point of scientific evidence: The blood spatters and the body fluids on the various surfaces, the finds in the ashes and in the industrial sized wood-burning stove, in which they found human fatty deposits, and traces of diesel used to create the enormous heat necessary to burn a body; the alibis, the sightings and witness statements, she had collected, the photographs from the cash point machines, which showed clearly a difference in height of Lucinda alive and her imposter; the wigs, the trench coat button, the tassels of an Indian bag, the peculiar purchase of contact lenses; Pier's Turner's history as a businessman and the state of his present company; the problems in their marriage and his tendencies to controlling every aspect of his wife's life; Ant reminds the judge and the jury of the dendrochronologist's report who managed to link a charred splinter of wood, smeared with Lucinda's blood and imbedded in a skull bone found in the mixture of saw-dust and ash in the Turner's barn, to the devil's mask in their sitting room - thus establishing it as the murder weapon; and finally the typically female bone and tooth fragments, which, luckily, had refused to disintegrate in Pier's Turner's inferno: They all bear Lucinda's DNA. They leave the most incriminating result of her work to last: the bloody fingerprint on the neck of a wine bottle which puts Piers and the dead or dying Lucinda together in the wine cellar. Ant makes a big effort not to sound triumphant. Before she leaves the witness stand, she has a quick look at the accused, who sits on his chair, flanked by officers, staring at her in disbelief.

Bex is there, when she is discharged, exhausted and empty.

'Are you going home tonight?' he asks.

She can only nod.

'I'll take you to the station. Will the divine Felix pick you up?' he teases gently, but it falls flat. She shakes her head.

'I have parked the car at the other end,' she says flatly.

'So, you will be all right?' he is looking for confirmation.

Another nod, a silent walk to his car and an even more silent drive to the station.

'Have you got a return ticket?'

She whispers: 'Yes, thank you', before getting out of his car and disappearing into the station.

Back home, she listens every day to the reports of the case on radio. After a few days, news of it dwindles. The novelty to the listeners has worn off. Ant doesn't hear from anybody and just concentrates on her life with Iolanthe, Persephone and Agatha, and their voluminous number of off-spring. Soon she will make a decision whether she should let the boar do his thing again. By now, the Girls almost ignore the piglets which have grown into great, lumbering animals, almost the size of their mothers.

Felix stops occasionally for a neighbourly chat, asking jokingly whether she will solve the next case. She shakes her head. Unlikely that she will be asked again; particularly now, that Bex soon retires!

'She thinks of him, when the first of April arrives. How will he cope? It's not easy to leave exciting and stressful jobs like theirs behind. Not many other things in life come anywhere close to filling the time. She has found her niche. Will he?

She hears shouting at the bottom of the hill. 'Must go,' she says to the Girls who only look up briefly. Ant trudges back down the hill, ready for her own dinner. The last few days were typical April weather: all four seasons in twenty-four hours; everything from sleet to rain to glorious sunshine. The thought of summer is exhilarating.

As she approaches her front door, she sees a figure standing at the garden gate. She knows that figure and is pleased to see him.

'Hello, stranger,' she shouts and he waves. 'Are you the bearer of good news?'

'You haven't heard then? Yes, I am indeed the bearer of excellent news!' he says, a broad smile on his face.

'Come on. Don't stand there smiling! What is it?'

'Would a magic word let me in?'

'Maybe,' she laughs.

'Just as well: It's GUILTY!'

'Life?' she asks.

'Yes, thirty years minimum. He will die in prison.'

'Come on in then, Bex.'

They talk over dinner and several glasses of wine.

'It was quite a spectacle,' Bex reports. 'Just before the summing-up by the prosecution, Turner demanded to speak to his solicitor. Everything stopped, and when they came back, his plea had changed to *guilty*. Of course, it overturned the entire schedule, and it took an extra day to get back on track.'

'He probably realised that he would be convicted anyway and tried something like plea bargaining. Luckily, it doesn't work in our country.'

'Quite! By the way, have you spoken to Lucinda's parents?'

'Yes, I have indeed. They said, they felt all along that their son-in-law was to blame; but they are very pleased that he is now behind bars. '

She grins at Bex without saying a word. He doesn't know what she finds so amusing.

'Spit it out!' he orders.

'I have an invitation for their family reunion in the summer; quite a posh affair!'

'You will of course, go in your piggy-outfit?' he hazards a cheeky guess.'

'Now, now,' she wags her finger at him, 'I am allowed to bring a guest, and it won't be you if you are disrespectful!'

She yawns and they both get up from the table.

'My first day of retirement wasn't bad at all,' he mutters wistfully, looking at the floor.

'There you are. You'll just have to get used to it.'

The next morning, after breakfast, she gives him a pair of old spare Wellingtons. They are a bit tight, but they will have to do. Luckily he has brought a pair of jeans, new by the looks of it. They won't be new for long. They climb slowly up to the pigs' enclosure and feed the animals.

'Refresh my memory: What are their names?'

'Iolanthe, Agatha, Persephone meet Bex,' she makes the introduction with an exaggerated bow. She empties her goodies into the trough and Bex gains in popularity by distributing three punnets of strawberries. Ant drags fresh straw out of the shed and sprinkles it over the ground. The Girls will sort it out themselves.

As Ant and Bex sit on the fence, watching and listening to the pigs' munching and snorting contentedly, she hears Bex next to her mutter, but she can't understand what he says.

She looks at him quizzically:

'Speak up! You are not an old man just yet,' she encourages him to repeat his words.

'I just wanted you to know that my wife died last year.'

The joke Ant had just thought off, got stuck in her throat.

'I am so sorry, Bex. That's awful, just before your retirement!'

'Yes, at least I could have looked after her myself now.'

'I know. That's rotten luck for you both.'

'How is your daughter?'

'Busy with her career and being courted.' It doesn't sound as if she has much time for dad.

'I really don't know what to do with myself every day all day.' He stares at the animals without seeing them.

Ant puts her hand on his arm: '…if it's any consolation: it will come to you. Maybe charity work? Maybe helping out in your old force when they are short staffed? Look at me. You called me back; and if you are really stuck, you can always help me out with the pigs.

He looks doubtful: 'Won't Felix mind?'

'Felix? Why?'

'Oh, I thought…'

'You thought wrong. …but you just reminded me that I owe his parents a dinner. How about tomorrow night? Then you can meet them all.'

'My social life is already improving,' he chuckles and they walk happily, arm in arm, down the hill. Only when they arrived at the house, does Bex notices that Ant must have ever so gently withdrawn her arm.

The End

BOOKS BY M. LINDSEY-NOBLE:

The R.F. Delderfield Biography: Butterfly Moments

The Bangla family saga;
The Green Sari
The Banyan Tree
The Flame

Mixed Blessings and other Love Stories

THE ANT MURDERS:
THE HUNCH (vol.1)